ATTACK OF THE STUFF

"The Life and Times of Bill Waddler"

BY JIM BENTON

PAPERCUTZ

NEW YORK

ATTACK OF THE STUFF

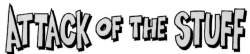

"The Life and Times of Bill Waddler"

BY JIM BENTON

I'm going to be a movie star!
or maybe a kitchen sink!
Everybody will know my name!
You have a name?

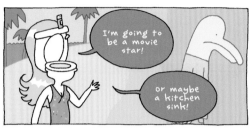

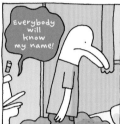

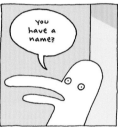

JEFF WHITMAN — Managing Editor
JIM SALICRUP
Editor-in-Chief

Special thanks to KRISTEN LeCLERC and Summer Benton

Hardcover ISBN: 978-1-5458-0498-8
Paperback ISBN: 978-1-5458-0499-5

Printed in Turkey
May 2020

Papercutz books may be purchased for business or promotional use.
For information on bulk purchases please contact Macmillan Corporate and Premium Sales Department at (800) 221-795 x5442.

Distributed by Macmillan
First printing

ATTACK OF THE STUFF

"The Life and Times of Bill Waddler"

BY JIM BENTON

PAPERCUTZ

THE SMURFS #21

BRINA THE CAT #1

CAT & CAT #1

THE SISTERS #1

ATTACK OF THE STUFF

GERONIMO STILTON #17

THEA STILTON #6

GERONIMO STILTON RREPORTER #1

THE MYTHICS #1

GUMBY #1

ANNE OF GREEN BAGELS #1

BLUEBEARD

THE RED SHOES

THE LITTLE MERMAID

FUZZY BASEBALL

HOTEL TRANSYLVANIA #1

THE LOUD HOUSE #1

MANOSAURS #1

THE ONLY LIVING BOY #5

THE ONLY LIVING GIRL #1

MORE GREAT GRAPHIC NOVEL SERIES AVAILABLE FROM

PAPERCUTƵ™

papercutz.com
All available where ebooks are sold.

CHAPTER ONE

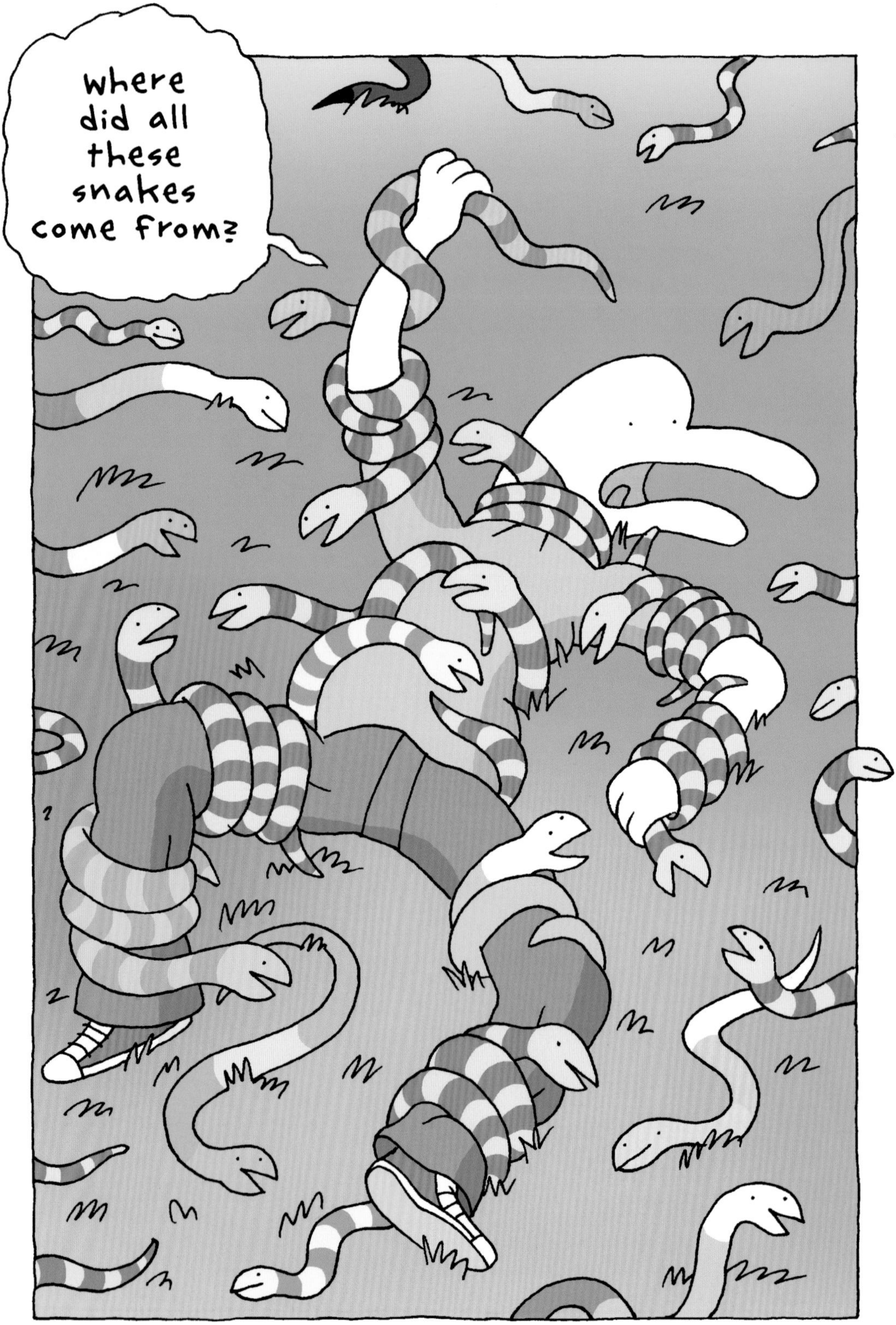
where did all these snakes come from?

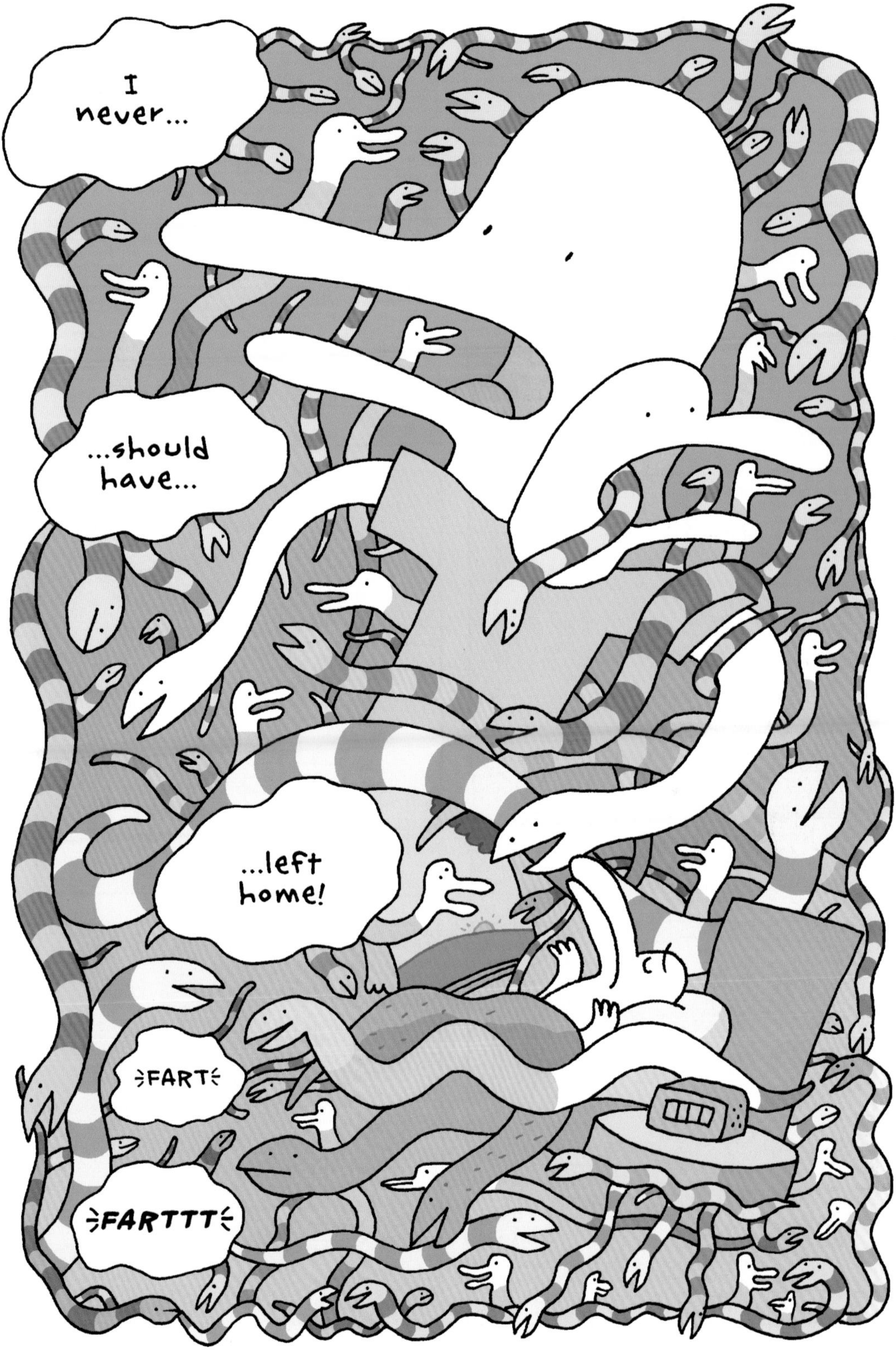
I never...
...should have...
...left home!
FART
FARTTT

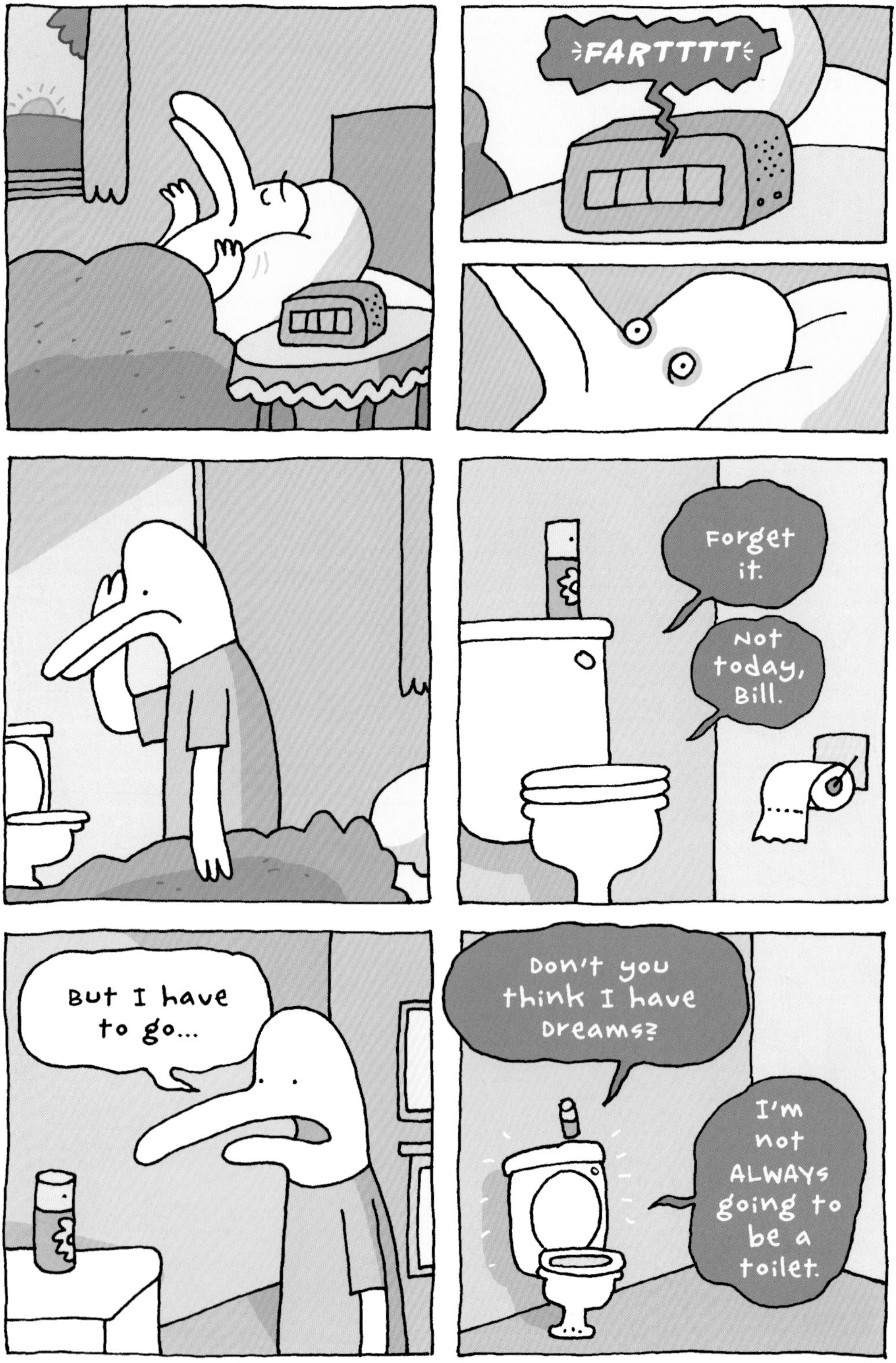
FARTTTT
Forget it.
Not today, Bill.
But I have to go...
Don't you think I have Dreams?
I'm not ALWAYS going to be a toilet.

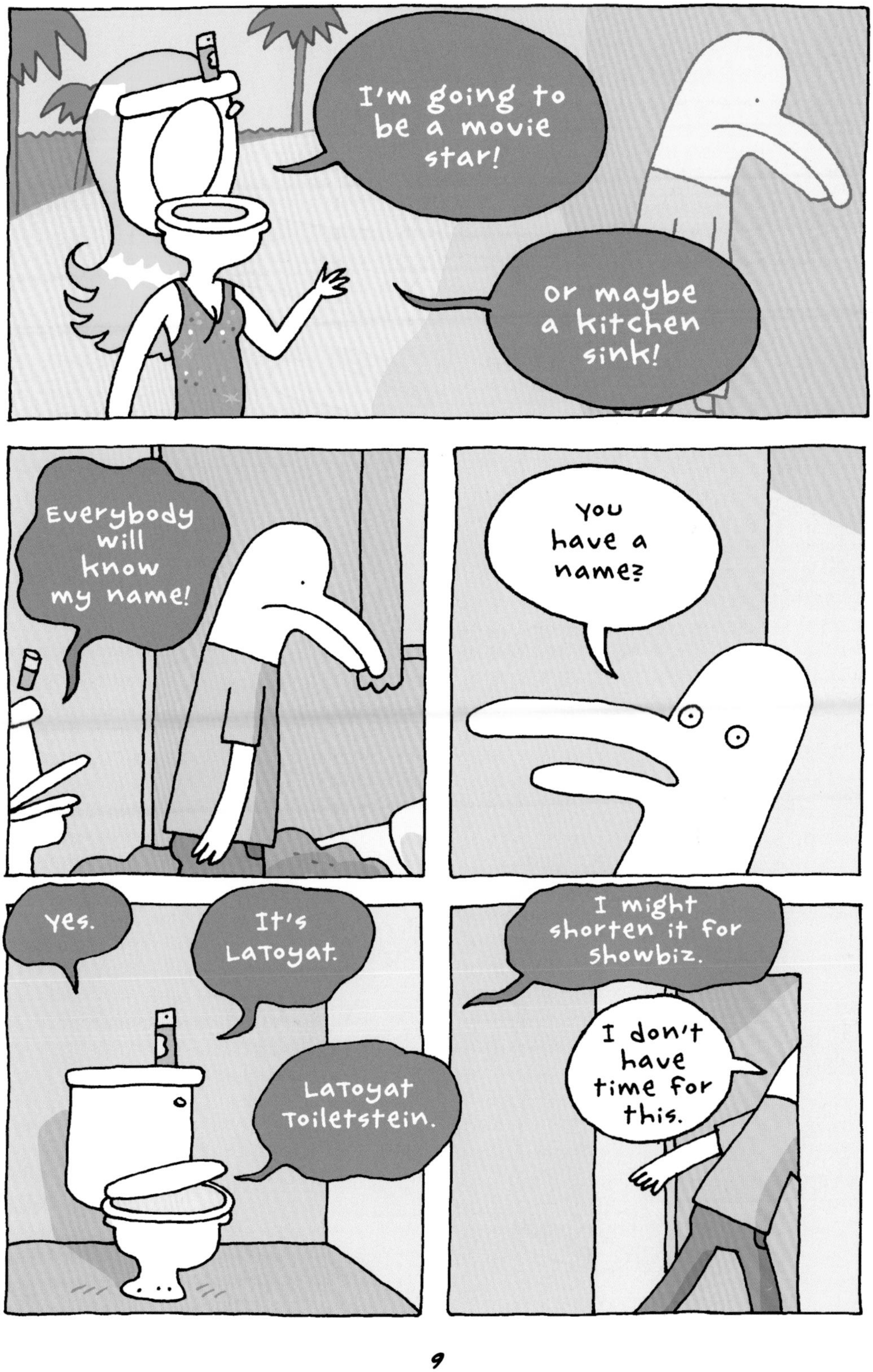
I'm going to be a movie star!
Or maybe a kitchen sink!
Everybody will know my name!
You have a name?
Yes.
It's LaToyat.
LaToyat Toiletstein.
I might shorten it for showbiz.
I don't have time for this.

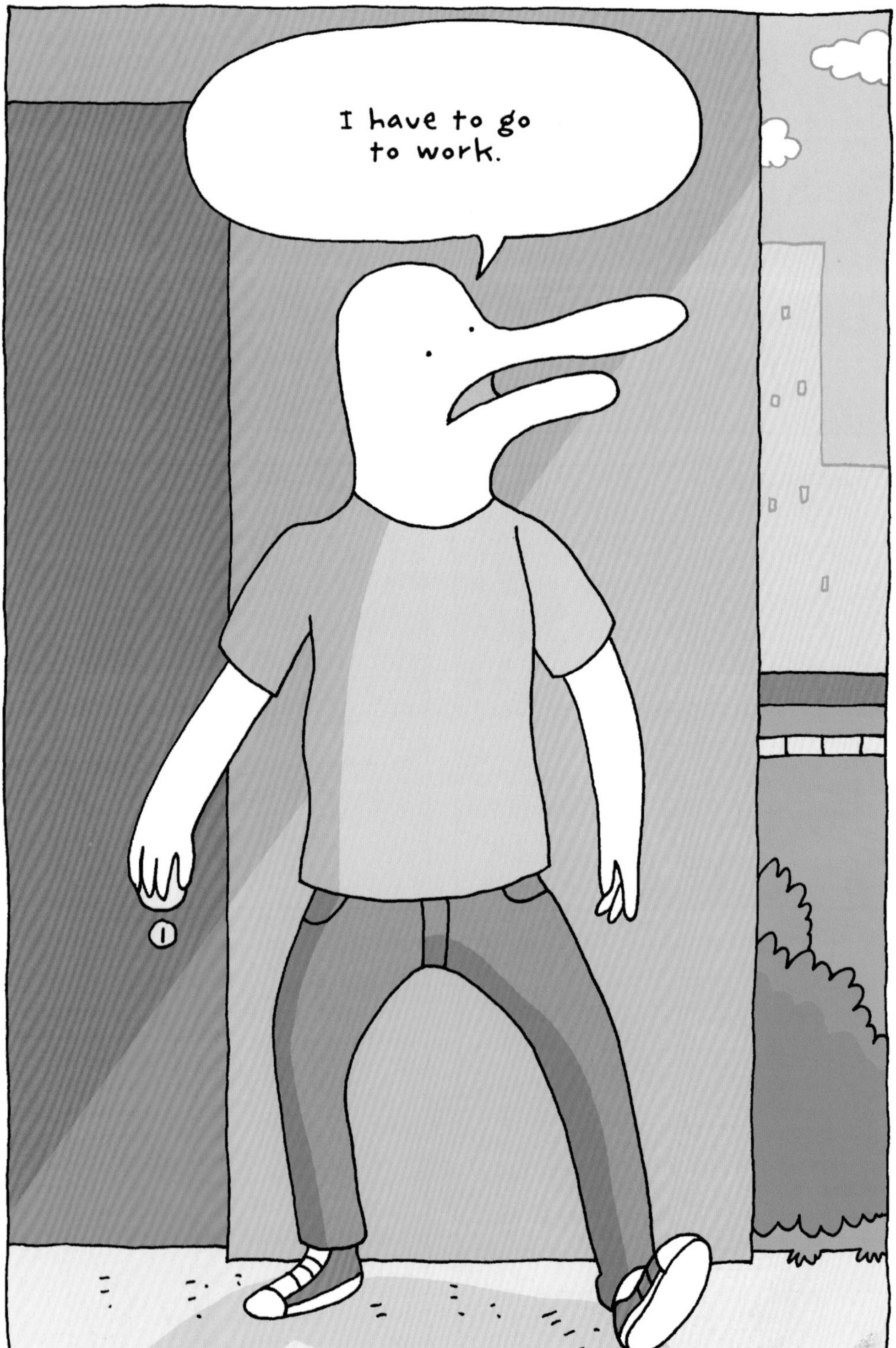
I have to go to work.

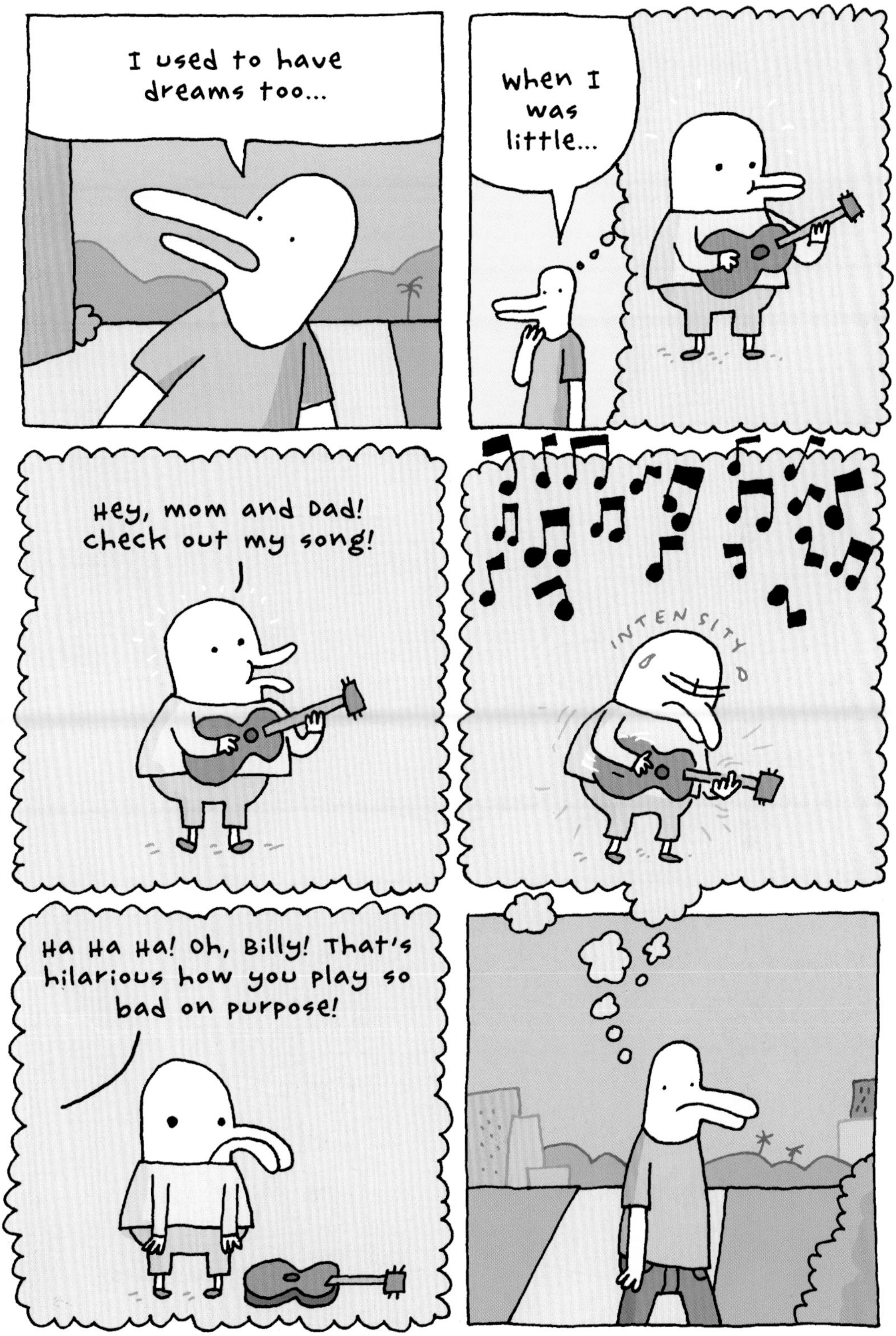

I used to have dreams too...
When I was little...
Hey, mom and Dad! check out my song!
INTENSITY
Ha Ha Ha! Oh, Billy! That's hilarious how you play so bad on purpose!

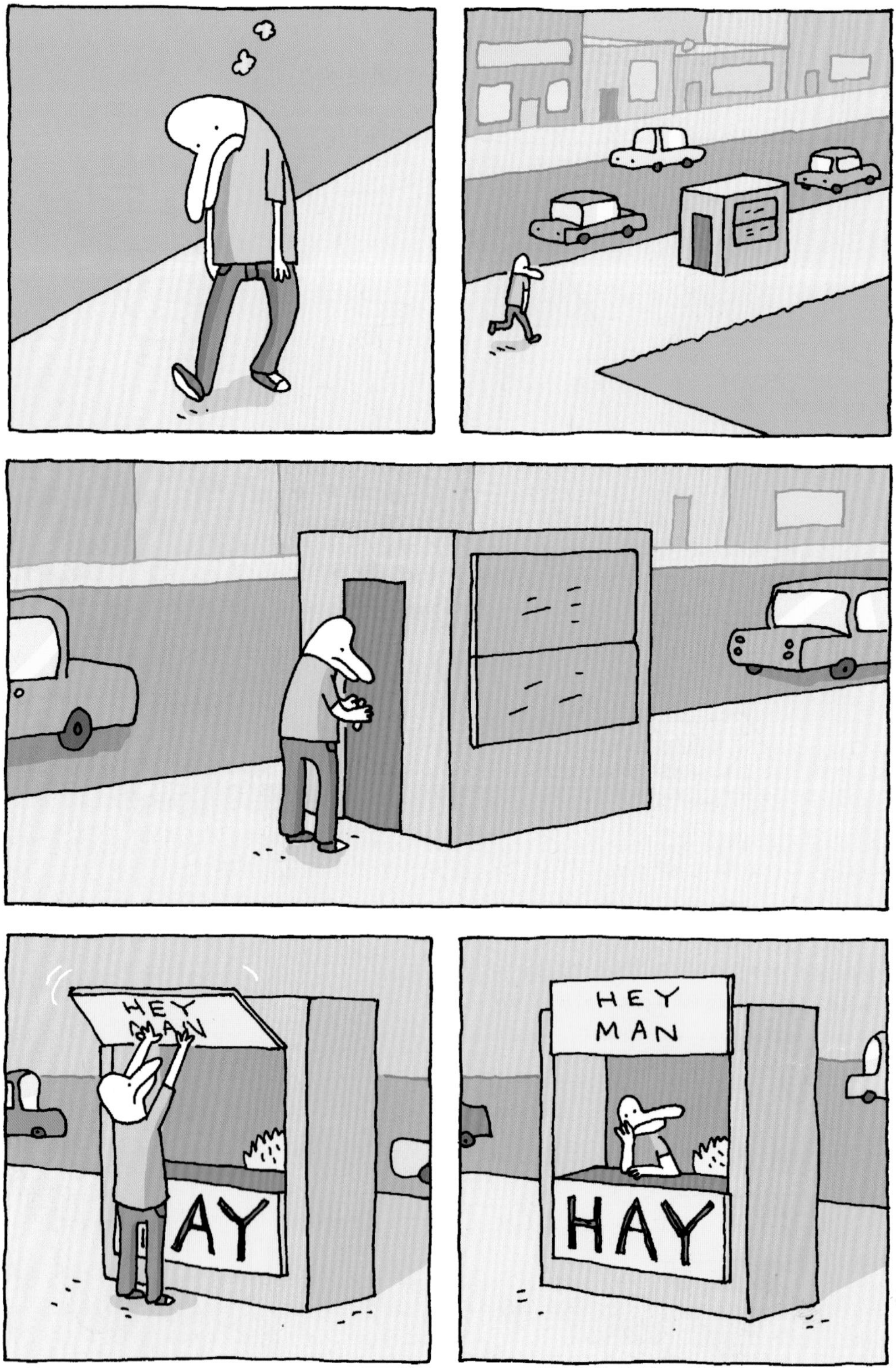
HEY MAN
AY
HEY MAN
HAY

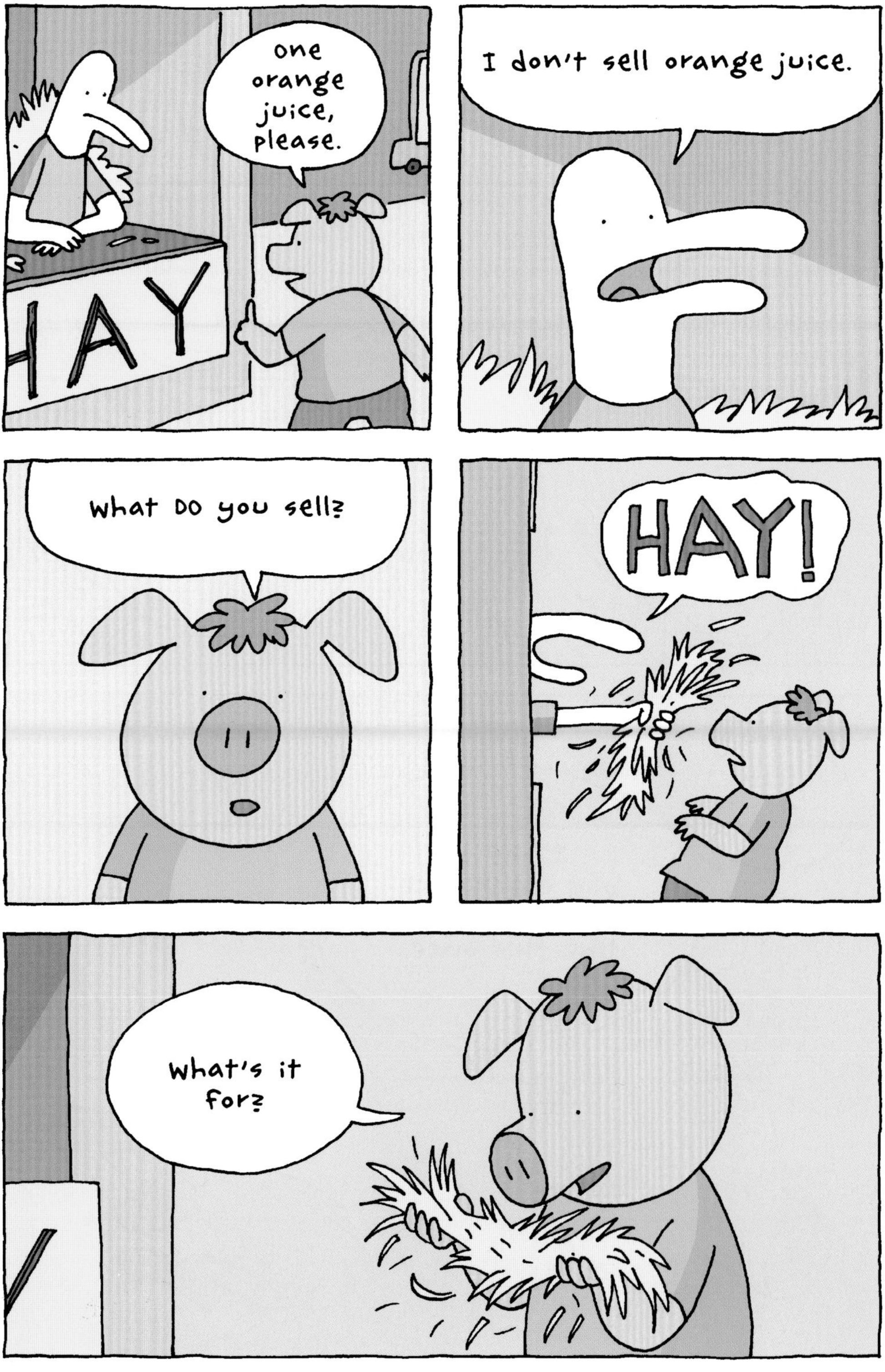
HAY
one orange juice, please.
I don't sell orange juice.
what DO you sell?
HAY!
what's it for?

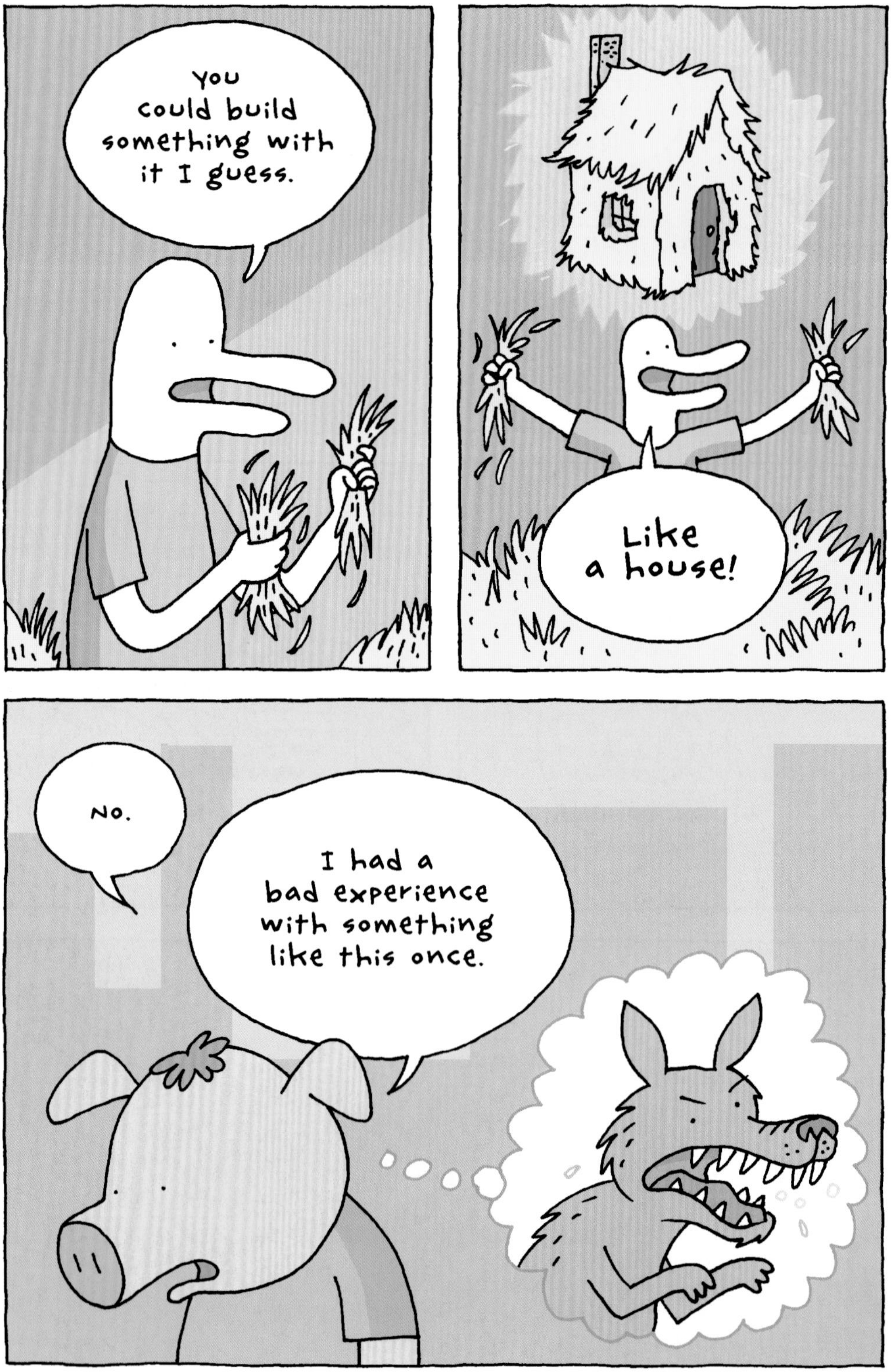

You could build something with it I guess.
Like a house!
No.
I had a bad experience with something like this once.

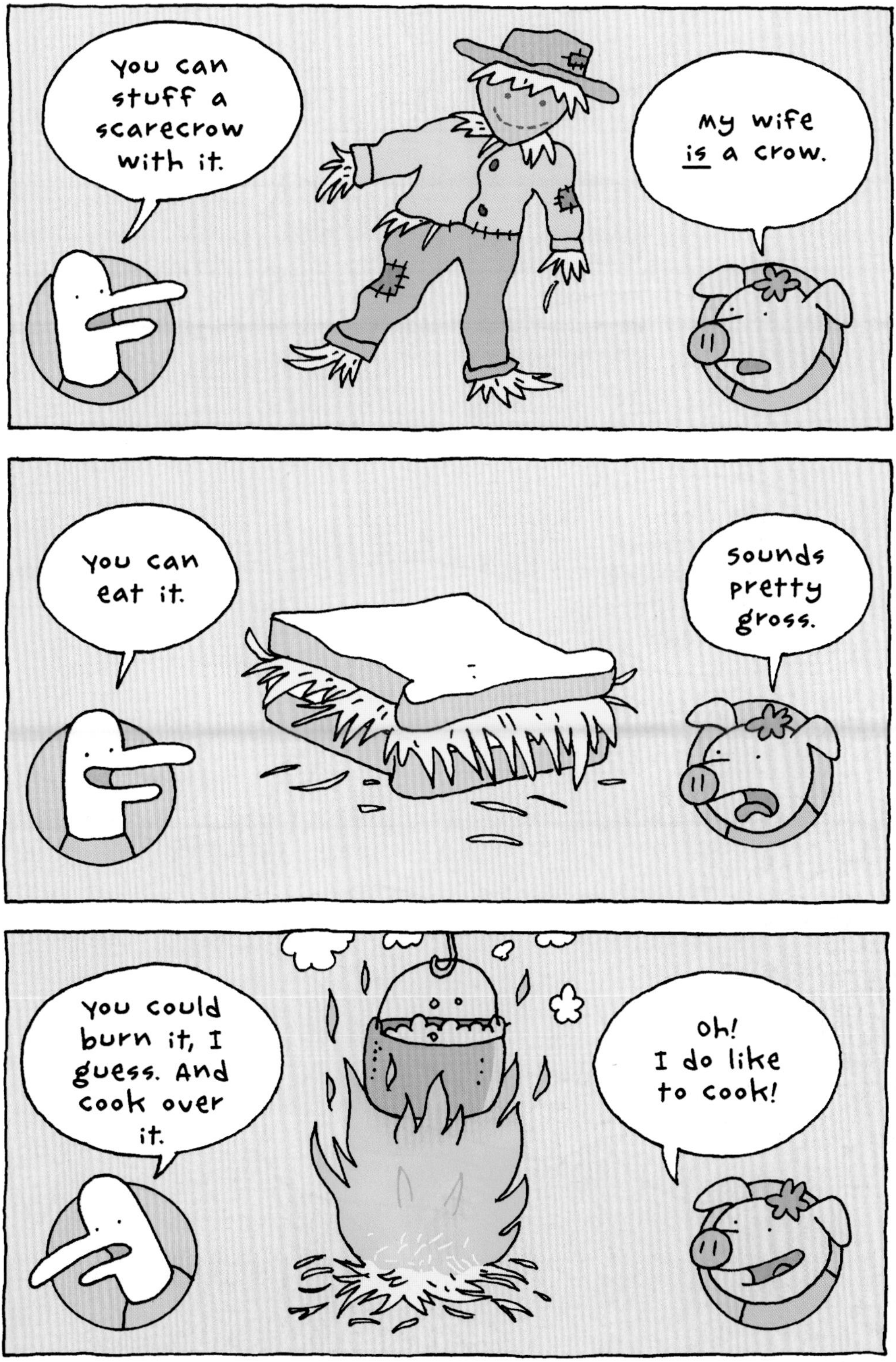
You can stuff a scarecrow with it.
My wife is a crow.
You can eat it.
Sounds pretty gross.
You could burn it, I guess. And cook over it.
Oh! I do like to cook!

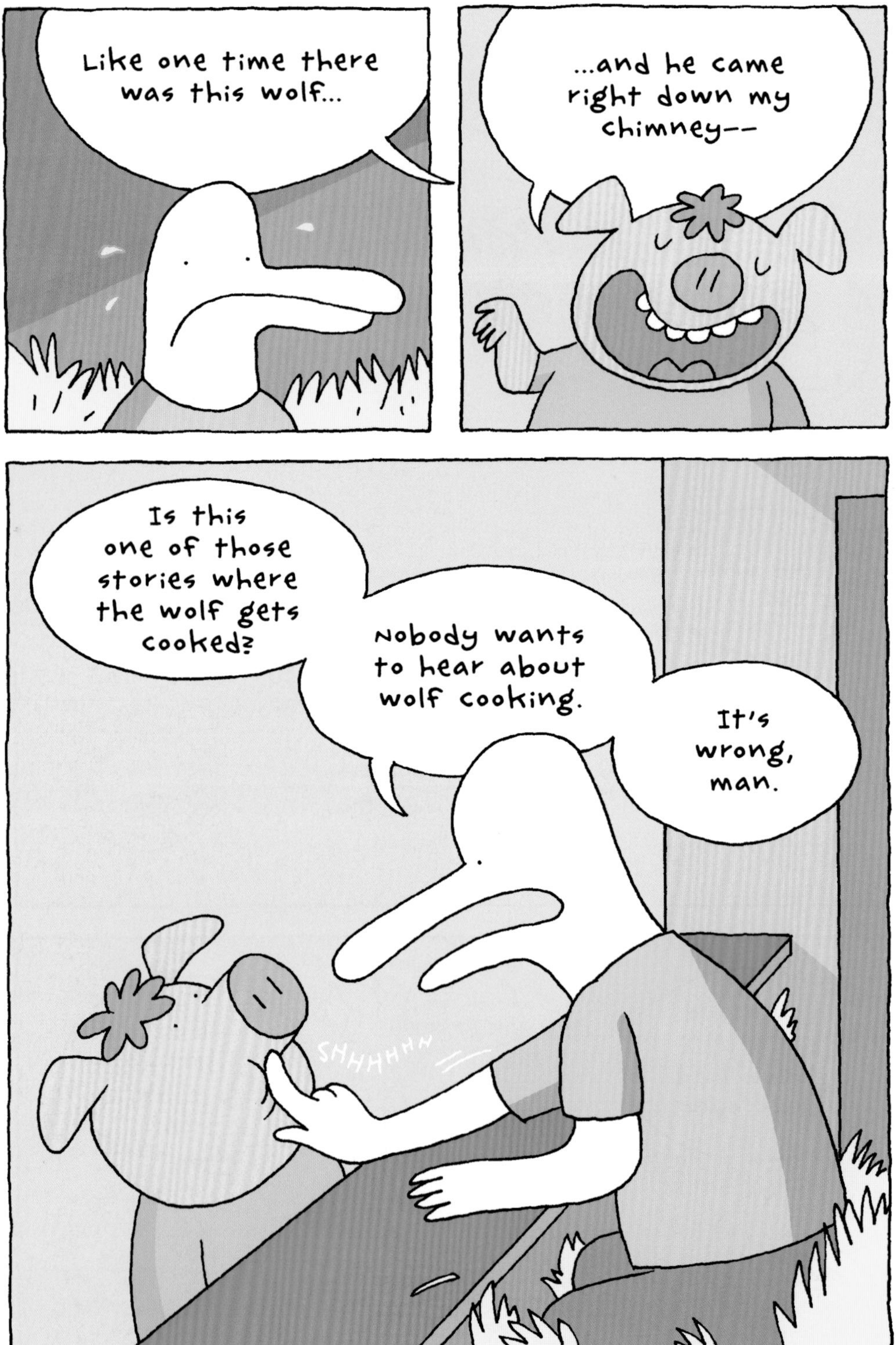
Like one time there was this wolf...
...and he came right down my chimney--
Is this one of those stories where the wolf gets cooked?
Nobody wants to hear about wolf cooking.
It's wrong, man.
SHHHHHH

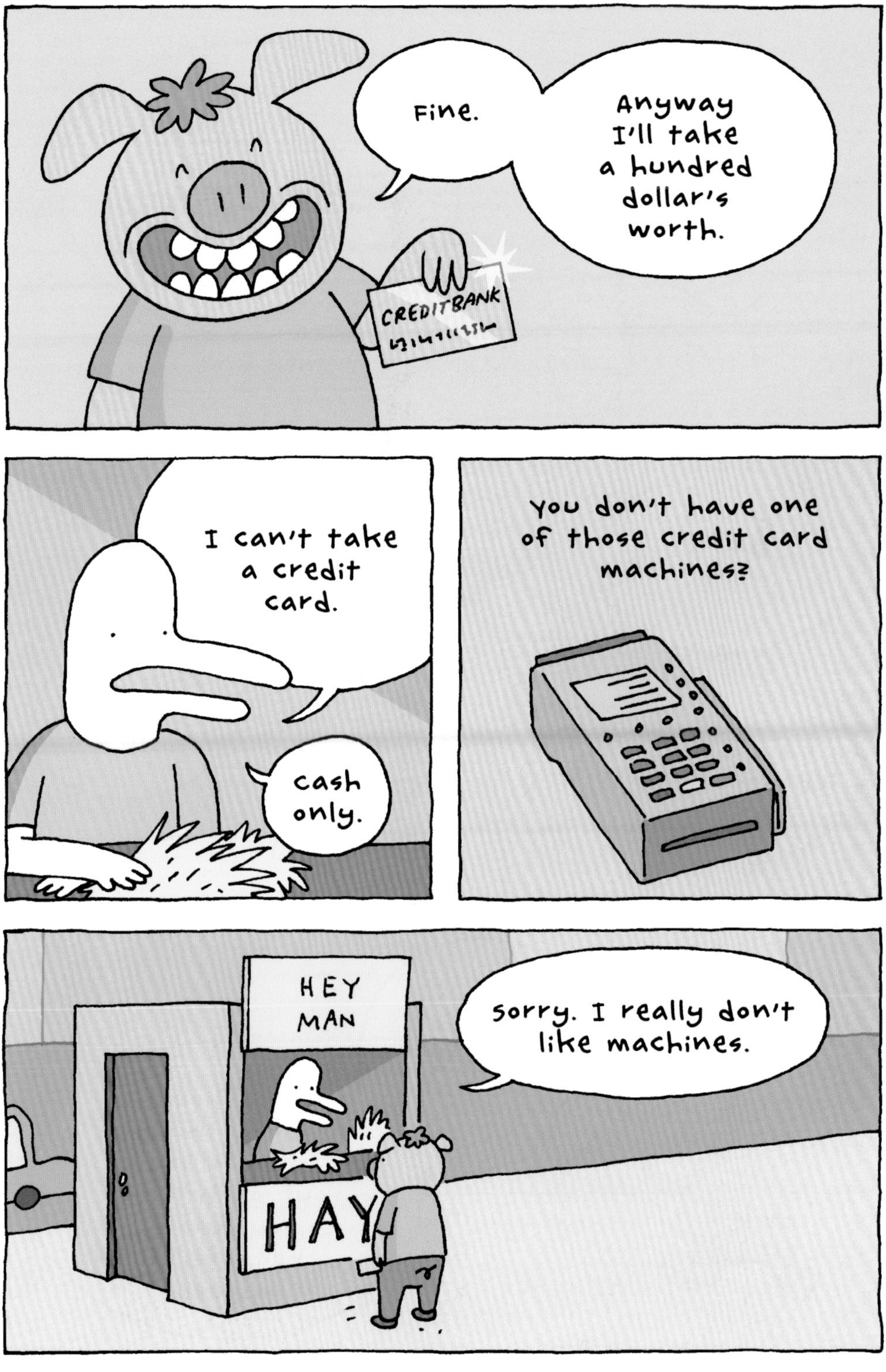
Fine.
Anyway I'll take a hundred dollar's worth.
CREDITBANK
I can't take a credit card.
cash only.
You don't have one of those credit card machines?
HEY MAN
Sorry. I really don't like machines.
HAY

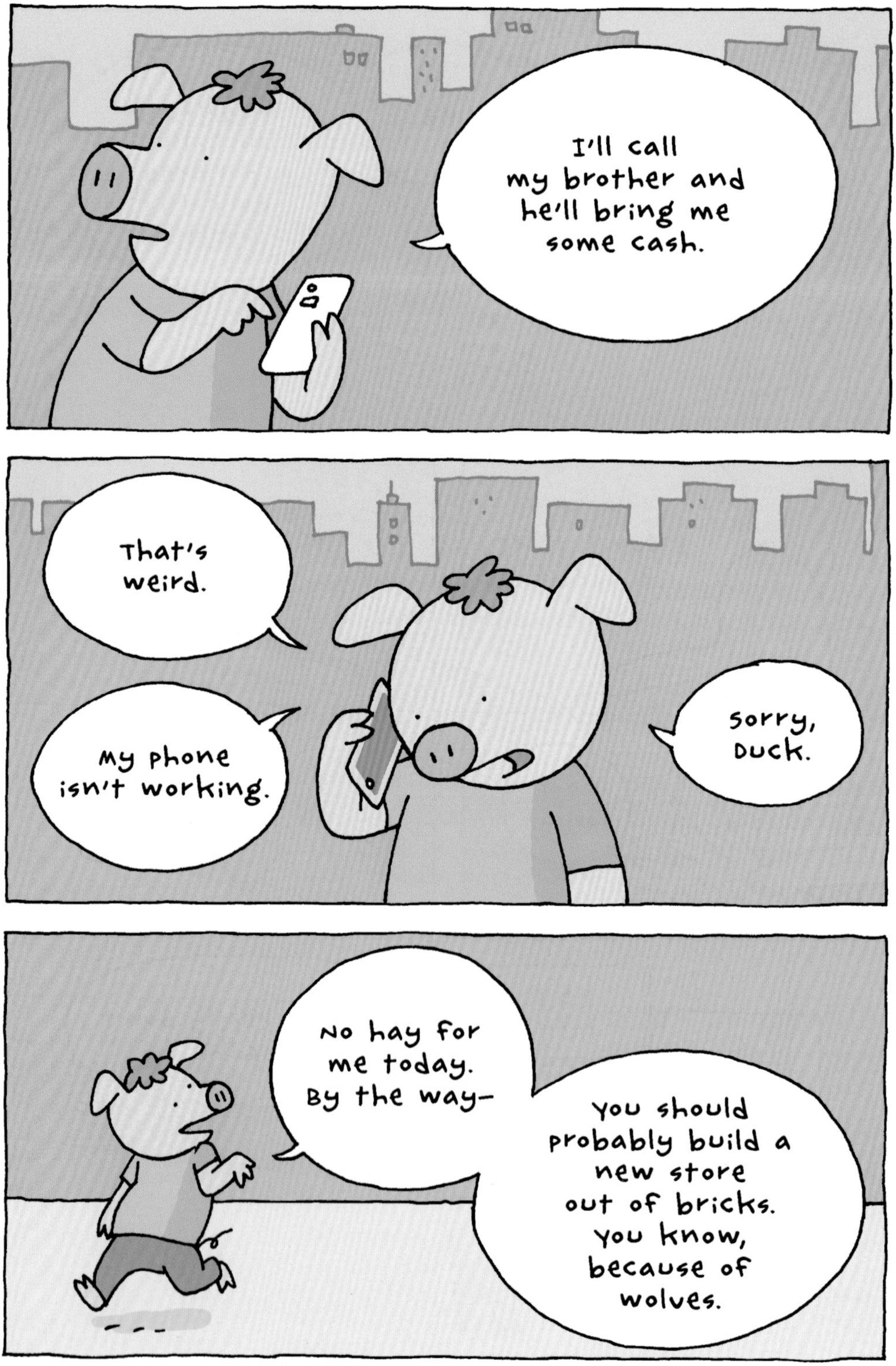
I'll call my brother and he'll bring me some cash.
That's weird.
My phone isn't working.
Sorry, Duck.
No hay for me today. By the way–
You should probably build a new store out of bricks. You know, because of wolves.

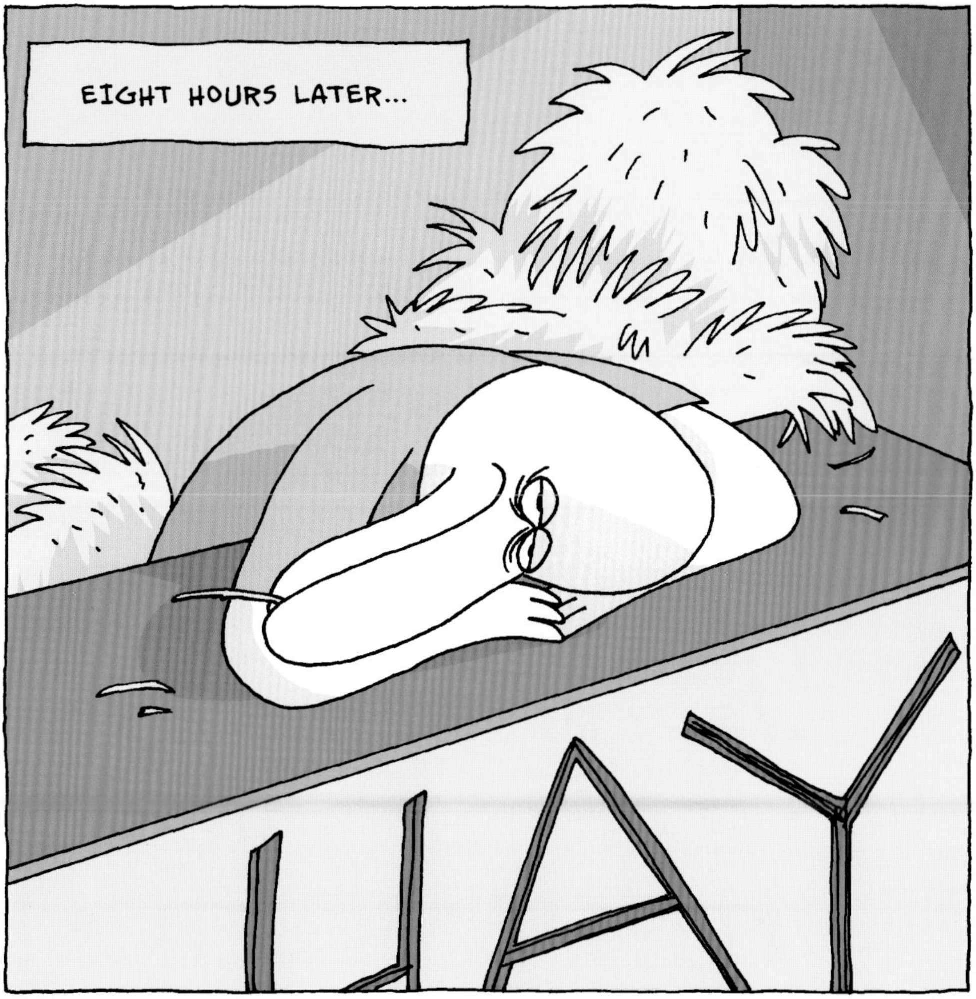
EIGHT HOURS LATER...

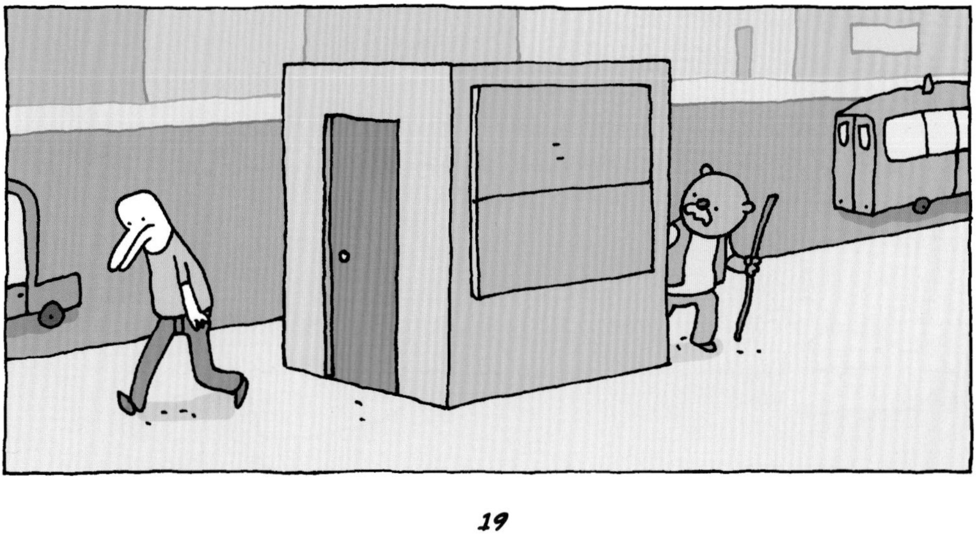

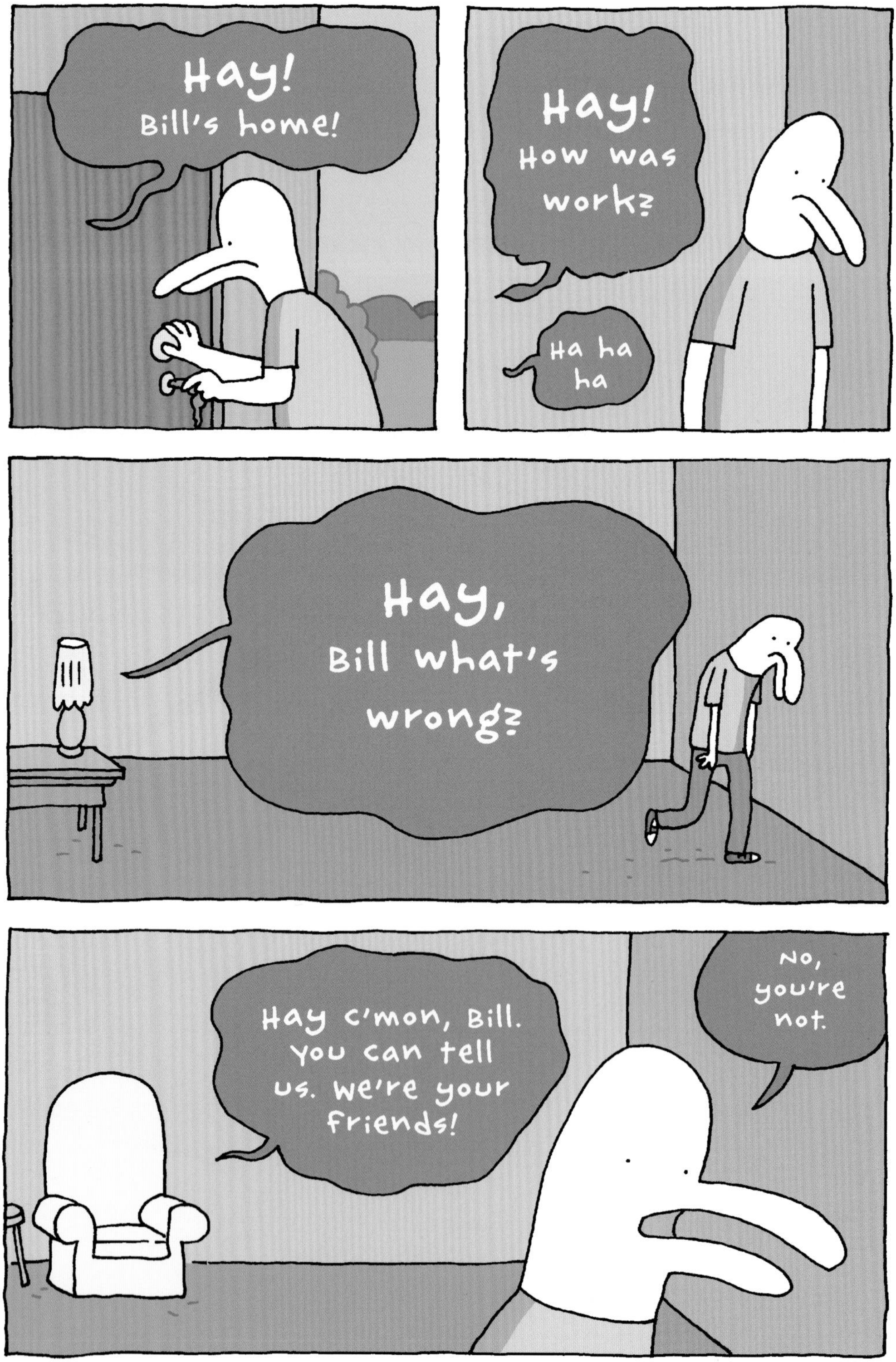
Hay! Bill's home!
Hay! How was work?
Ha ha ha
Hay, Bill what's wrong?
Hay c'mon, Bill. You can tell us. We're your friends!
No, you're not.

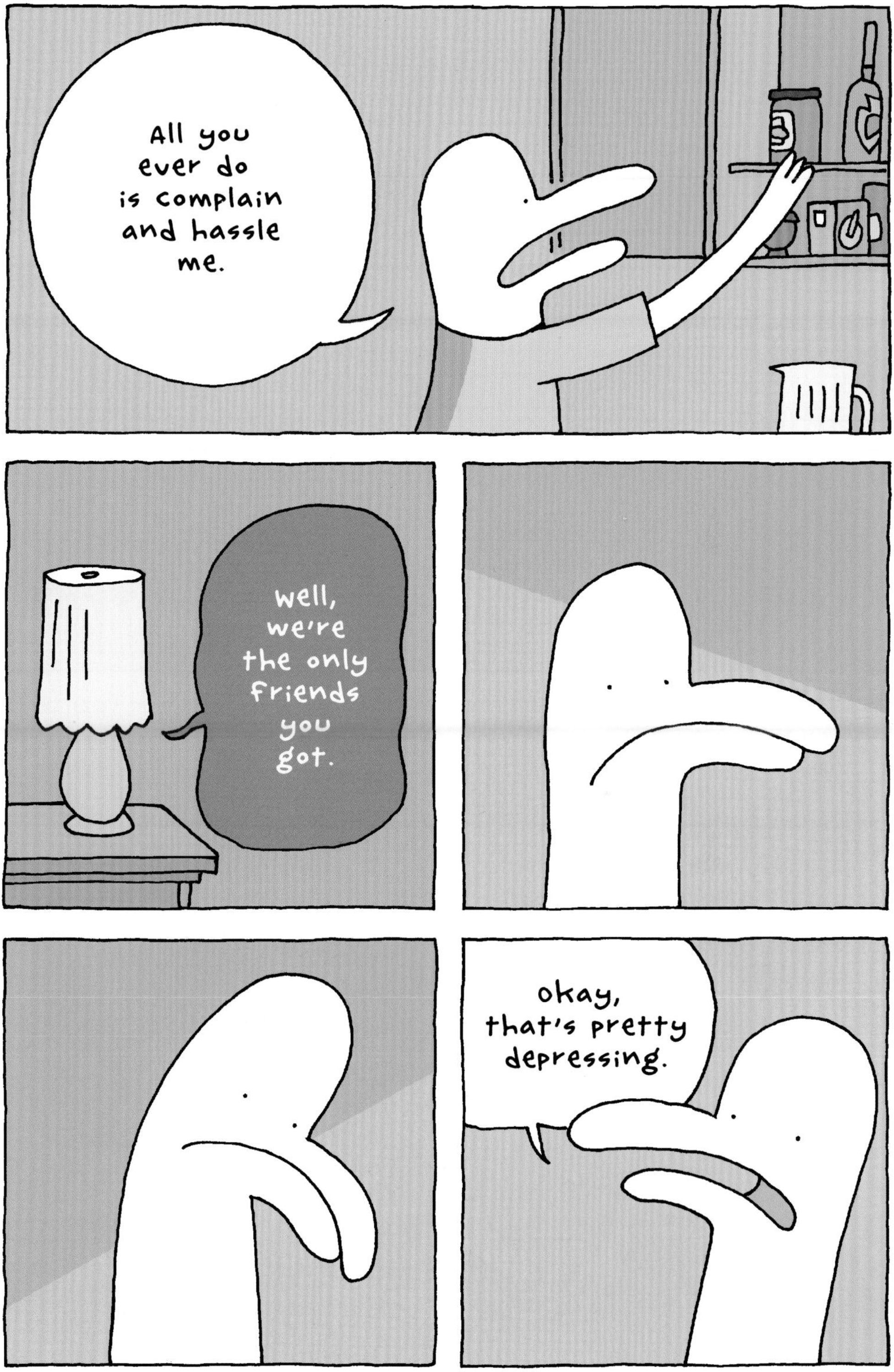
All you ever do is complain and hassle me.
well, we're the only friends you got.
okay, that's pretty depressing.

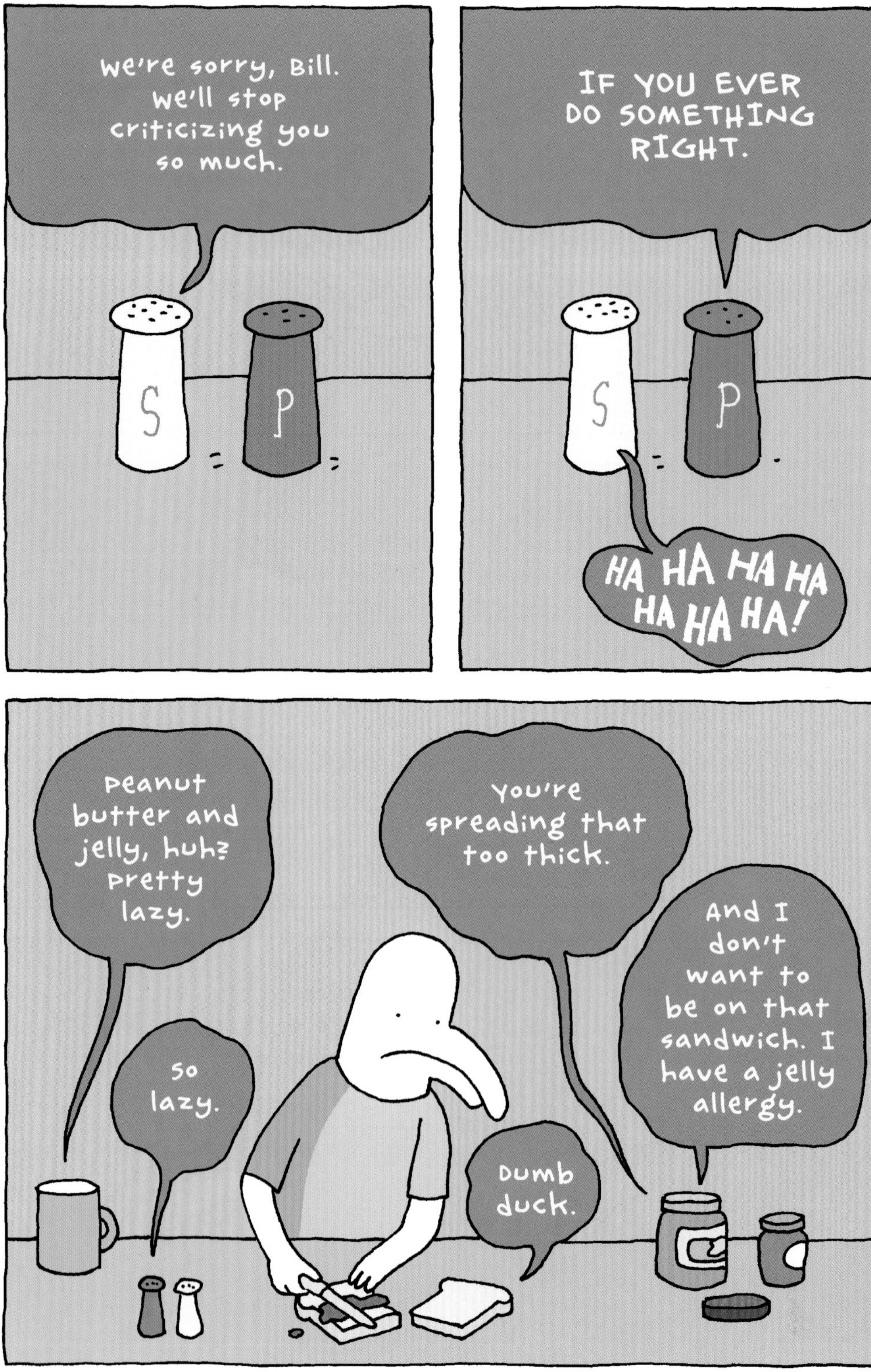
We're sorry, Bill. We'll stop criticizing you so much.
IF YOU EVER DO SOMETHING RIGHT.
HA HA HA HA HA HA HA!
Peanut butter and jelly, huh? Pretty lazy.
So lazy.
You're spreading that too thick.
Dumb duck.
And I don't want to be on that sandwich. I have a jelly allergy.

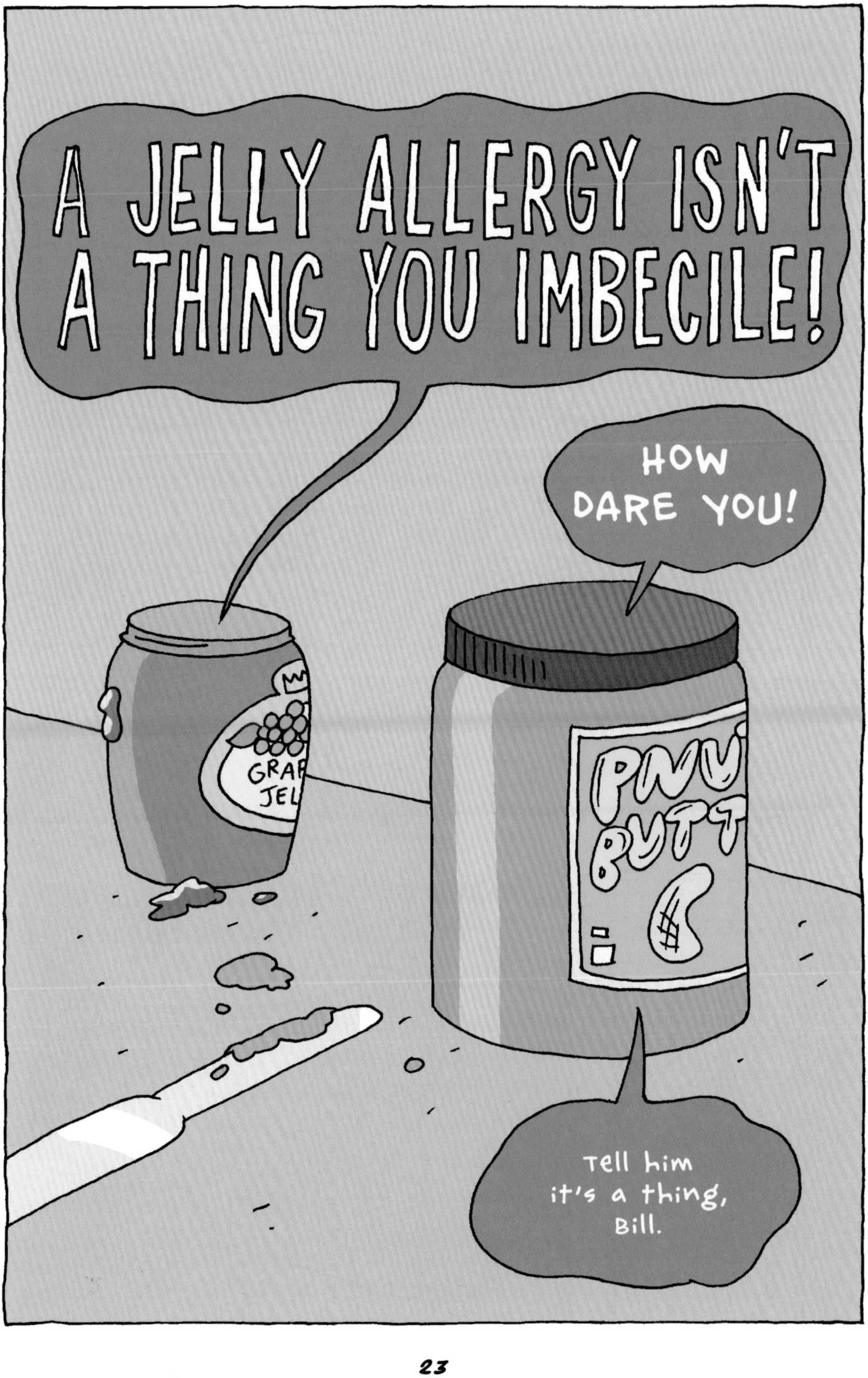
A JELLY ALLERGY ISN'T A THING YOU IMBECILE!
HOW DARE YOU!
Tell him it's a thing, Bill.
GRAP JEL
PNUT BUTT

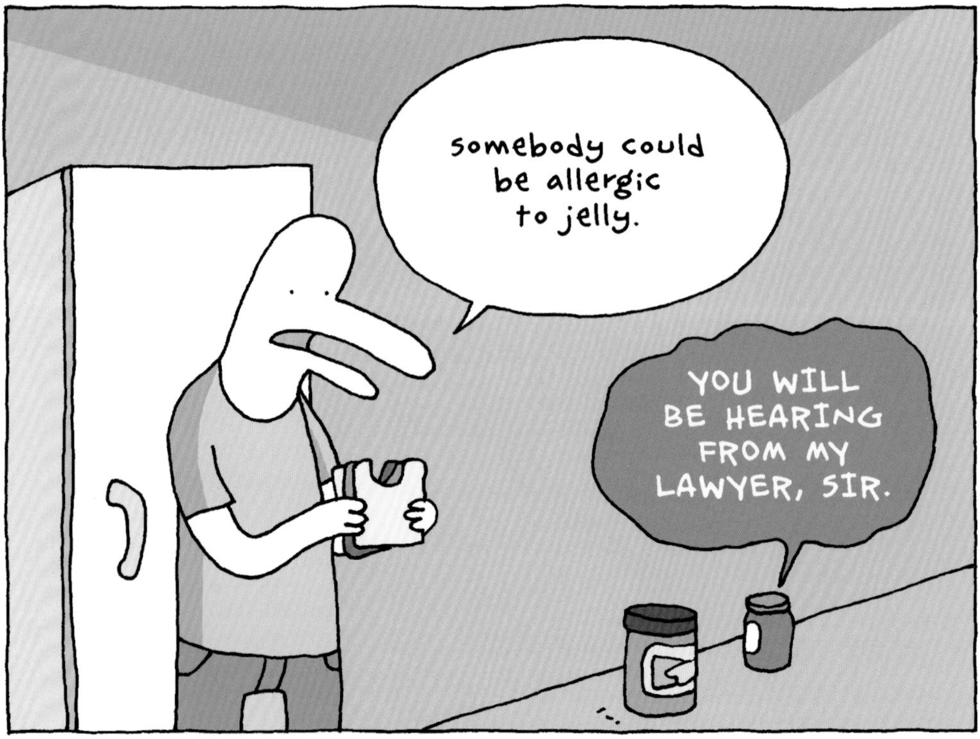
somebody could be allergic to jelly.
YOU WILL BE HEARING FROM MY LAWYER, SIR.

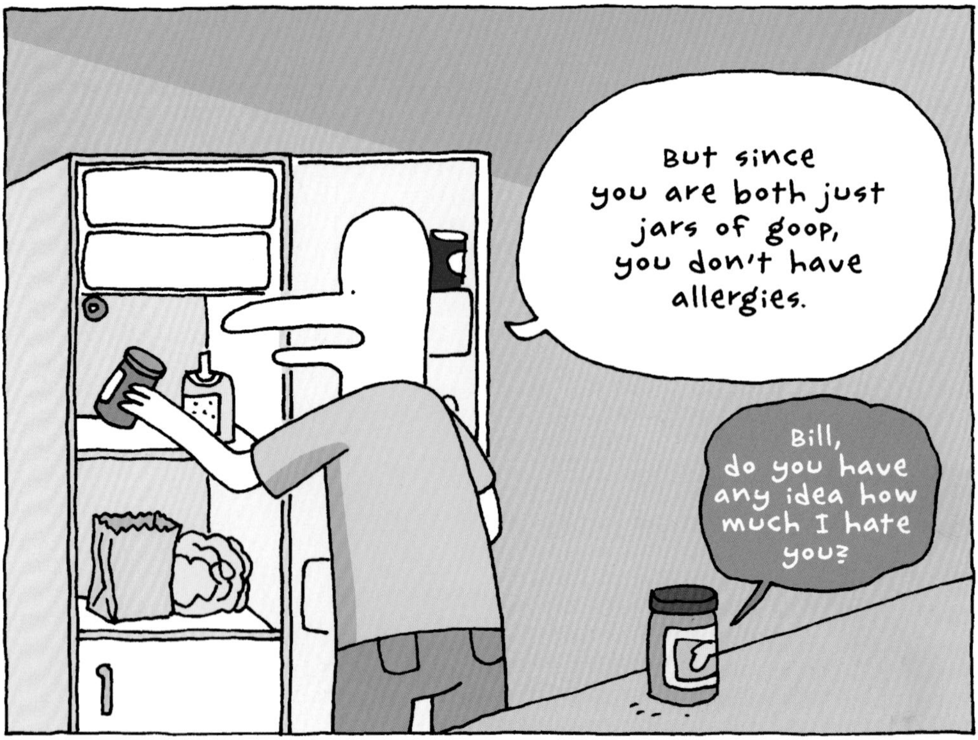
But since you are both just jars of goop, you don't have allergies.
Bill, do you have any idea how much I hate you?

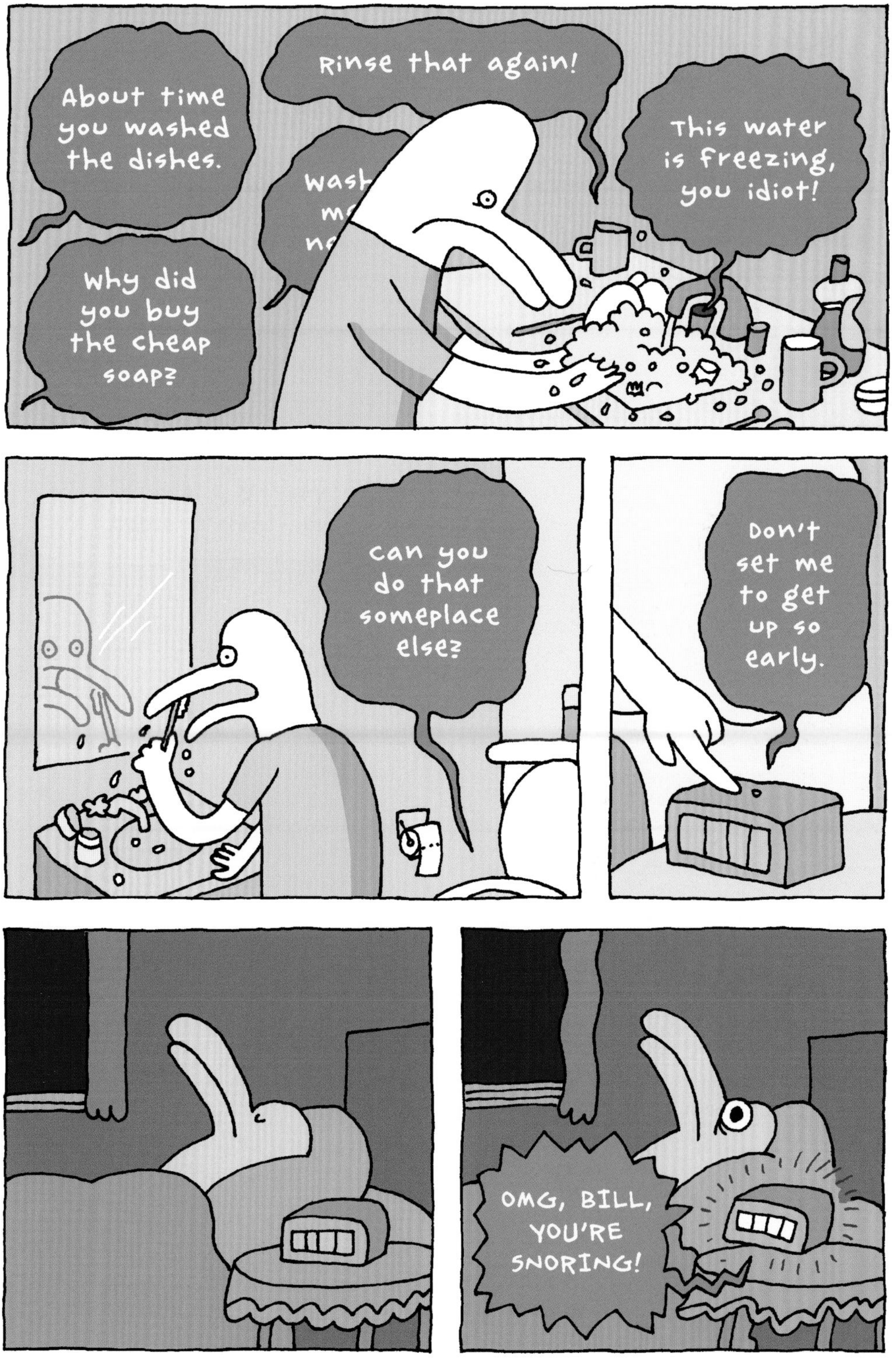
About time you washed the dishes.
Rinse that again!
This water is freezing, you idiot!
Why did you buy the cheap soap?
Can you do that someplace else?
Don't set me to get up so early.
OMG, BILL, YOU'RE SNORING!

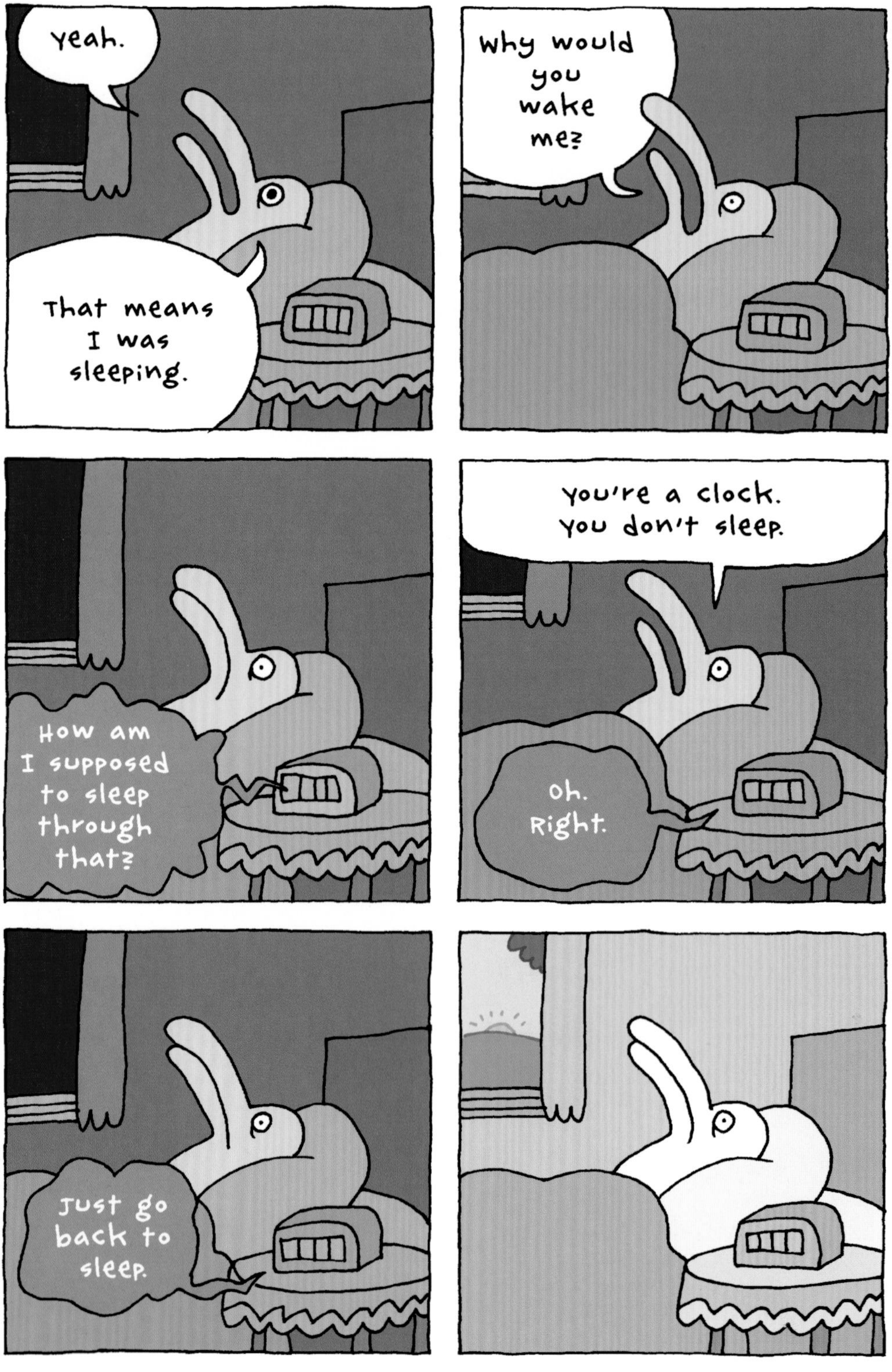
yeah.
That means I was sleeping.
Why would you wake me?
How am I supposed to sleep through that?
You're a clock. You don't sleep.
Oh. Right.
Just go back to sleep.

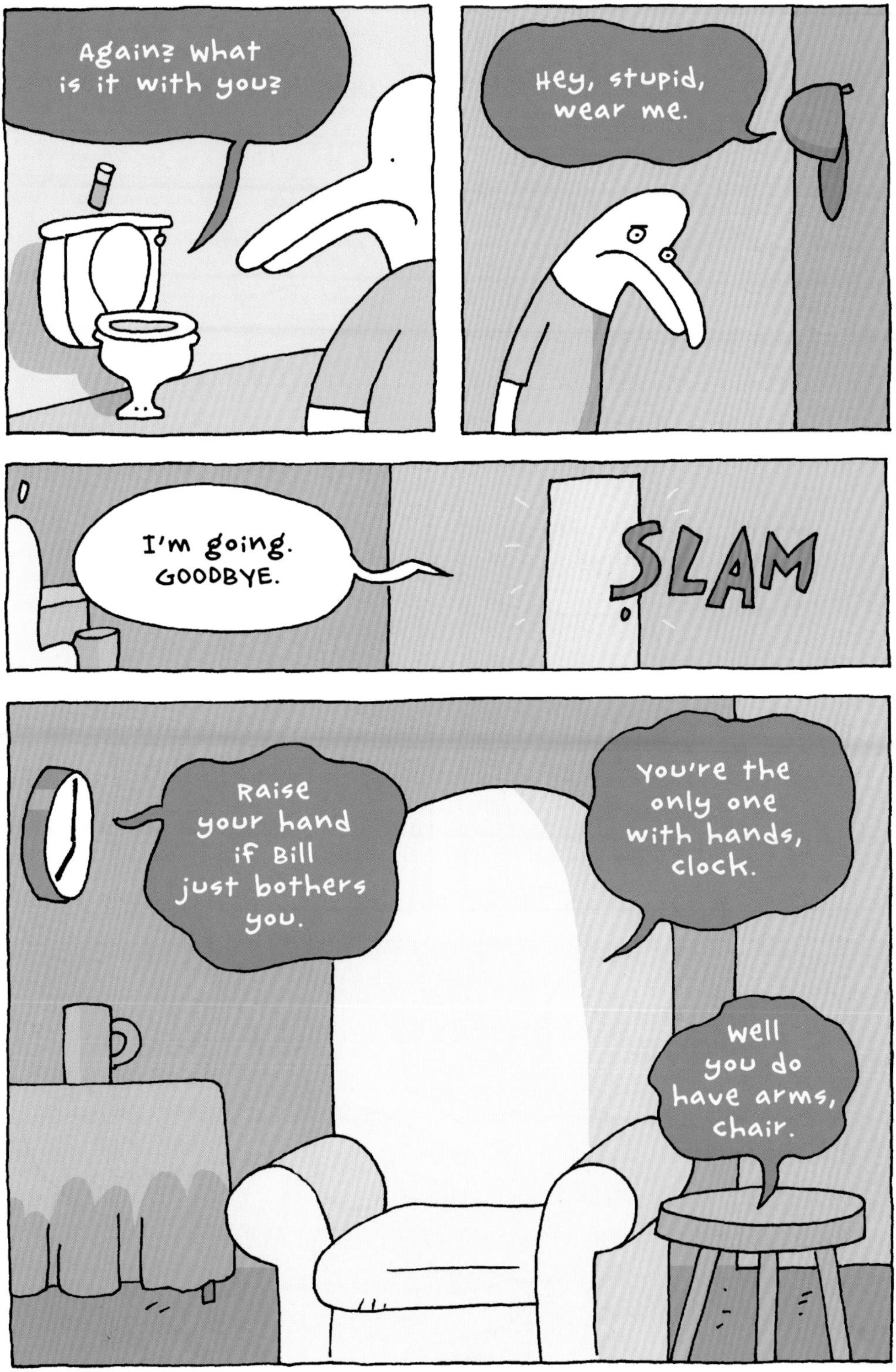
Again? What is it with you?
Hey, stupid, wear me.
I'm going. GOODBYE.
SLAM
Raise your hand if Bill just bothers you.
You're the only one with hands, clock.
Well you do have arms, chair.

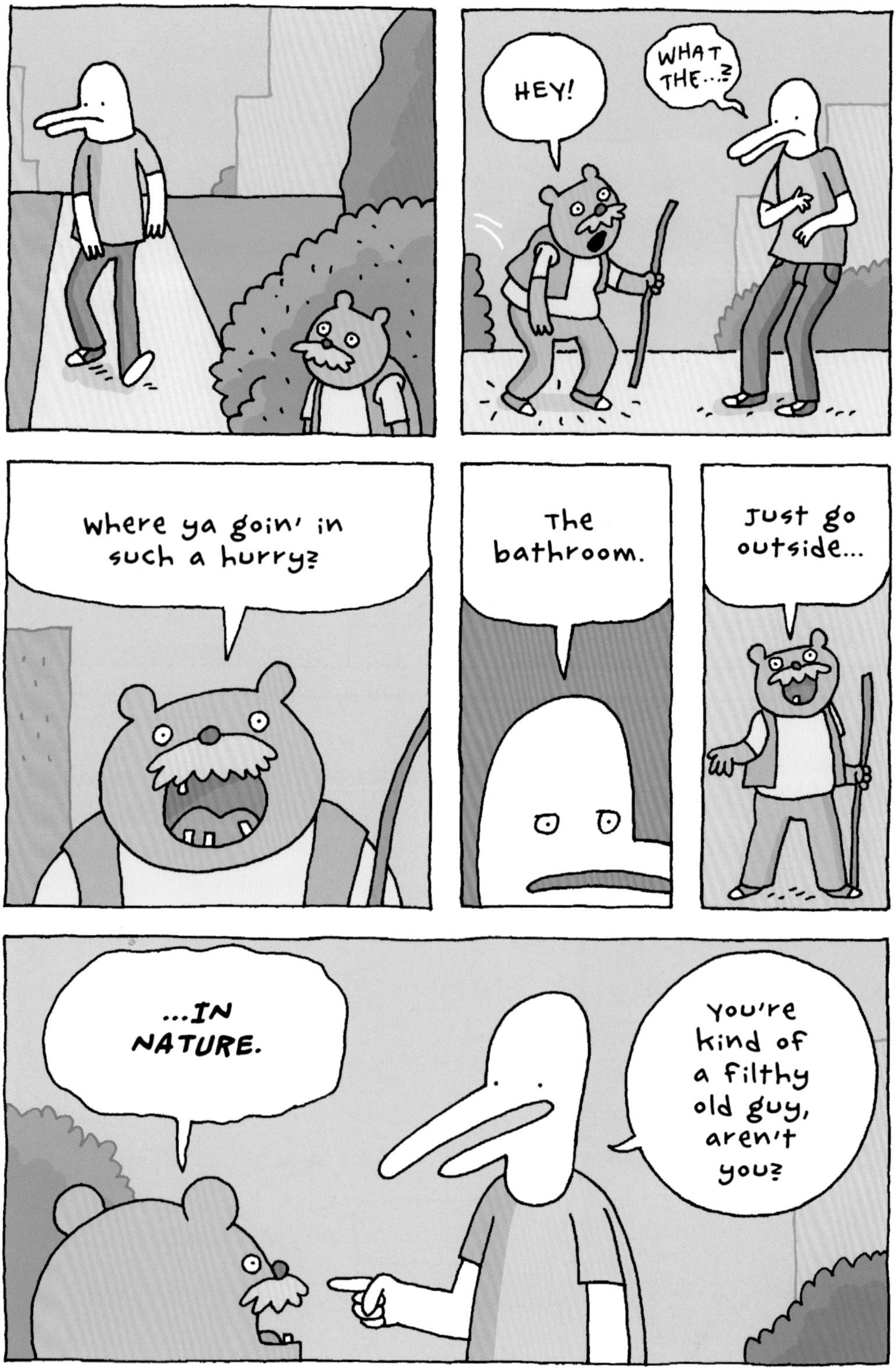
HEY!
WHAT THE...?
Where ya goin' in such a hurry?
The bathroom.
Just go outside...
...IN NATURE.
You're kind of a filthy old guy, aren't you?

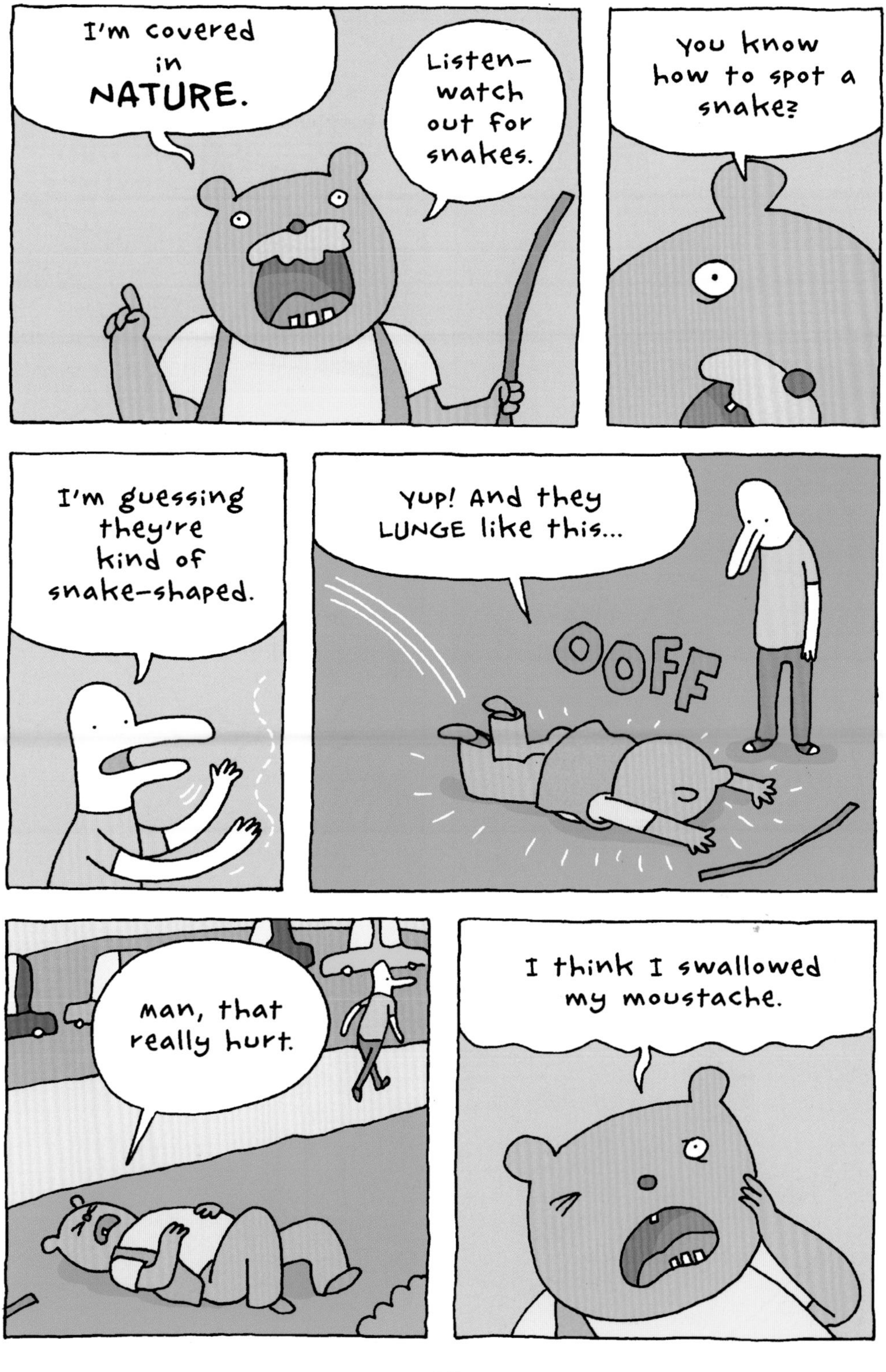
I'm covered in NATURE.
Listen— watch out for snakes.
You know how to spot a snake?
I'm guessing they're kind of snake-shaped.
YUP! And they LUNGE like this...
OOFF
Man, that really hurt.
I think I swallowed my moustache.

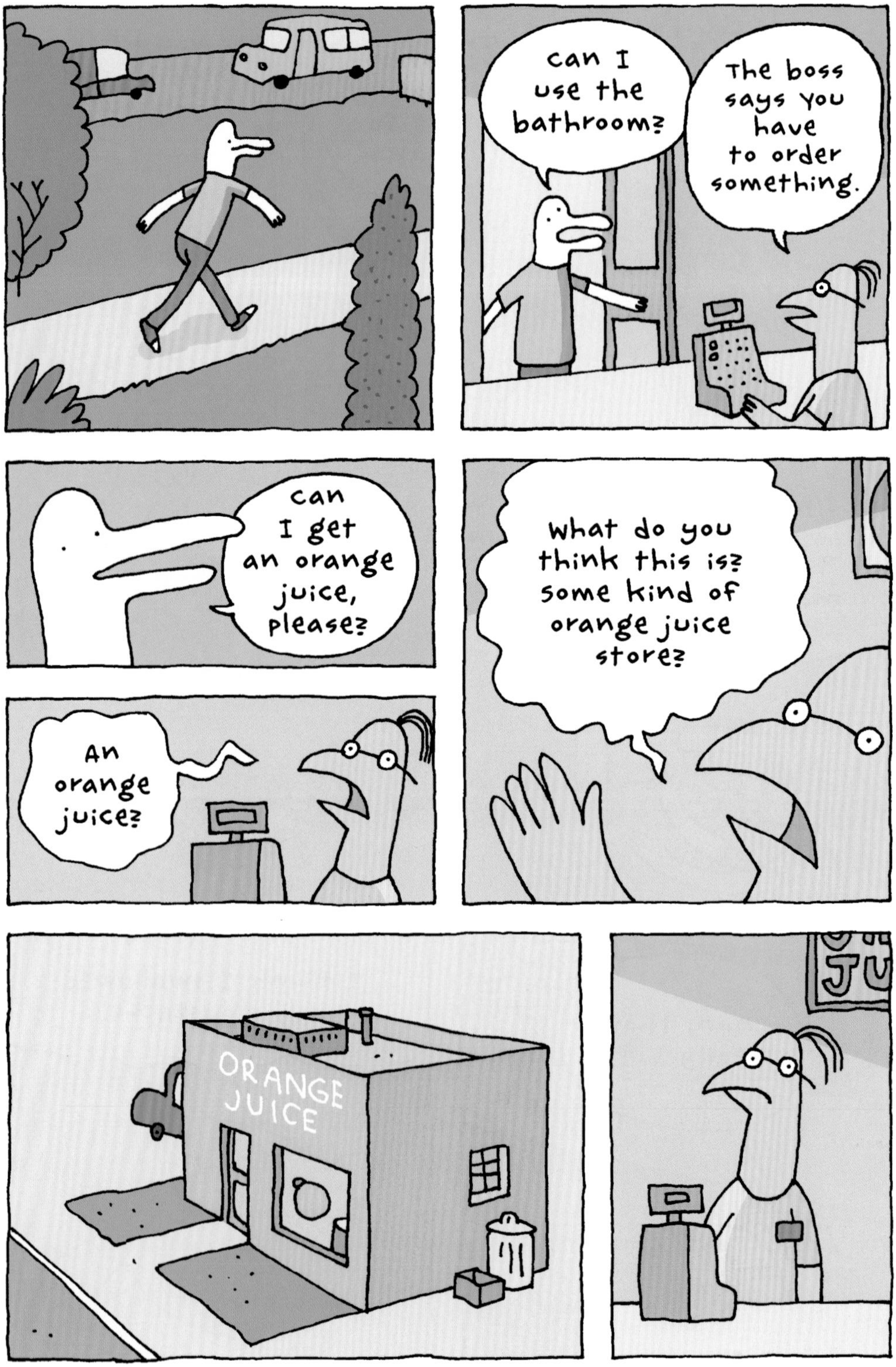
can I use the bathroom?
The boss says you have to order something.
can I get an orange juice, please?
An orange juice?
What do you think this is? some kind of orange juice store?
ORANGE JUICE

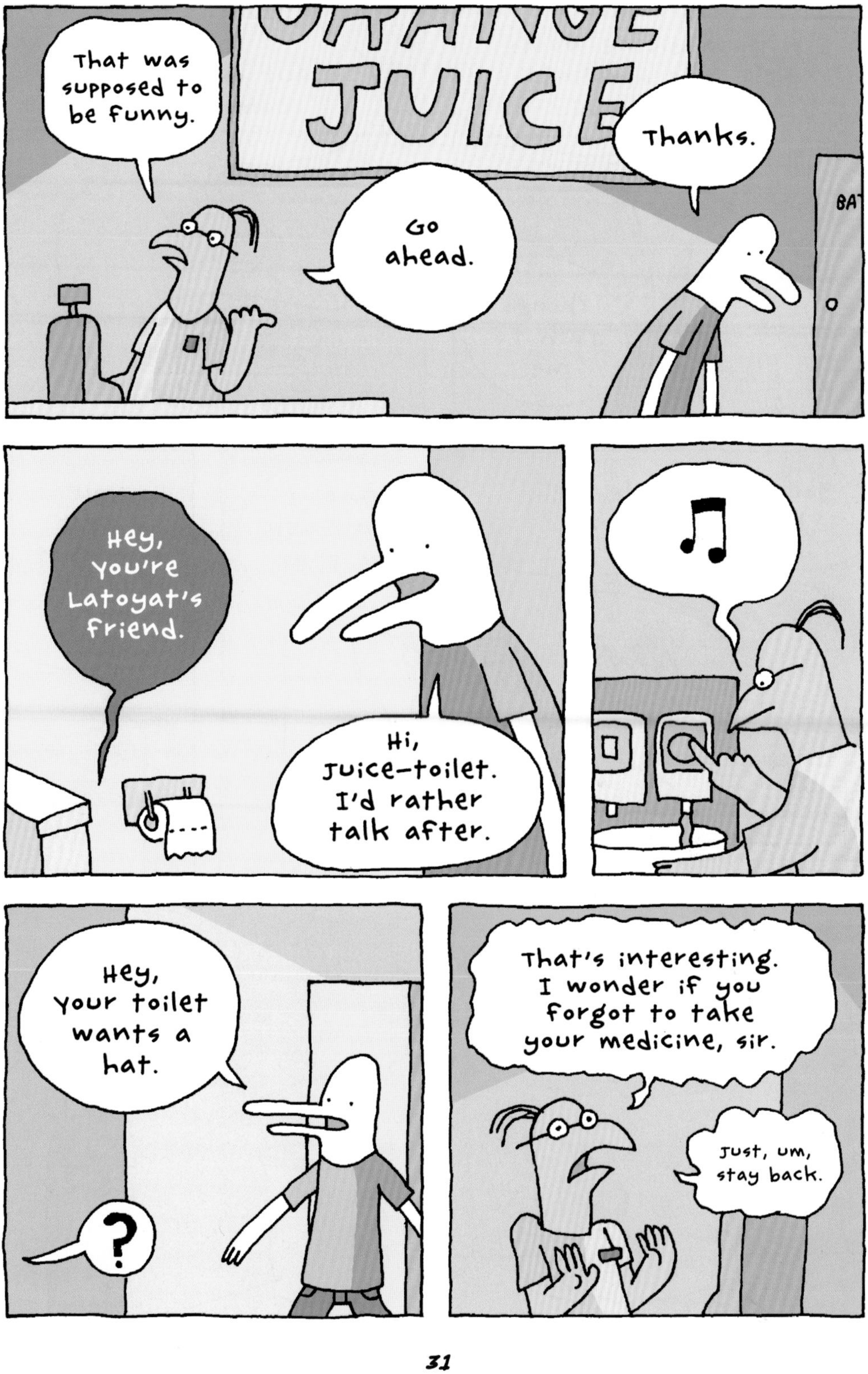
ORANGE
JUICE
That was supposed to be funny.
Thanks.
Go ahead.
BAT
Hey, you're Latoyat's friend.
Hi, Juice-toilet. I'd rather talk after.
Hey, your toilet wants a hat.
?
That's interesting. I wonder if you forgot to take your medicine, sir.
Just, um, stay back.

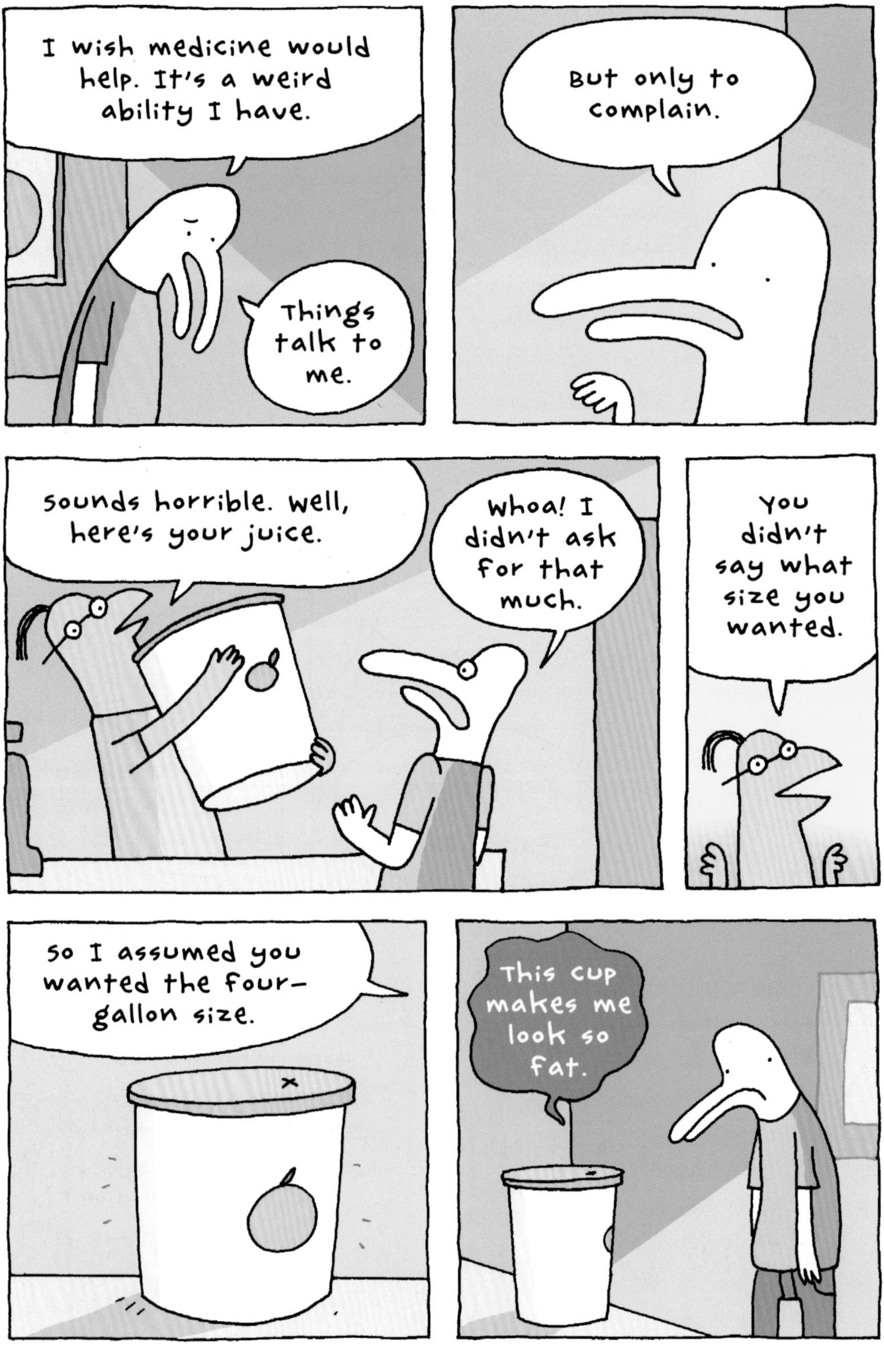
I wish medicine would help. It's a weird ability I have.
Things talk to me.
But only to complain.
Sounds horrible. Well, here's your juice.
Whoa! I didn't ask for that much.
You didn't say what size you wanted.
So I assumed you wanted the four-gallon size.
This cup makes me look so fat.

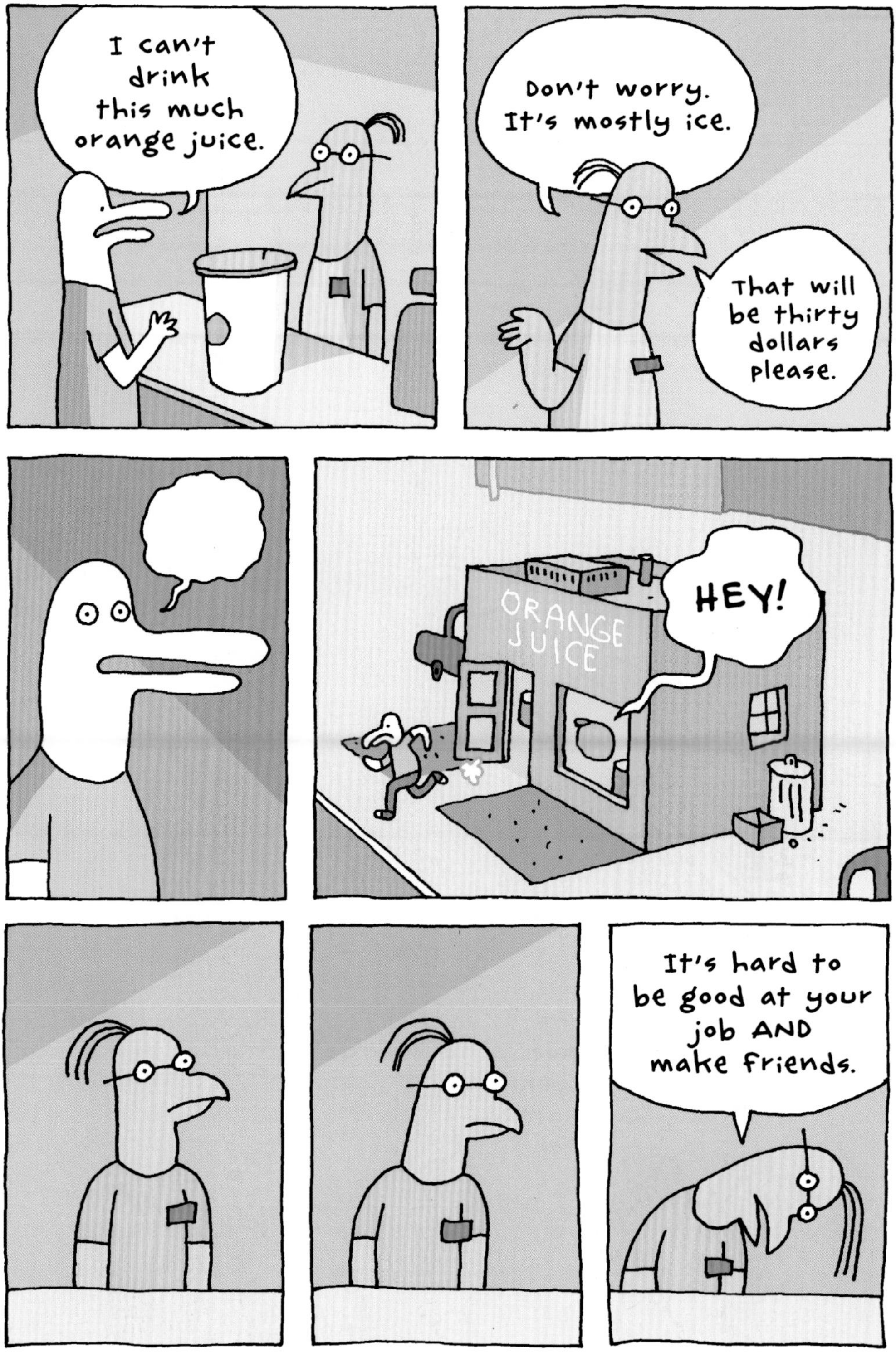
I can't drink this much orange juice.
Don't worry. It's mostly ice.
That will be thirty dollars please.
ORANGE JUICE
HEY!
It's hard to be good at your job AND make friends.

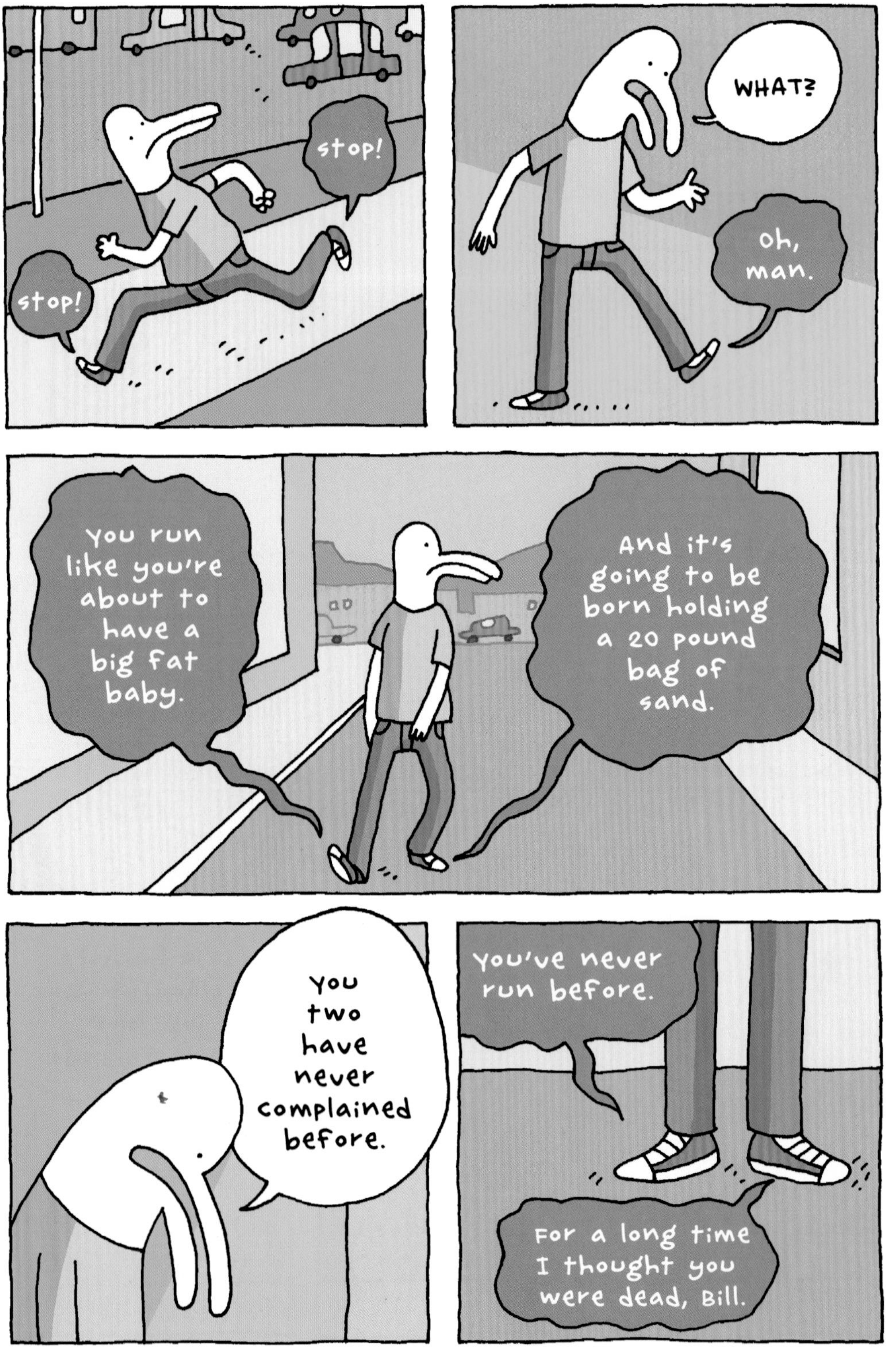
stop!
stop!
WHAT?
oh, man.
you run like you're about to have a big fat baby.
And it's going to be born holding a 20 pound bag of sand.
You two have never complained before.
You've never run before.
For a long time I thought you were dead, Bill.

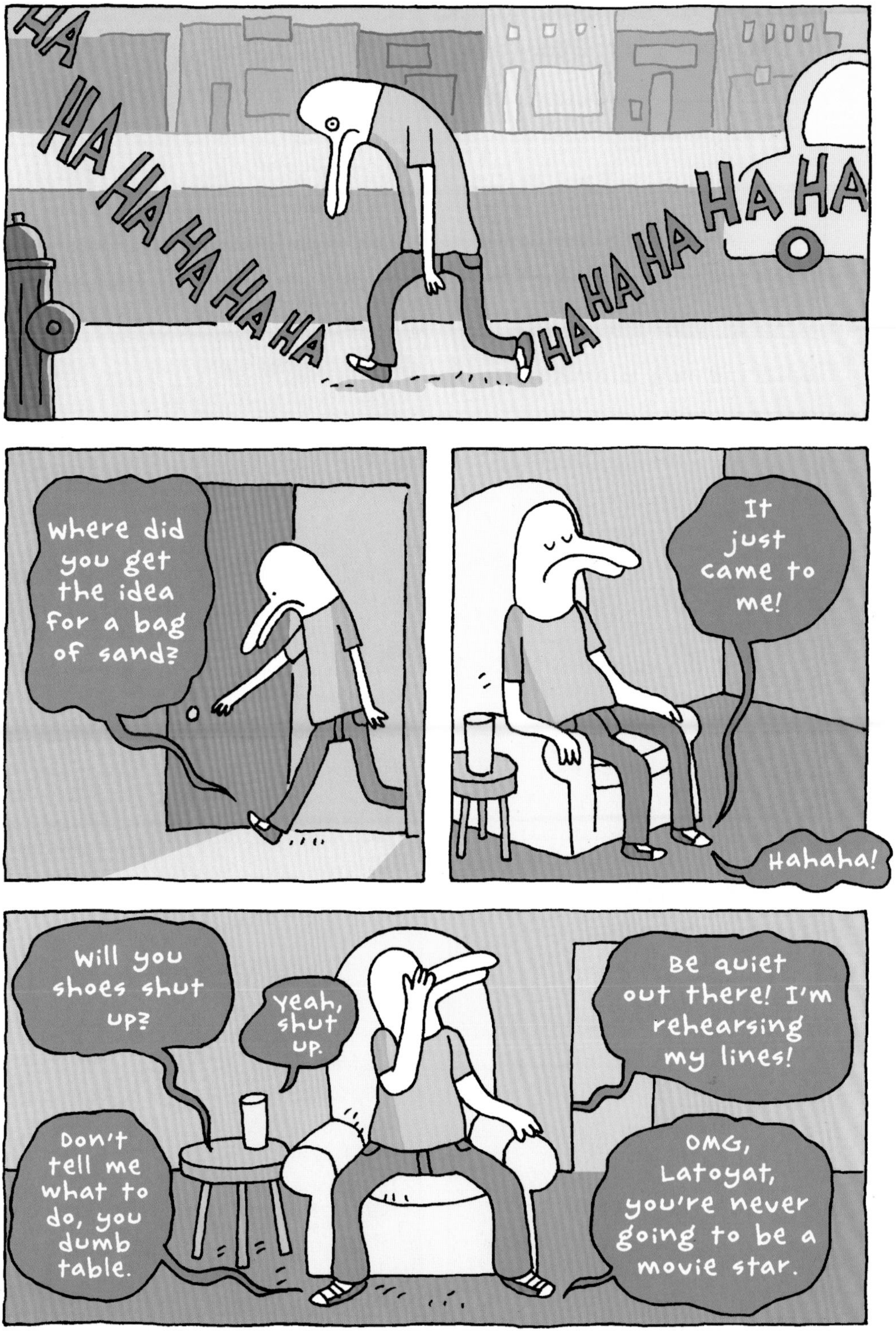
HA HA HA HA HA HA HA HA
HA HA HA HA HA HA HA
Where did you get the idea for a bag of sand?
It just came to me!
Hahaha!
Will you shoes shut up?
Yeah, shut up.
Be quiet out there! I'm rehearsing my lines!
Don't tell me what to do, you dumb table.
OMG, Latoyat, you're never going to be a movie star.

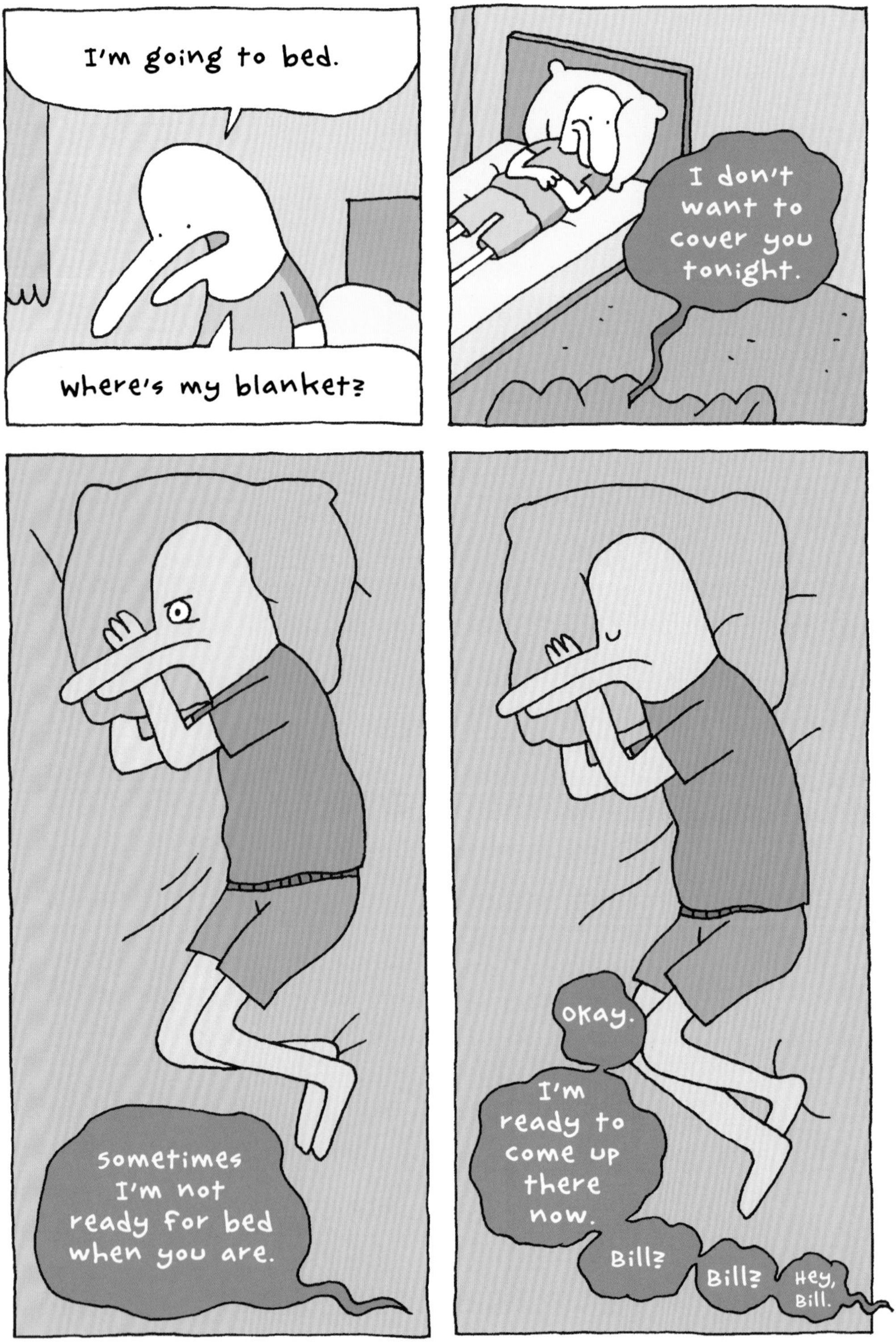
I'm going to bed.
Where's my blanket?
I don't want to cover you tonight.
Sometimes I'm not ready for bed when you are.
Okay.
I'm ready to come up there now.
Bill?
Bill?
Hey, Bill.

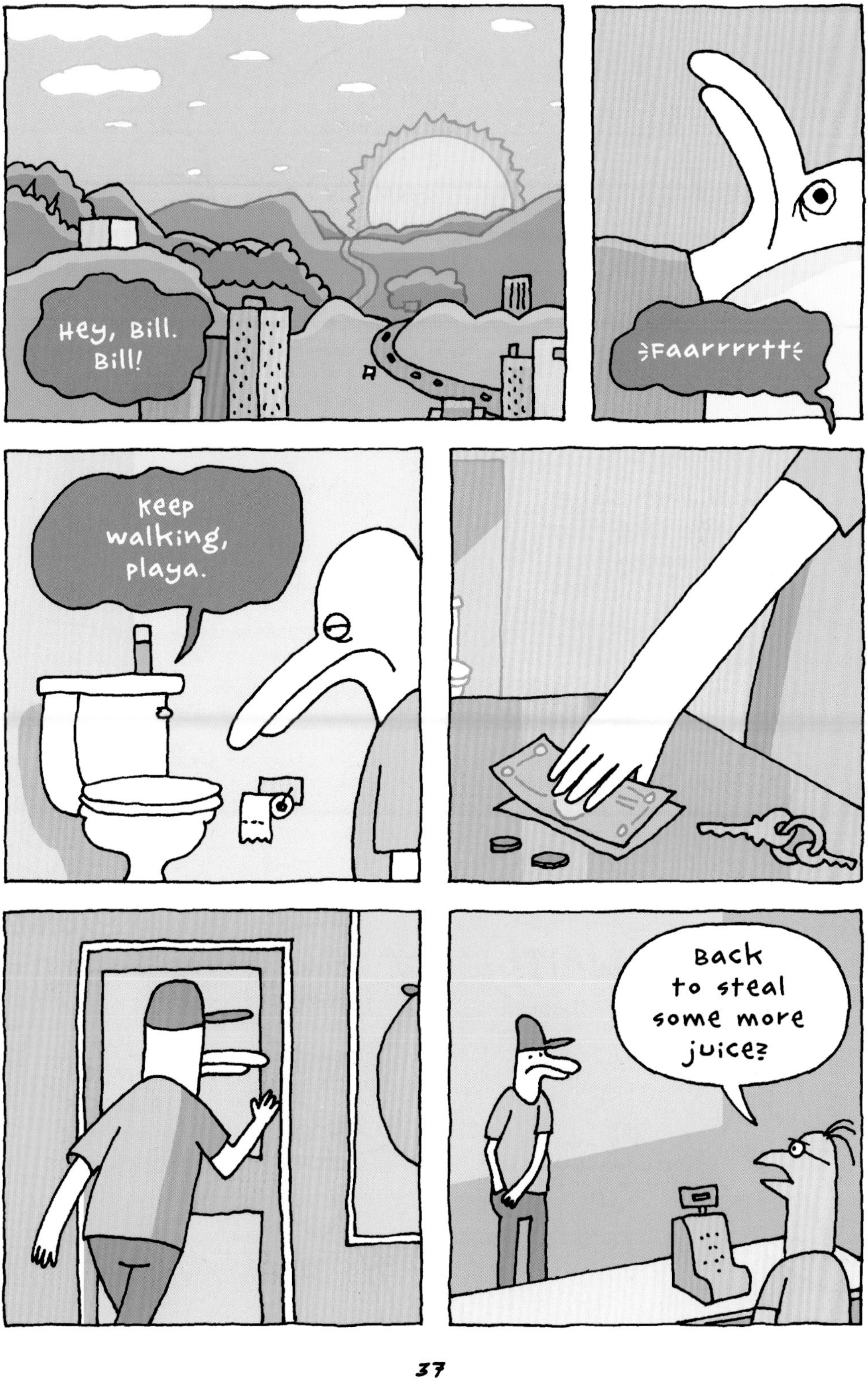
Hey, Bill.
Bill!
Faarrrrtt
Keep walking, playa.
Back to steal some more juice?

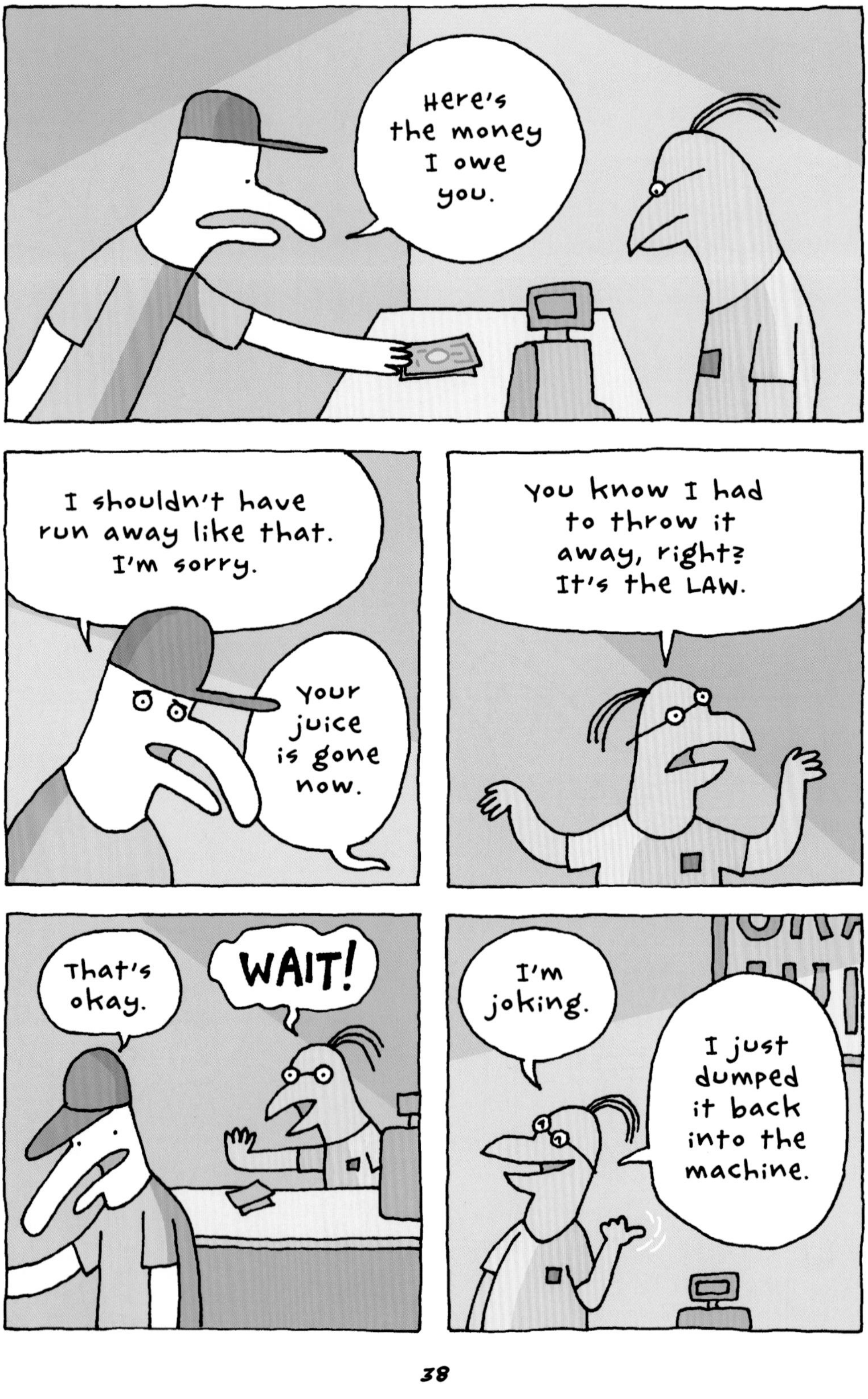
Here's the money I owe you.
I shouldn't have run away like that. I'm sorry.
Your juice is gone now.
You know I had to throw it away, right? It's the LAW.
That's okay.
WAIT!
I'm joking.
I just dumped it back into the machine.

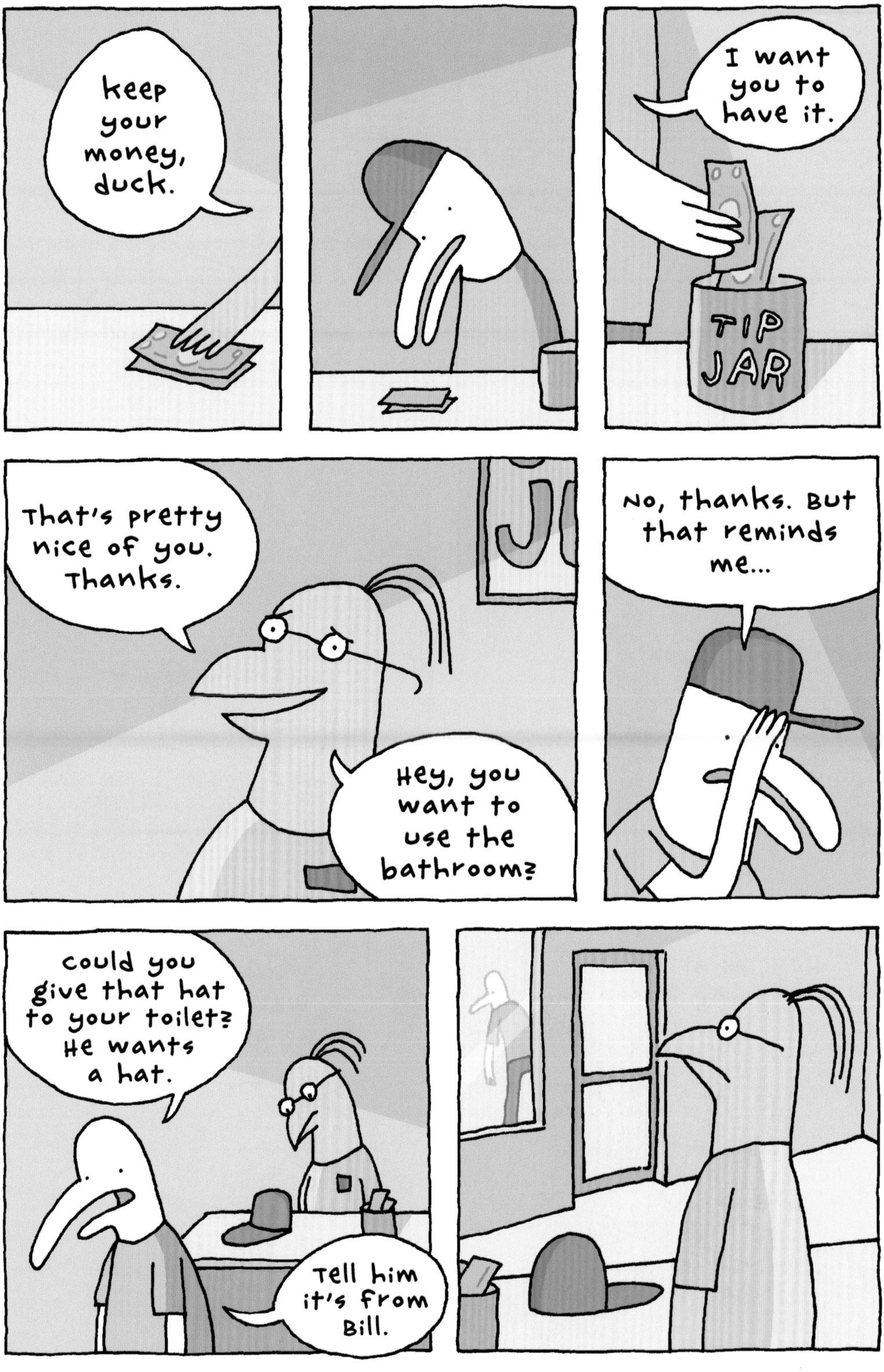
keep your money, duck.
I want you to have it.
TIP JAR
That's pretty nice of you. Thanks.
Hey, you want to use the bathroom?
No, thanks. But that reminds me...
could you give that hat to your toilet? He wants a hat.
Tell him it's from Bill.

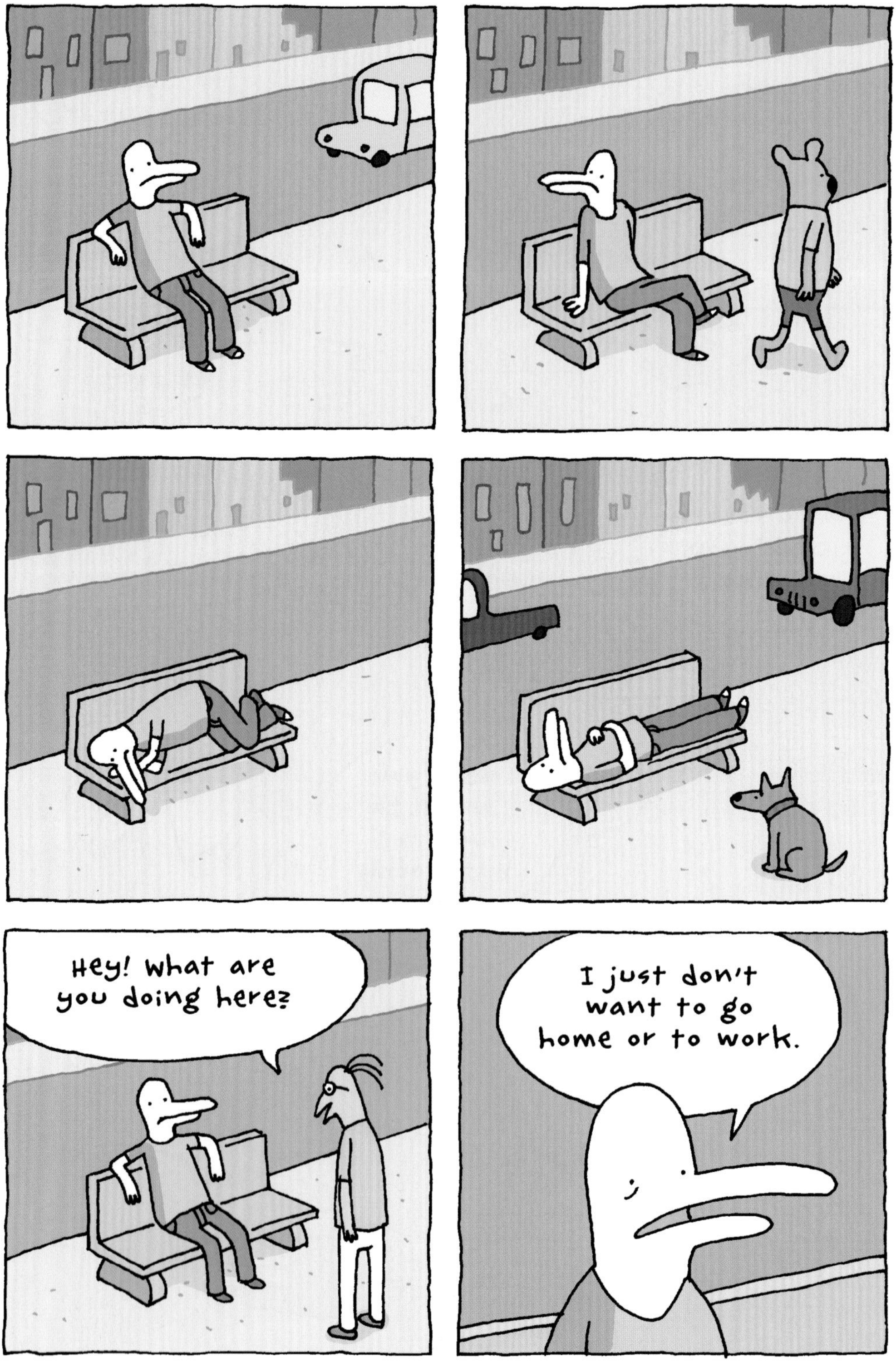
Hey! What are
you doing here?
I just don't
want to go
home or to work.

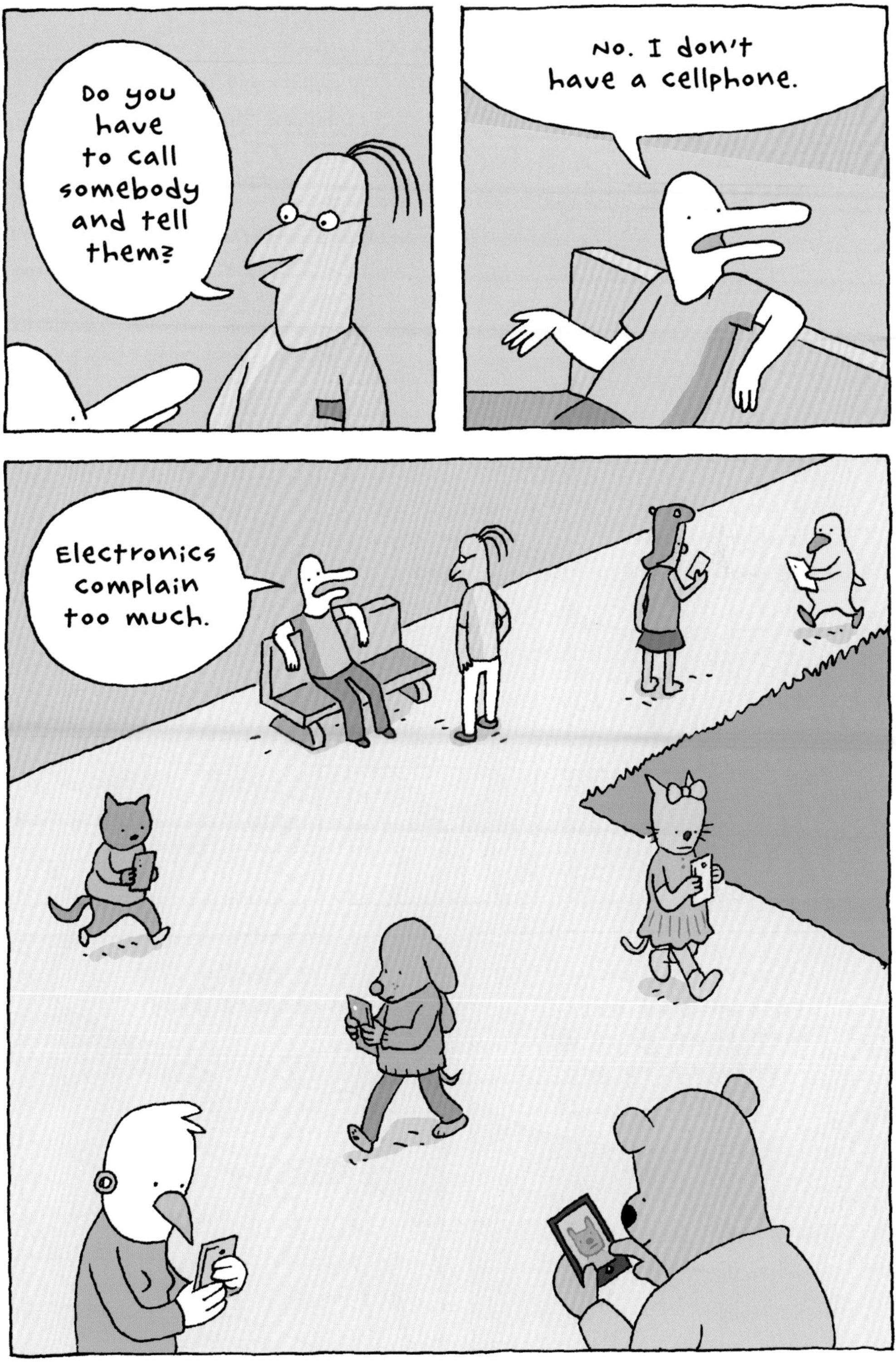
Do you have to call somebody and tell them?
No. I don't have a cellphone.
Electronics complain too much.

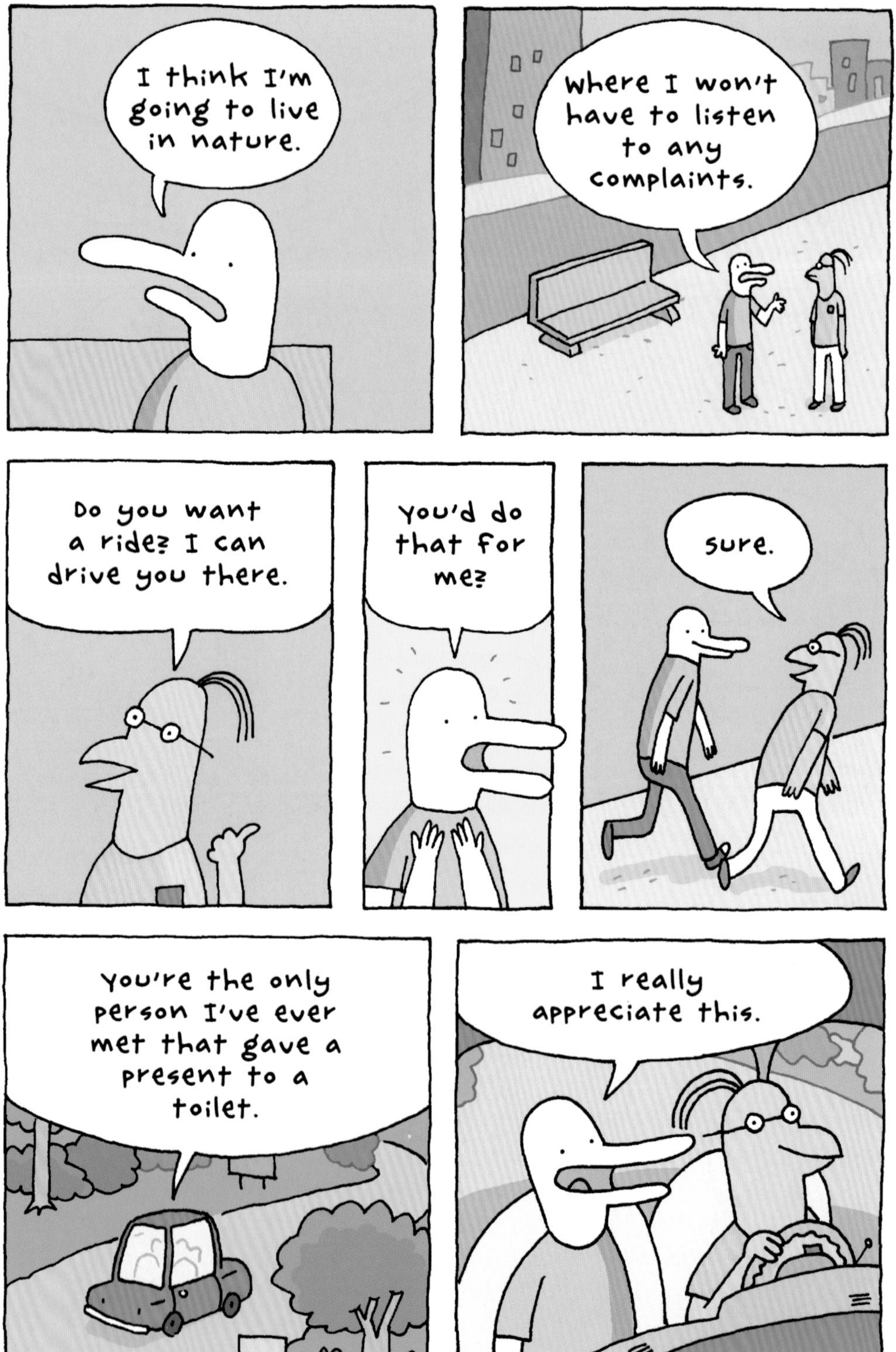
I think I'm going to live in nature.
Where I won't have to listen to any complaints.
Do you want a ride? I can drive you there.
You'd do that for me?
Sure.
You're the only person I've ever met that gave a present to a toilet.
I really appreciate this.

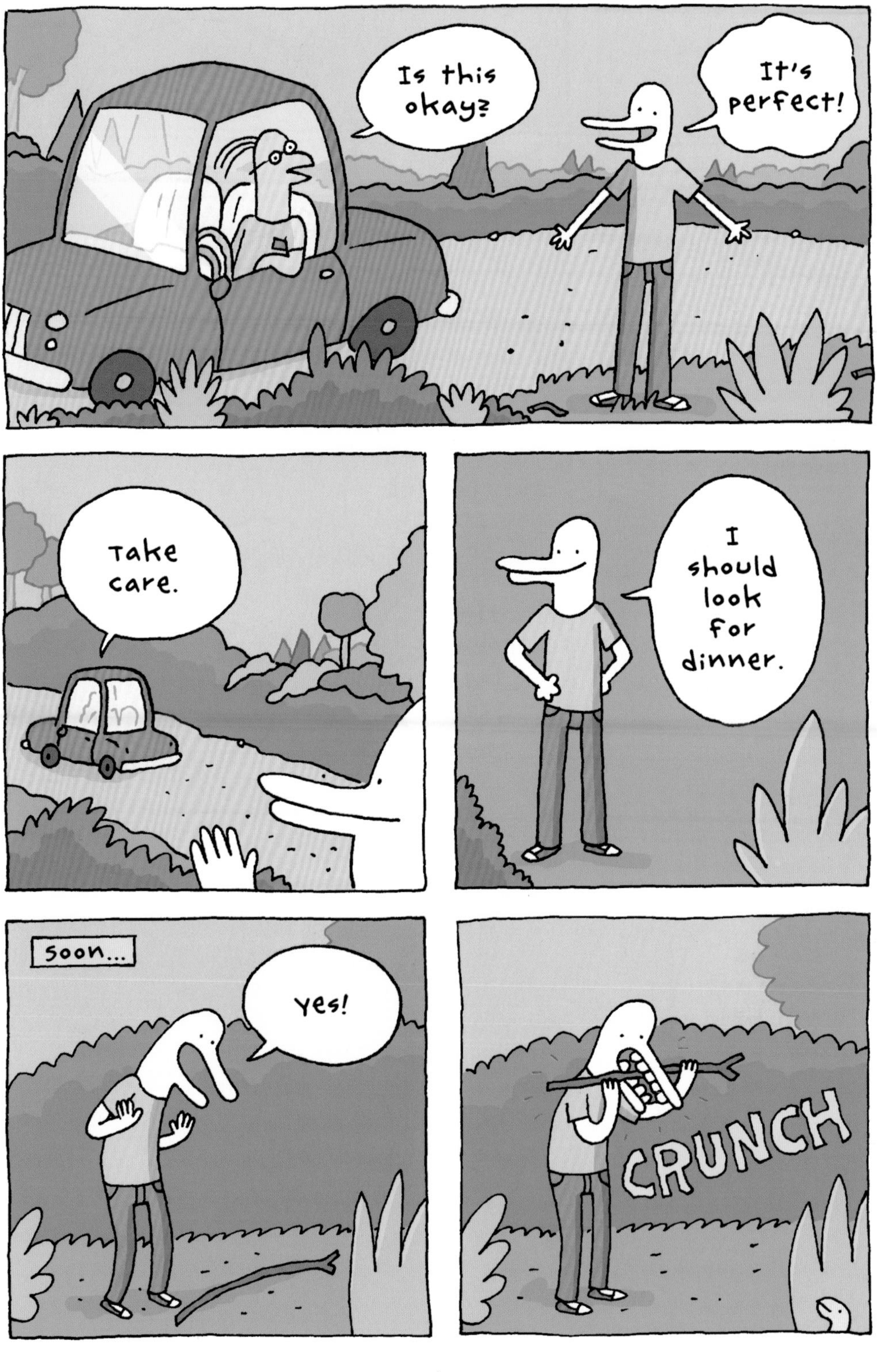
Is this okay?
It's perfect!
Take care.
I should look for dinner.
soon...
yes!
CRUNCH

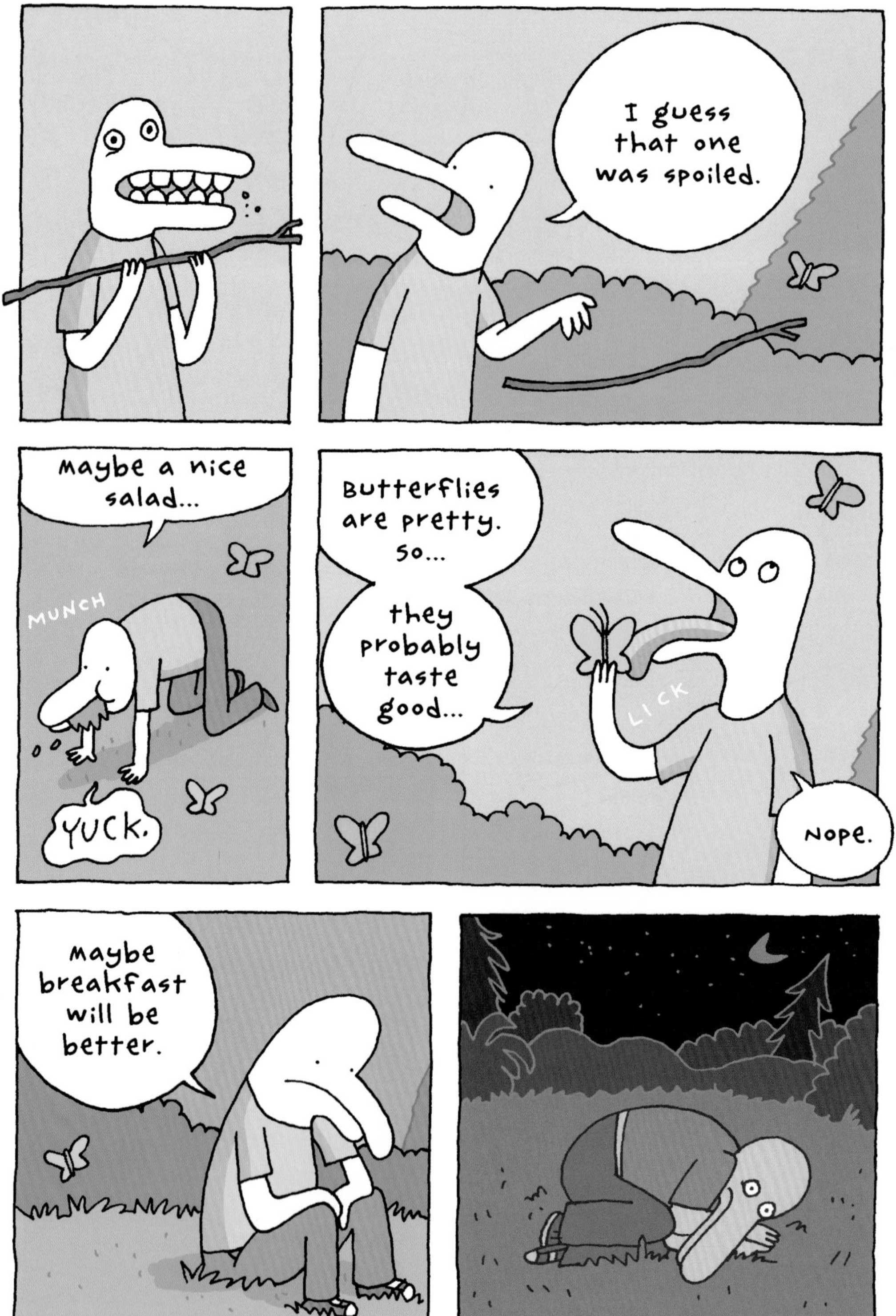
I guess that one was spoiled.
Maybe a nice salad...
MUNCH
YUCK.
Butterflies are pretty. So...
they probably taste good...
LICK
Nope.
Maybe breakfast will be better.

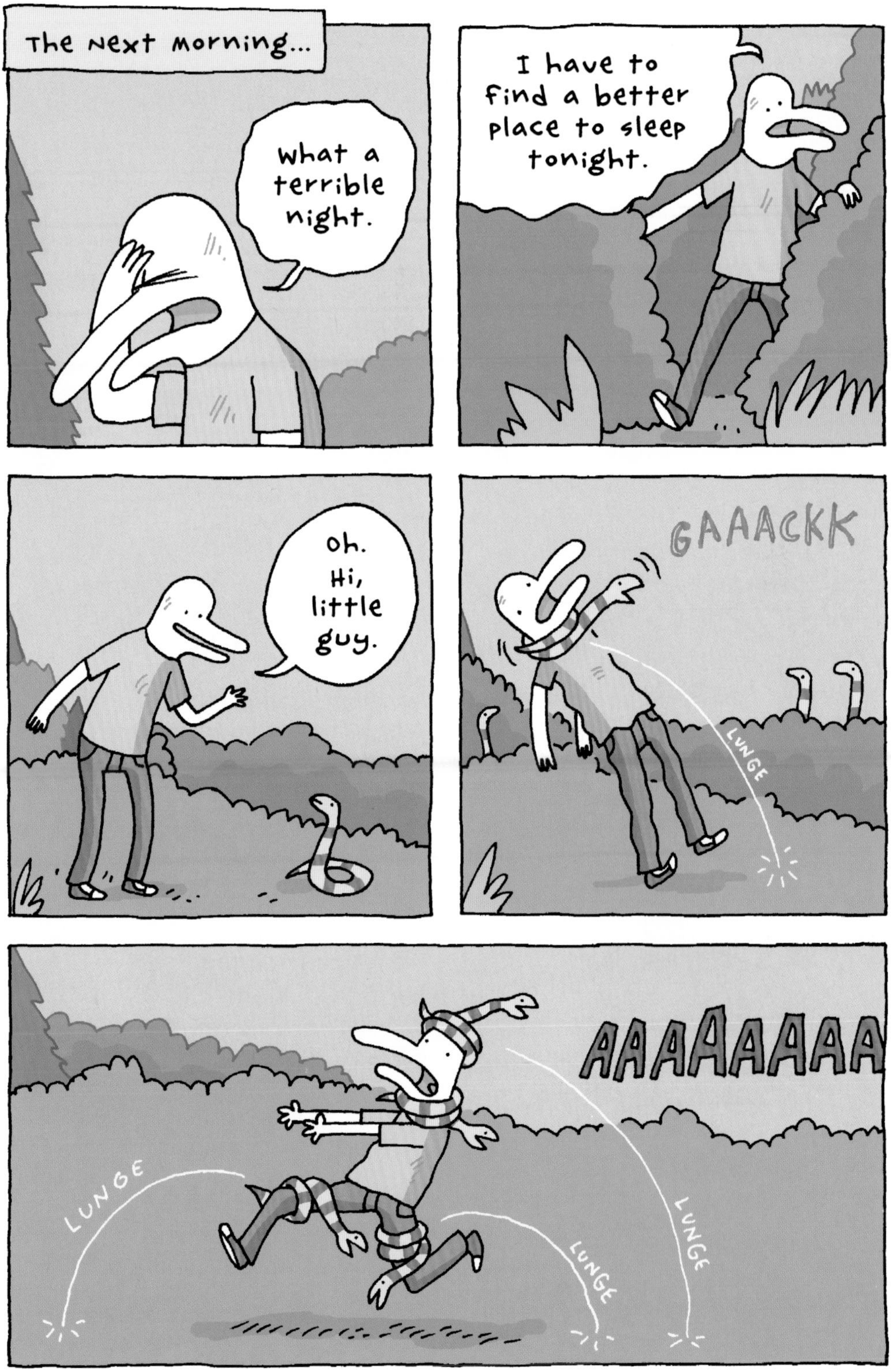
The next morning...
What a terrible night.
I have to find a better place to sleep tonight.
Oh. Hi, little guy.
GAAACKK
LUNGE
AAAAAAAA
LUNGE
LUNGE
LUNGE

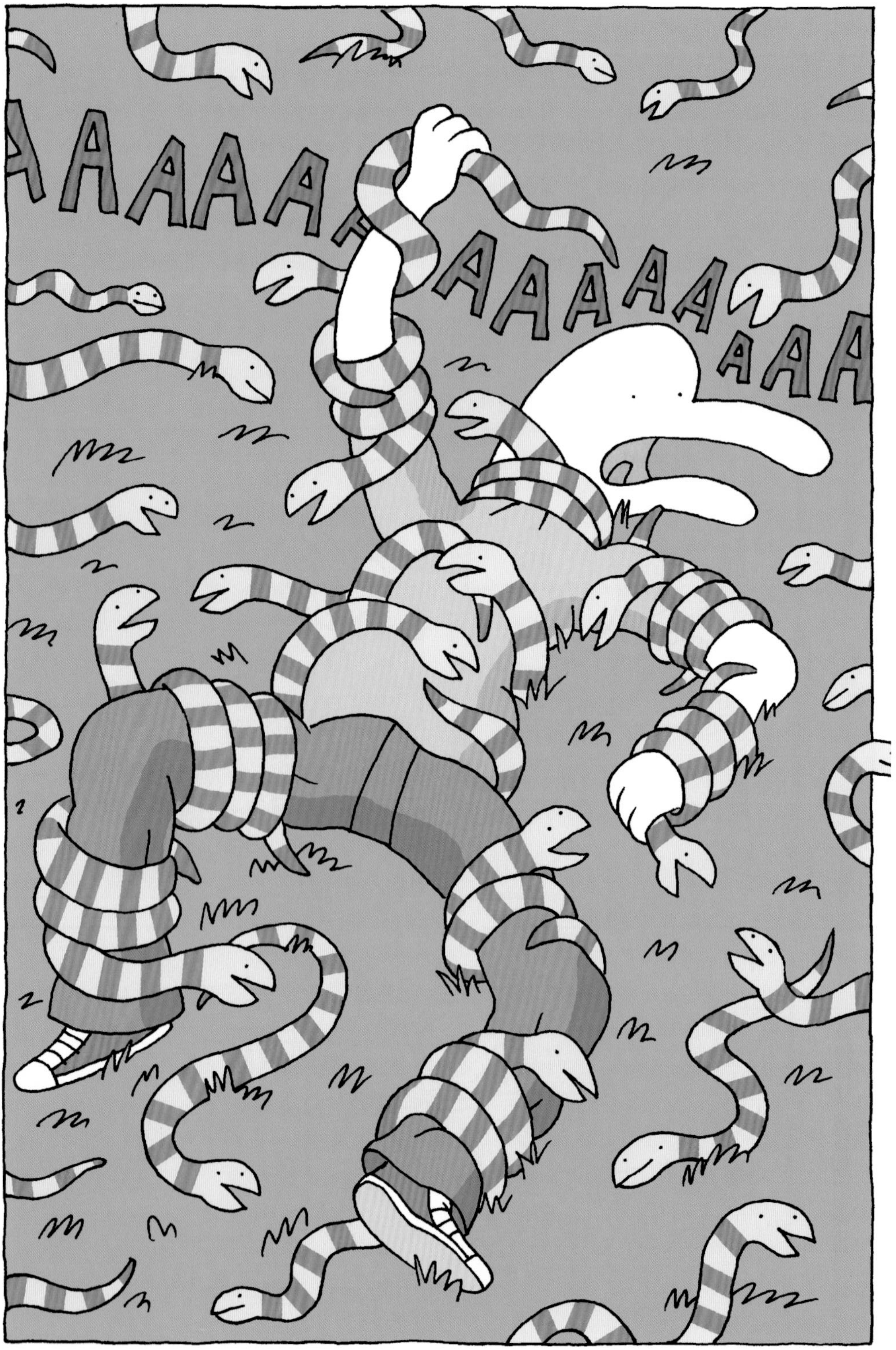
AAAAAAAAAAAAAA

CHAPTER TWO

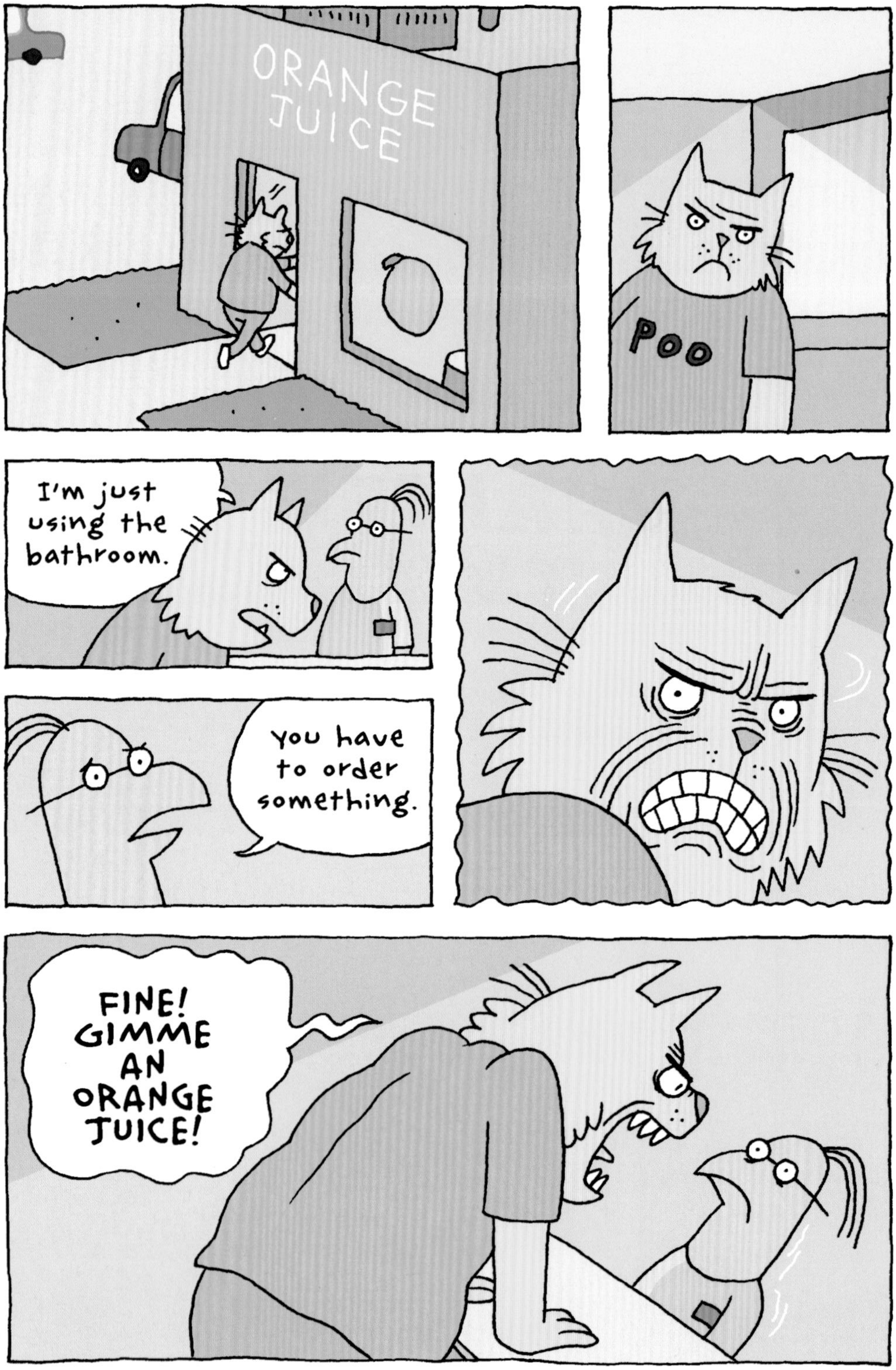
ORANGE JUICE
POO
I'm just using the bathroom.
you have to order something.
FINE! GIMME AN ORANGE JUICE!

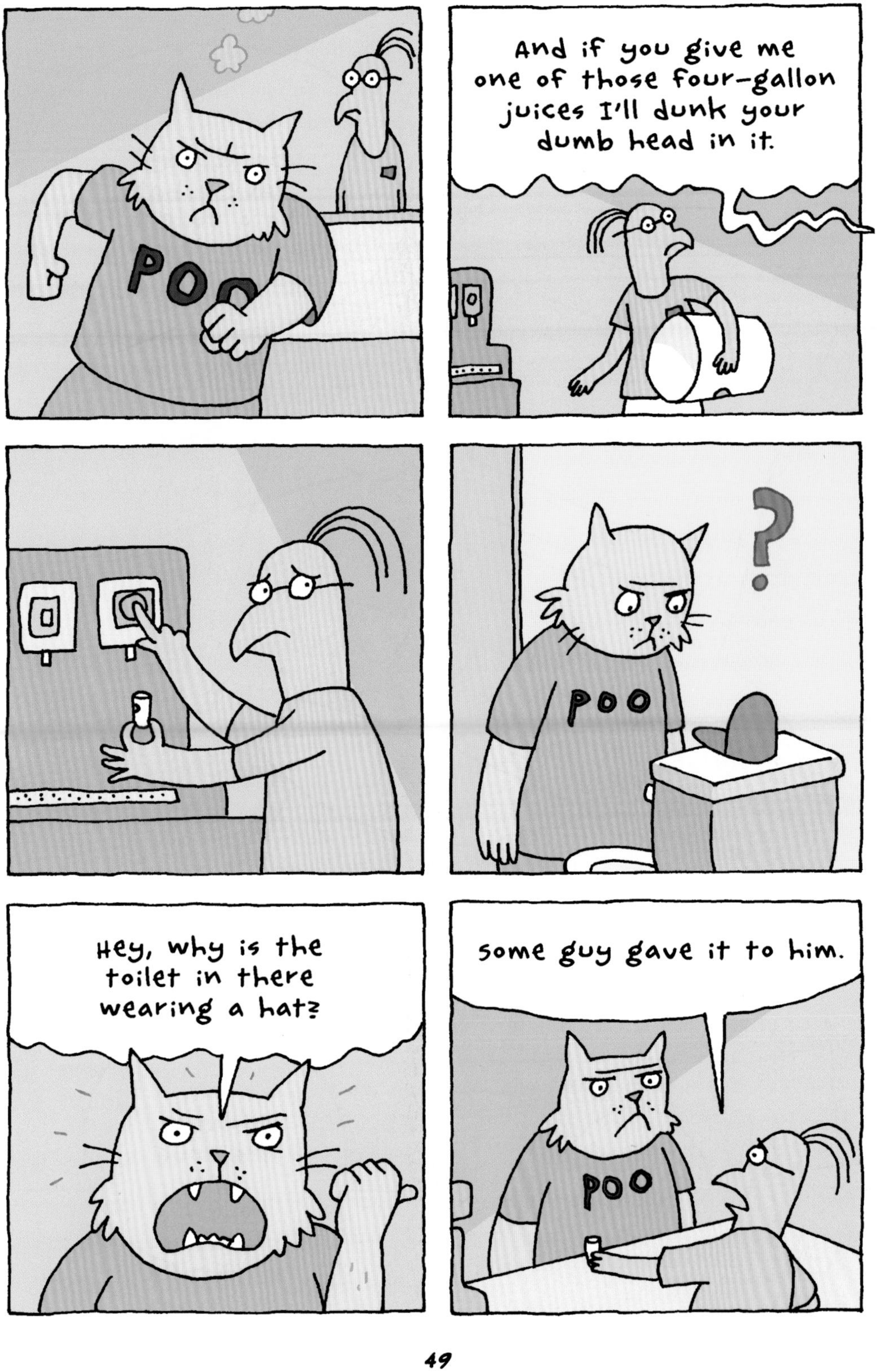
POO
And if you give me one of those four-gallon juices I'll dunk your dumb head in it.
?
POO
Hey, why is the toilet in there wearing a hat?
Some guy gave it to him.
POO

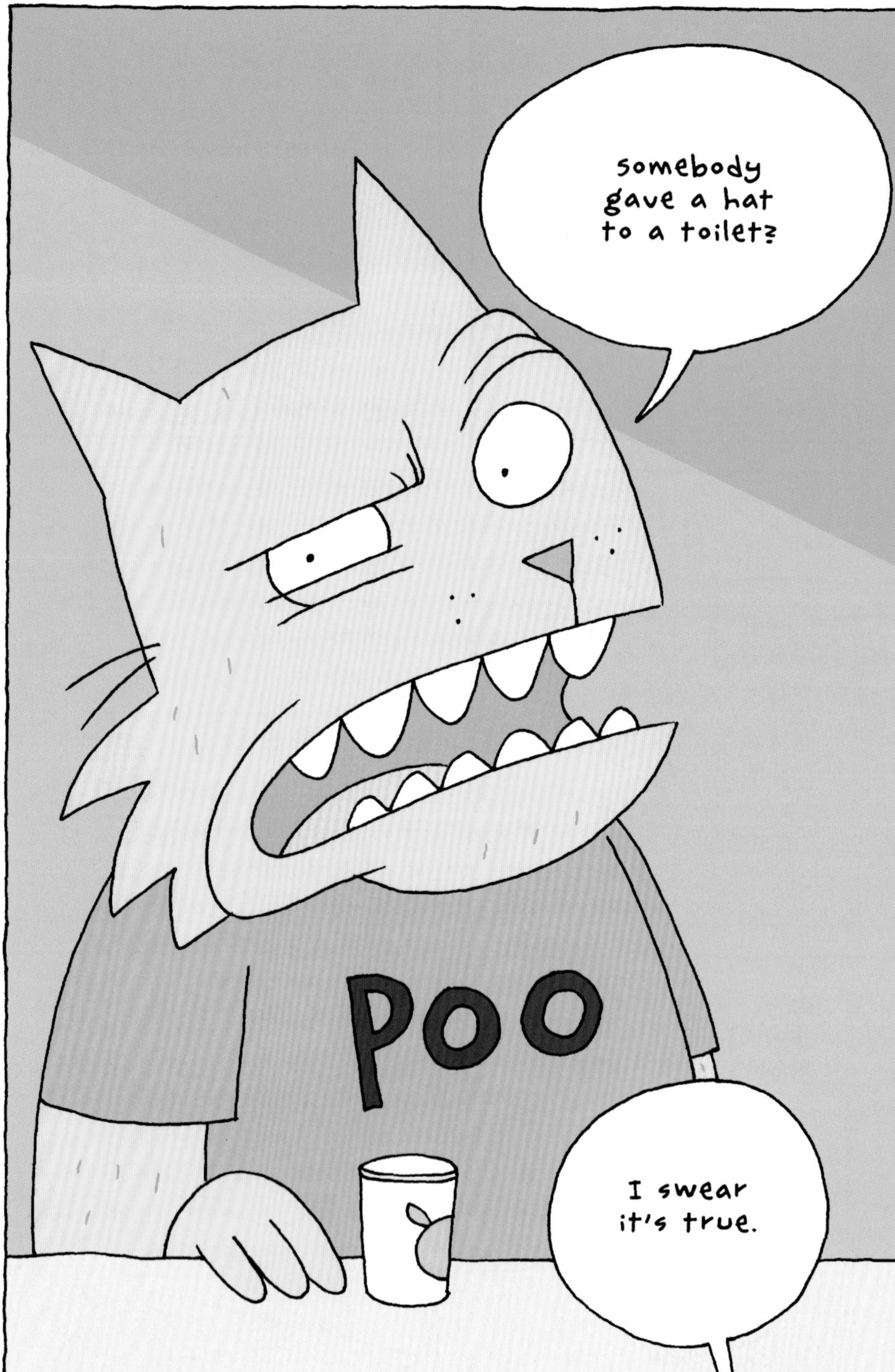
somebody gave a hat to a toilet?
POO
I swear it's true.

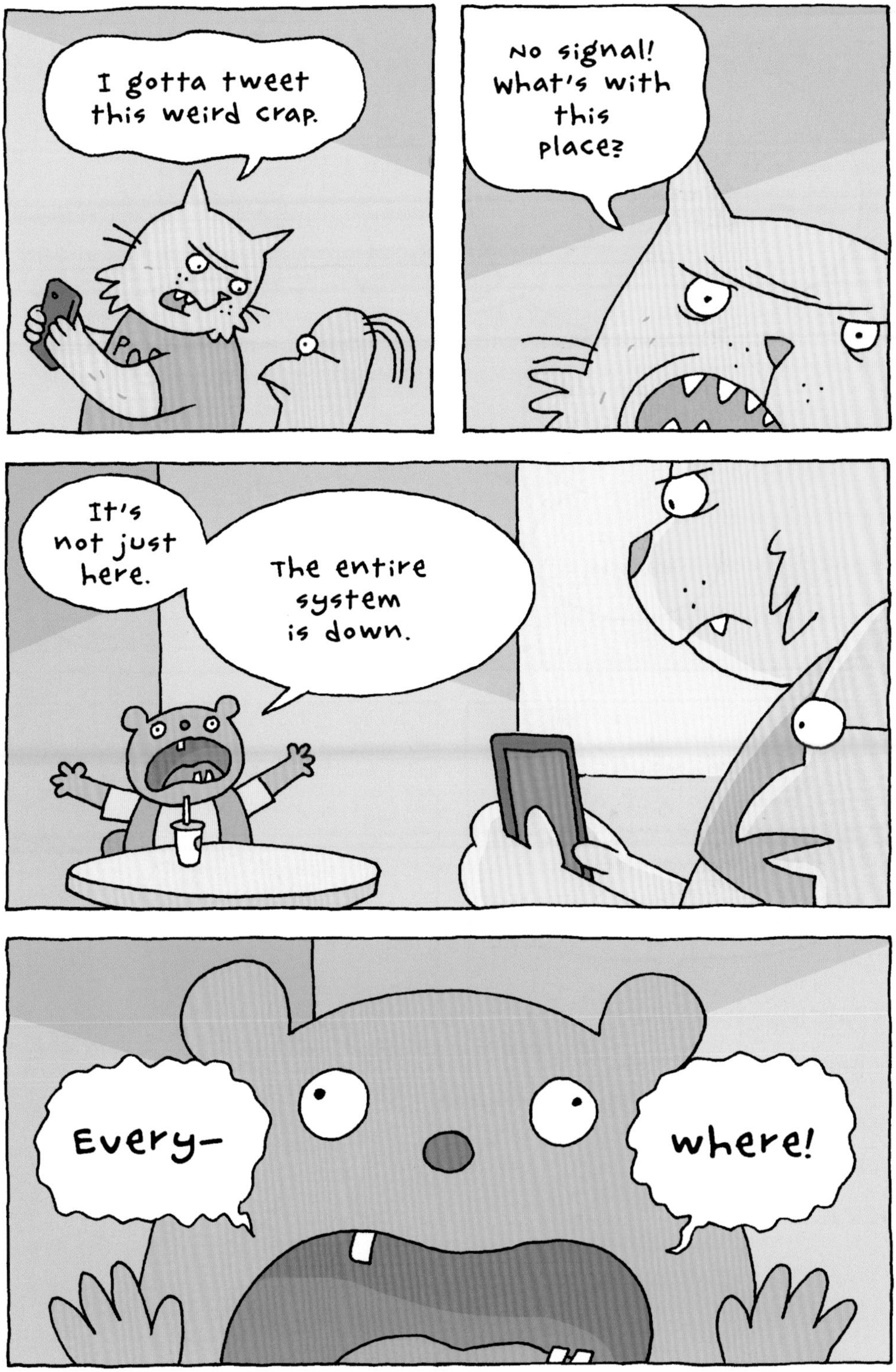
I gotta tweet this weird crap.
No signal! What's with this place?
It's not just here.
The entire system is down.
Every-
where!

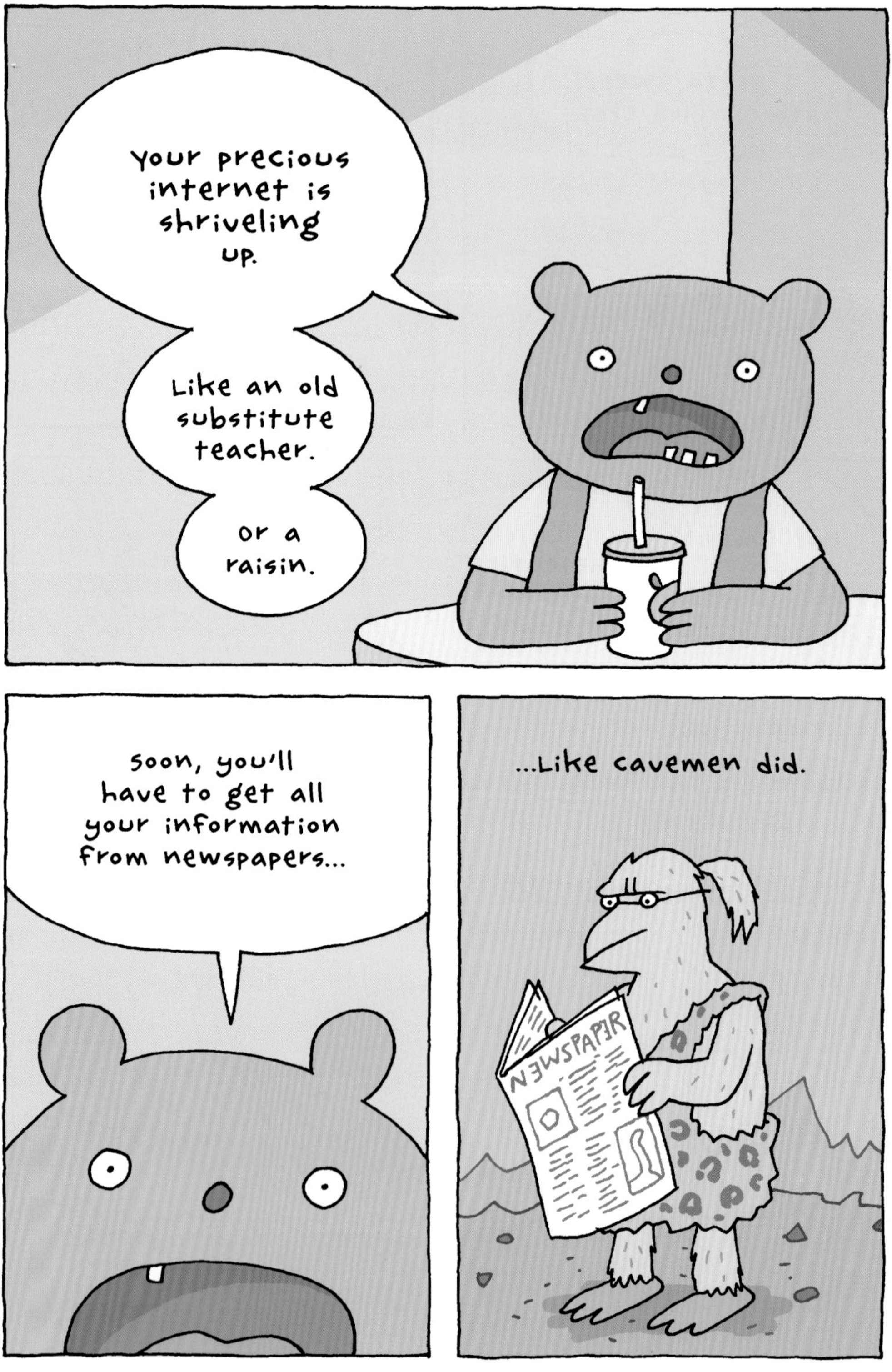
Your precious internet is shriveling up.
Like an old substitute teacher.
Or a raisin.
Soon, you'll have to get all your information from newspapers...
...Like cavemen did.
NEWSPAPER

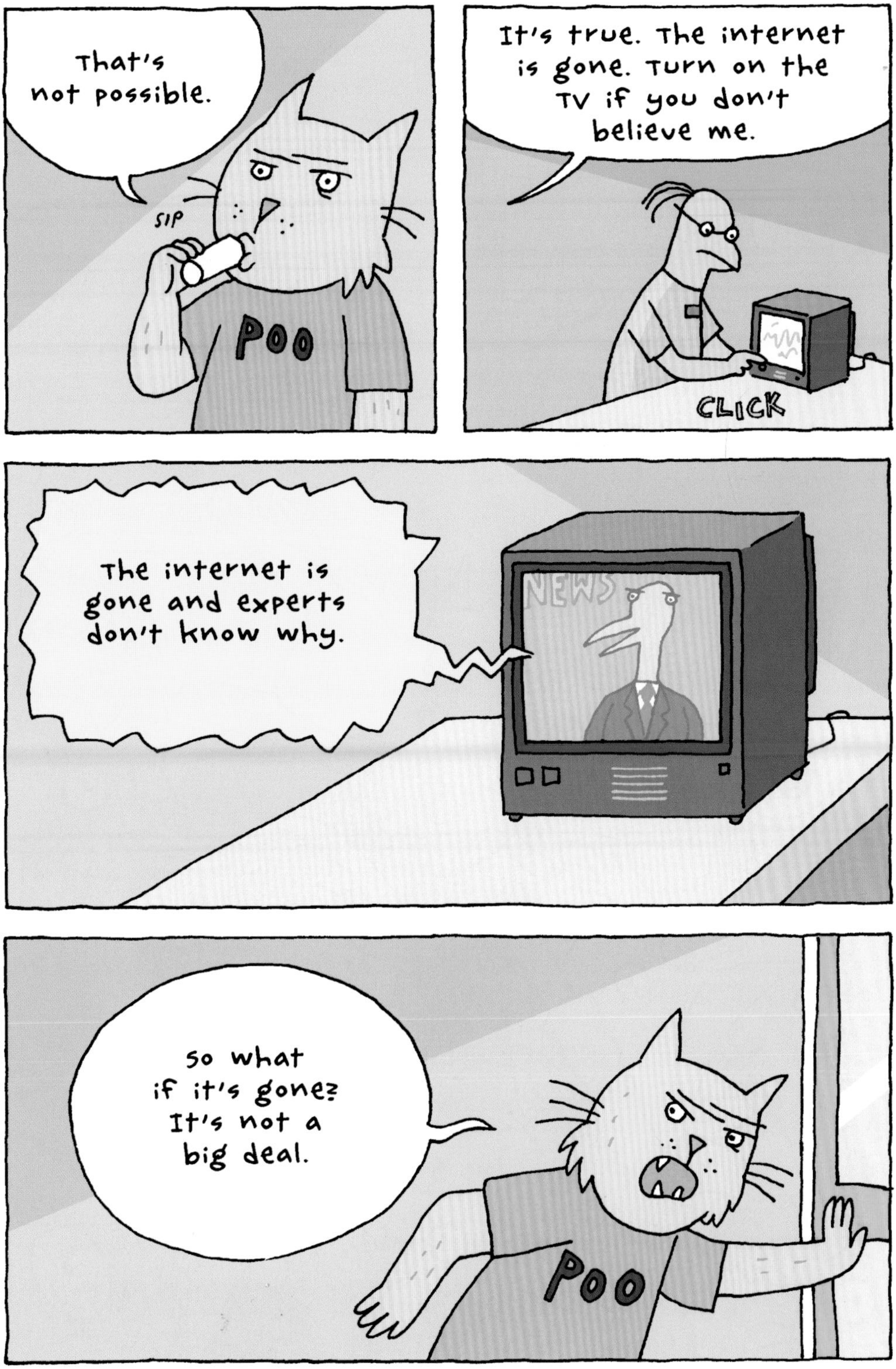
That's not possible.
SIP
POO
It's true. The internet is gone. Turn on the TV if you don't believe me.
CLICK
NEWS
The internet is gone and experts don't know why.
So what if it's gone? It's not a big deal.
POO

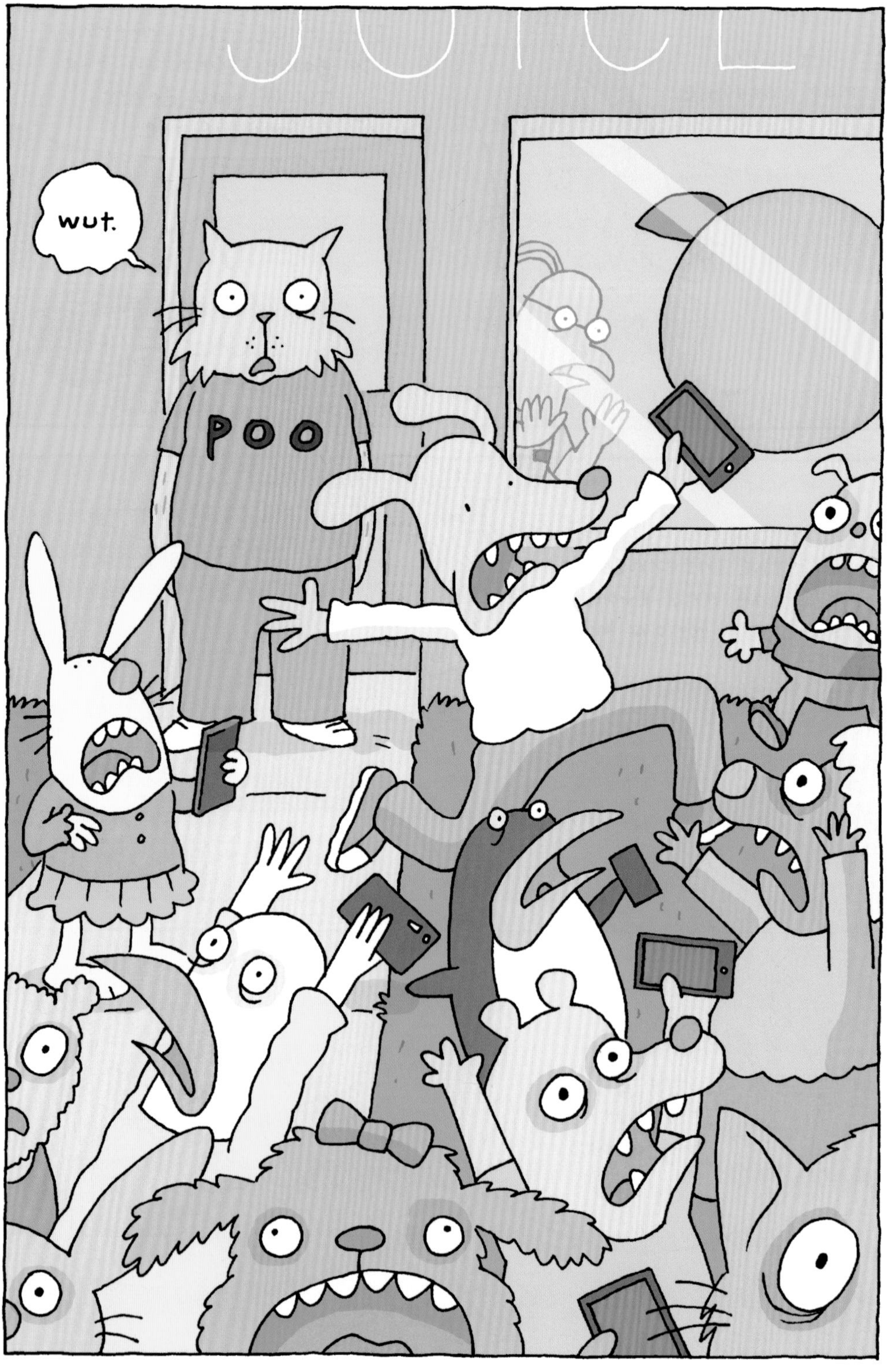
JUICE
wut.
POO

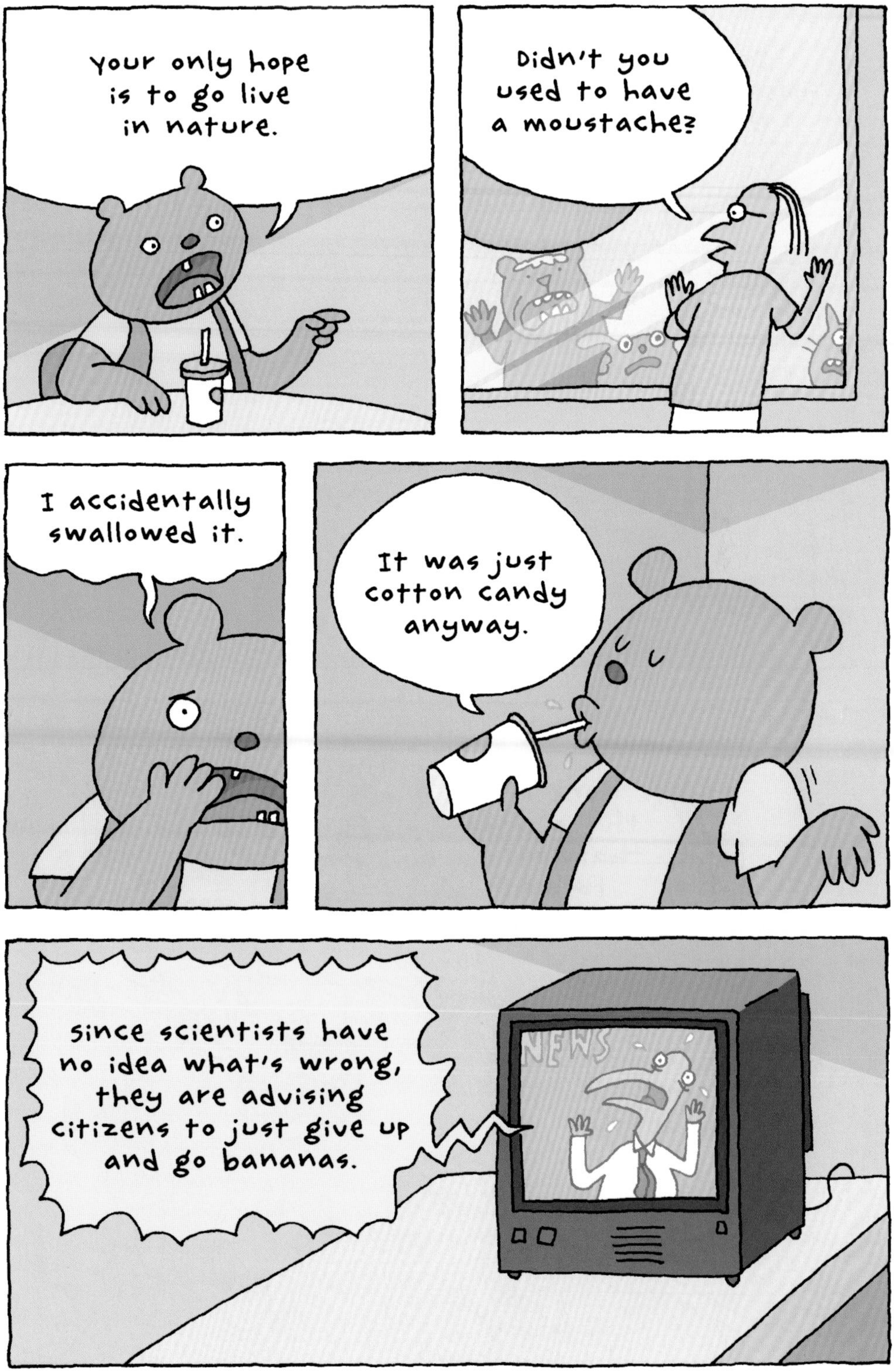

your only hope is to go live in nature.
Didn't you used to have a moustache?
I accidentally swallowed it.
It was just cotton candy anyway.
since scientists have no idea what's wrong, they are advising citizens to just give up and go bananas.
NEWS

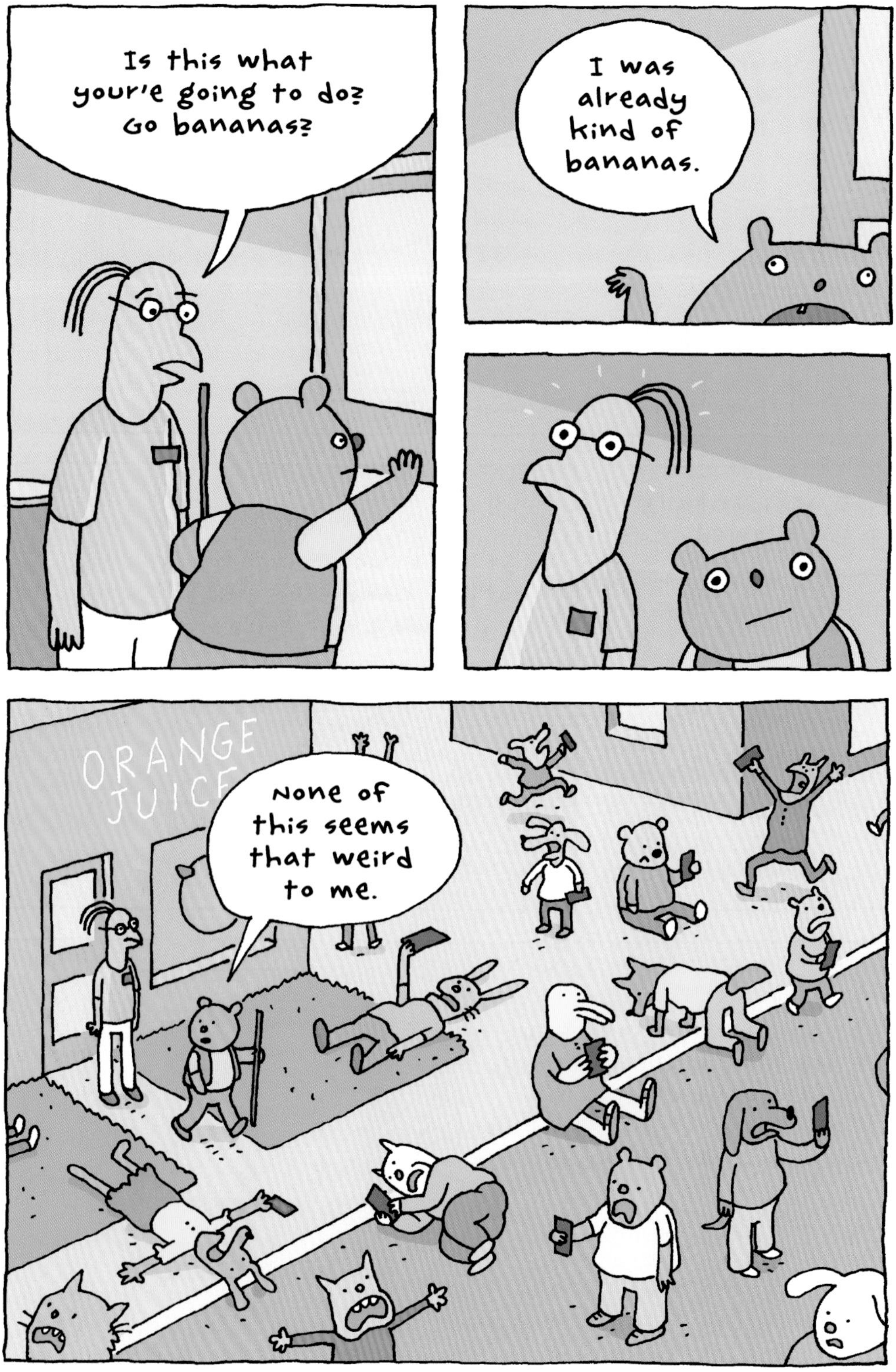
Is this what your'e going to do? Go bananas?
I was already kind of bananas.
ORANGE JUICE
None of this seems that weird to me.

I bet this is like when the electricity goes out. They'll get it fixed soon.

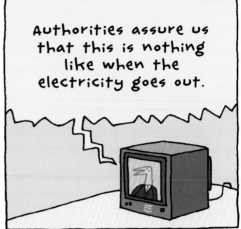

Authorities assure us that this is nothing like when the electricity goes out.

And it won't be fixed soon.

And since pretty much everything is connected to the internet, it won't be long before everything just shuts down.

SPUTTER FIZZLE CLICK

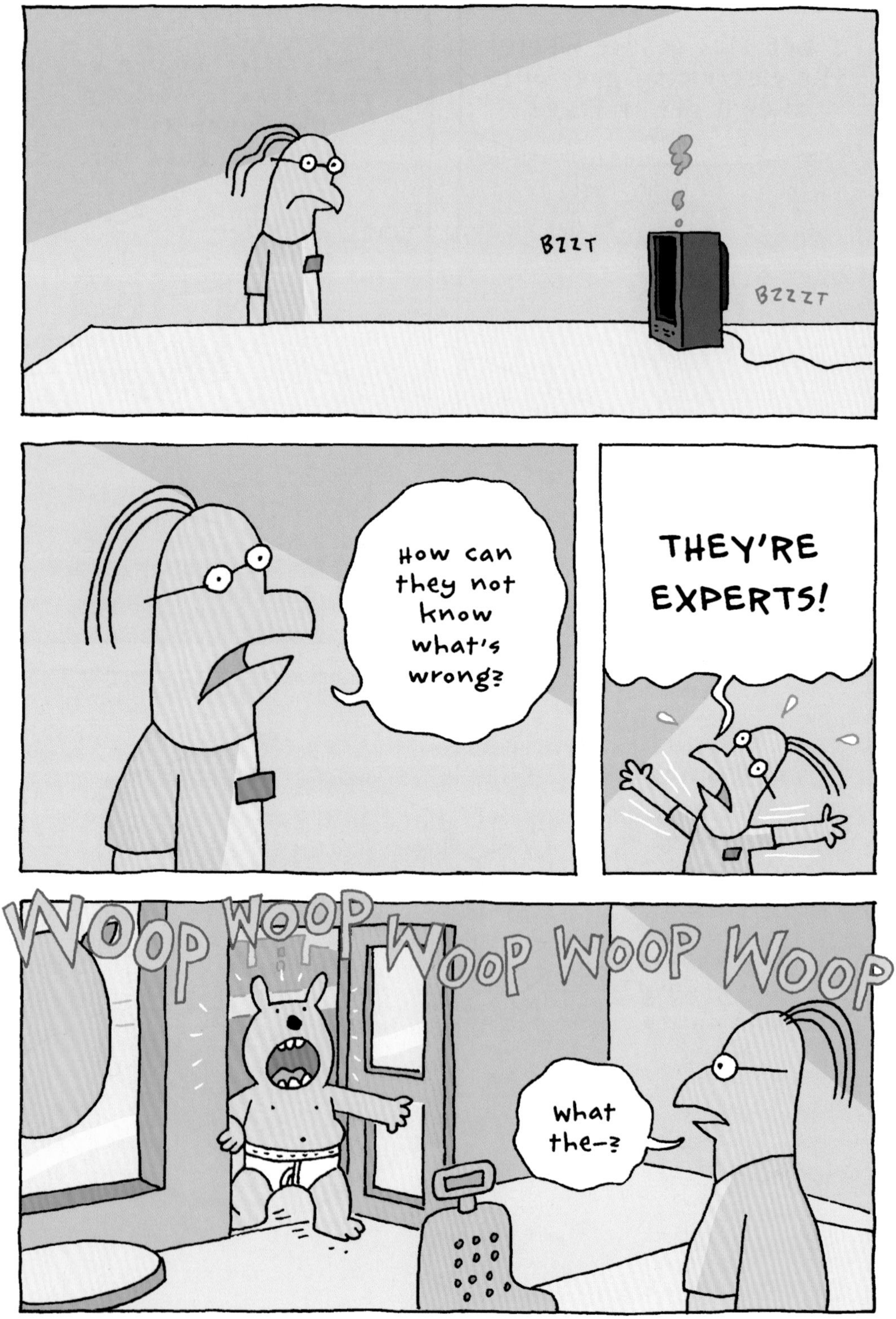
BZZT
BZZZT
How can they not know what's wrong?
THEY'RE EXPERTS!
WOOP WOOP WOOP WOOP WOOP
What the-?

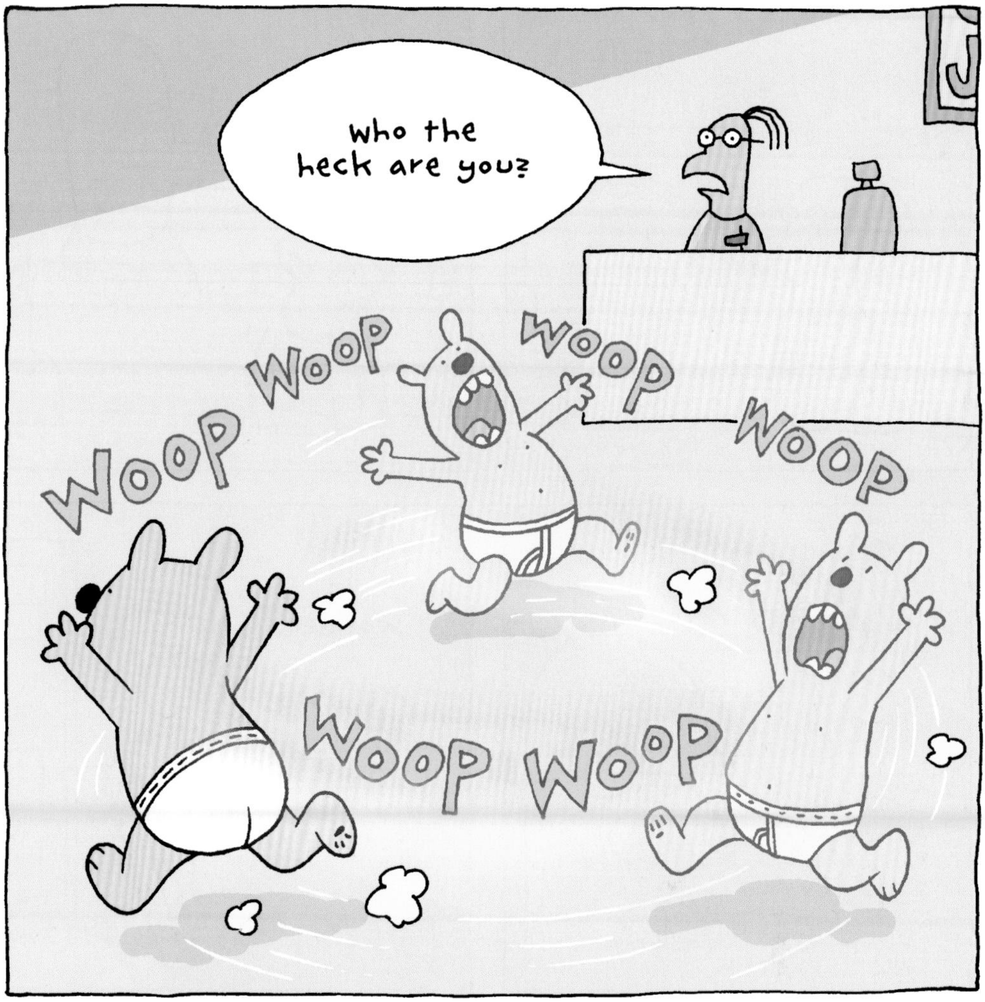
who the heck are you?
WOOP WOOP WOOP WOOP
WOOP WOOP

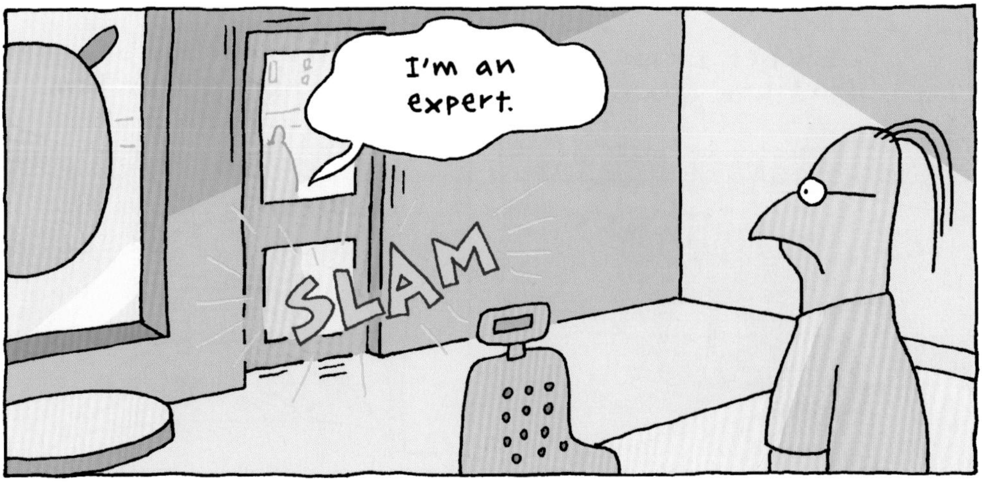
I'm an expert.
SLAM

I wonder...

I'll bet I can
find him again.

He'll probably be
right where I left him.

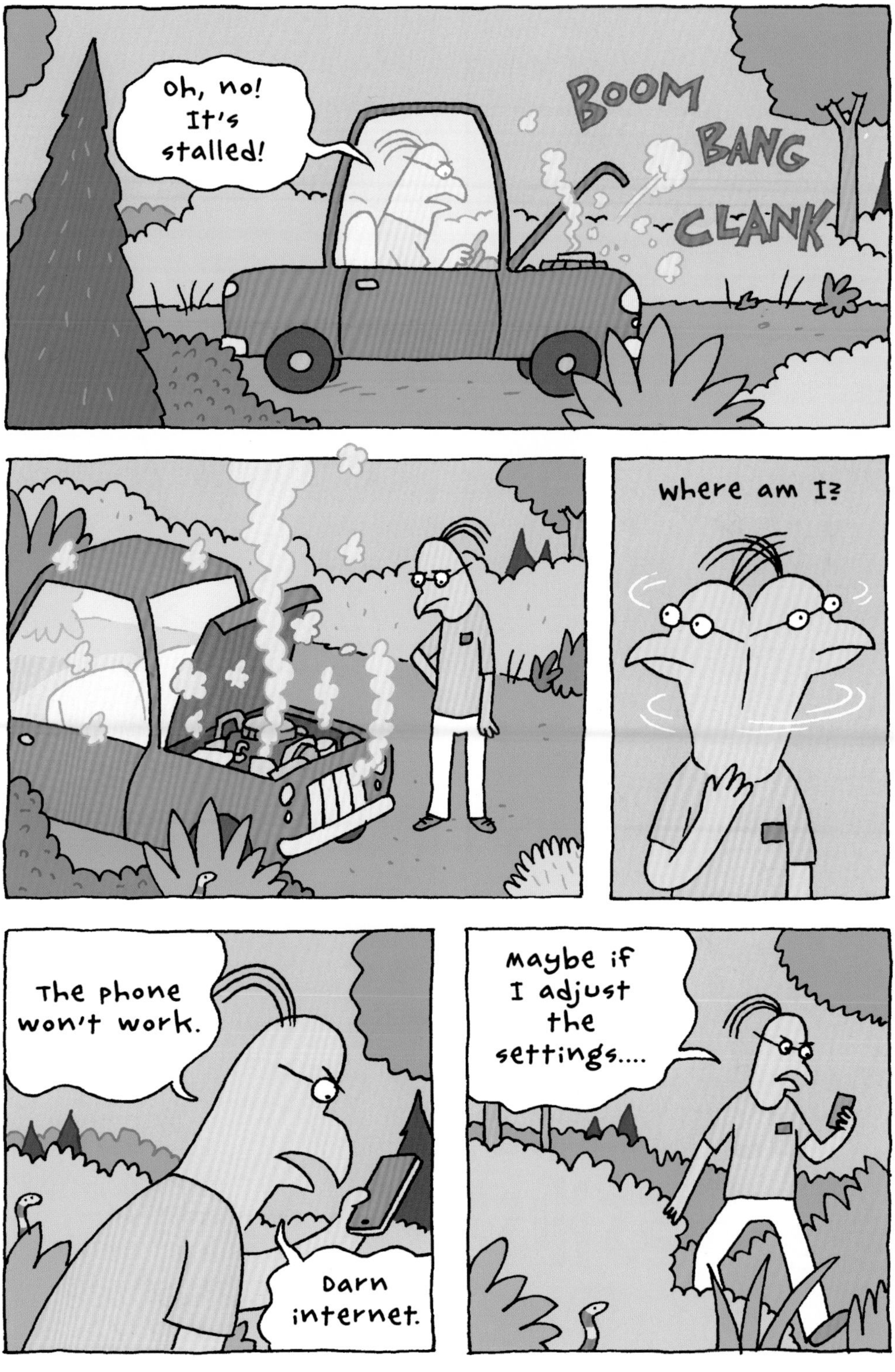
Oh, no! It's stalled!
BOOM
BANG
CLANK
Where am I?
The phone won't work.
Darn internet.
Maybe if I adjust the settings....

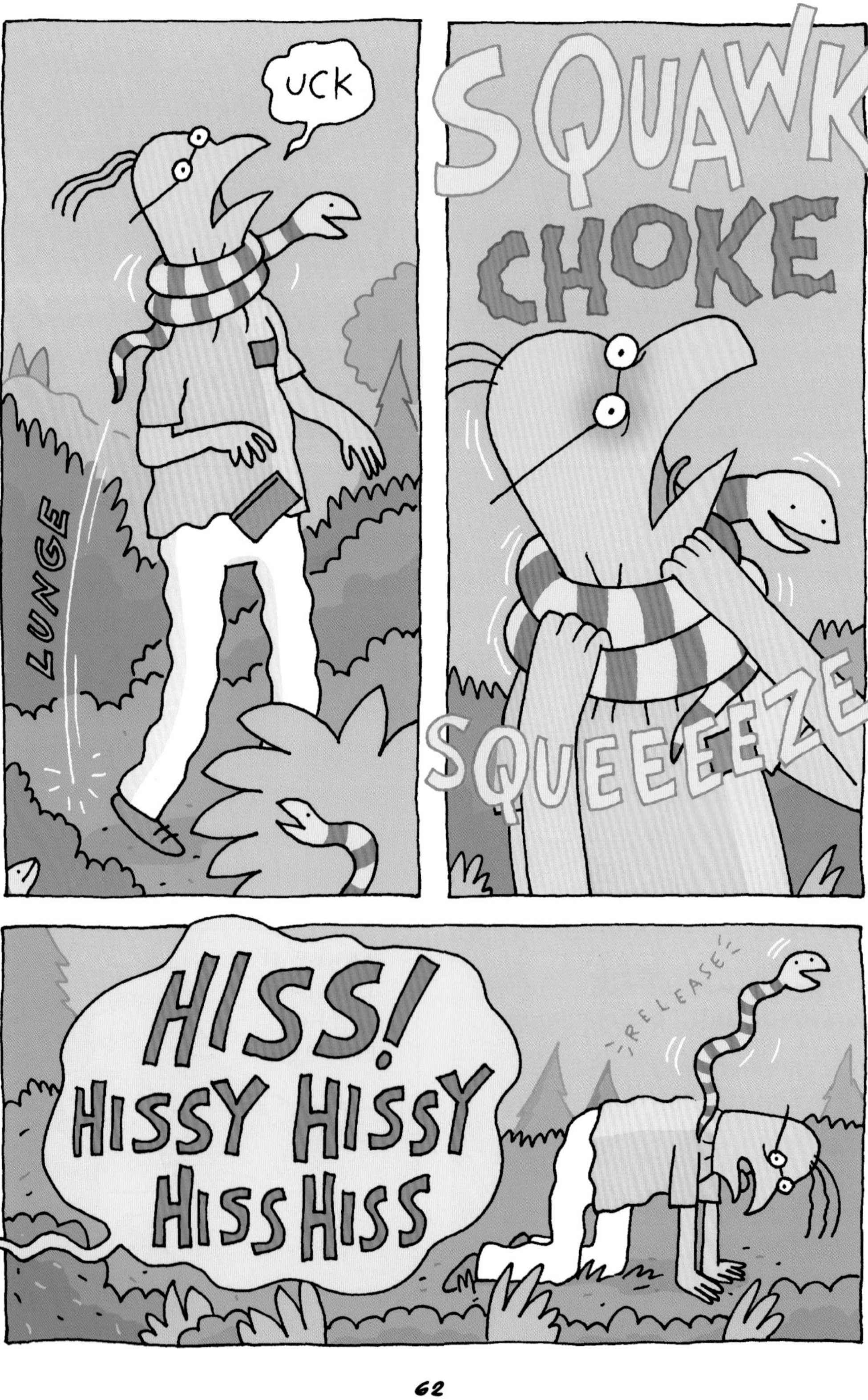
UCK
LUNGE
SQUAWK
CHOKE
SQUEEEEZE
HISS!
HISSY HISSY
HISS HISS
RELEASE

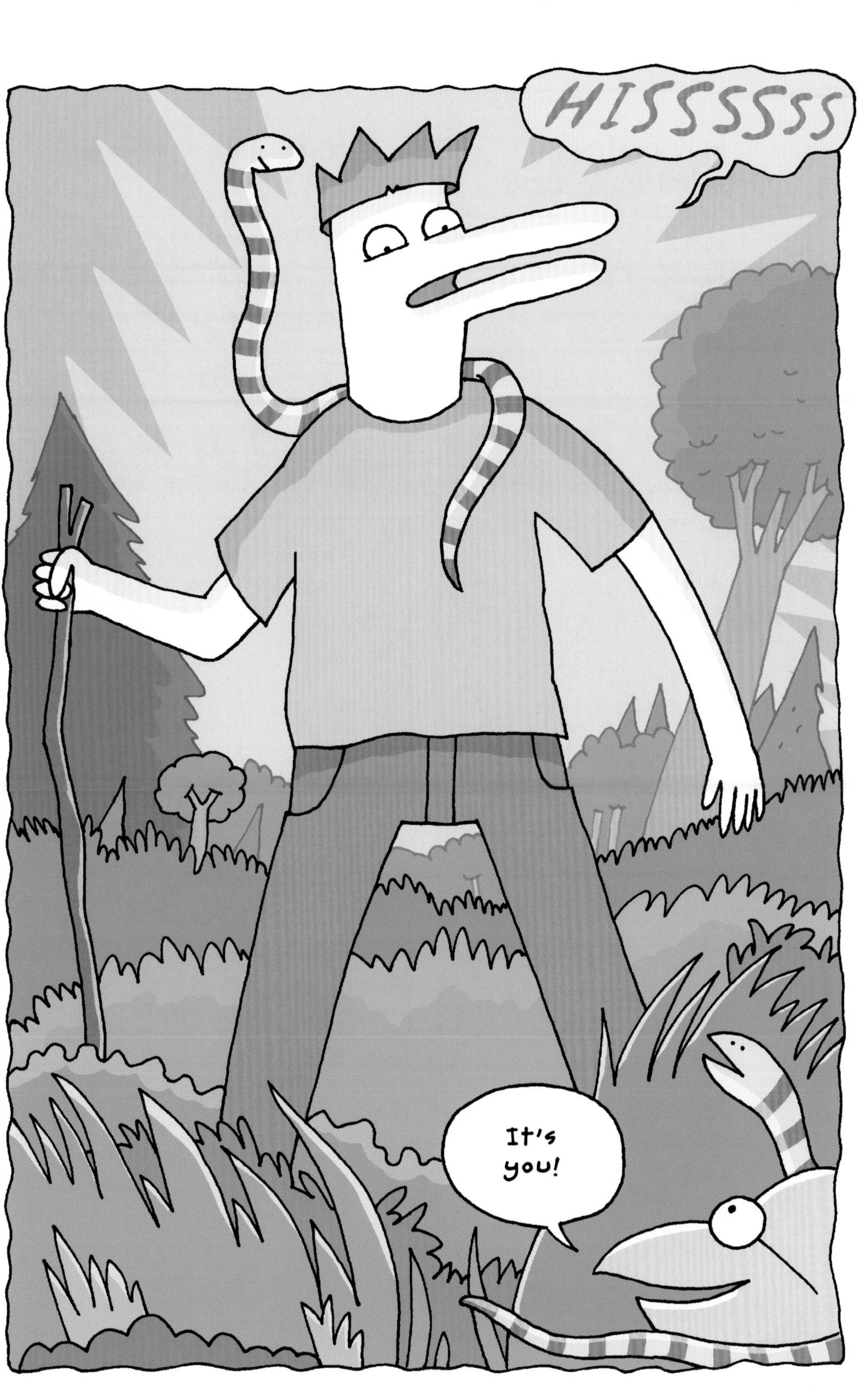
HISSSSS
It's you!

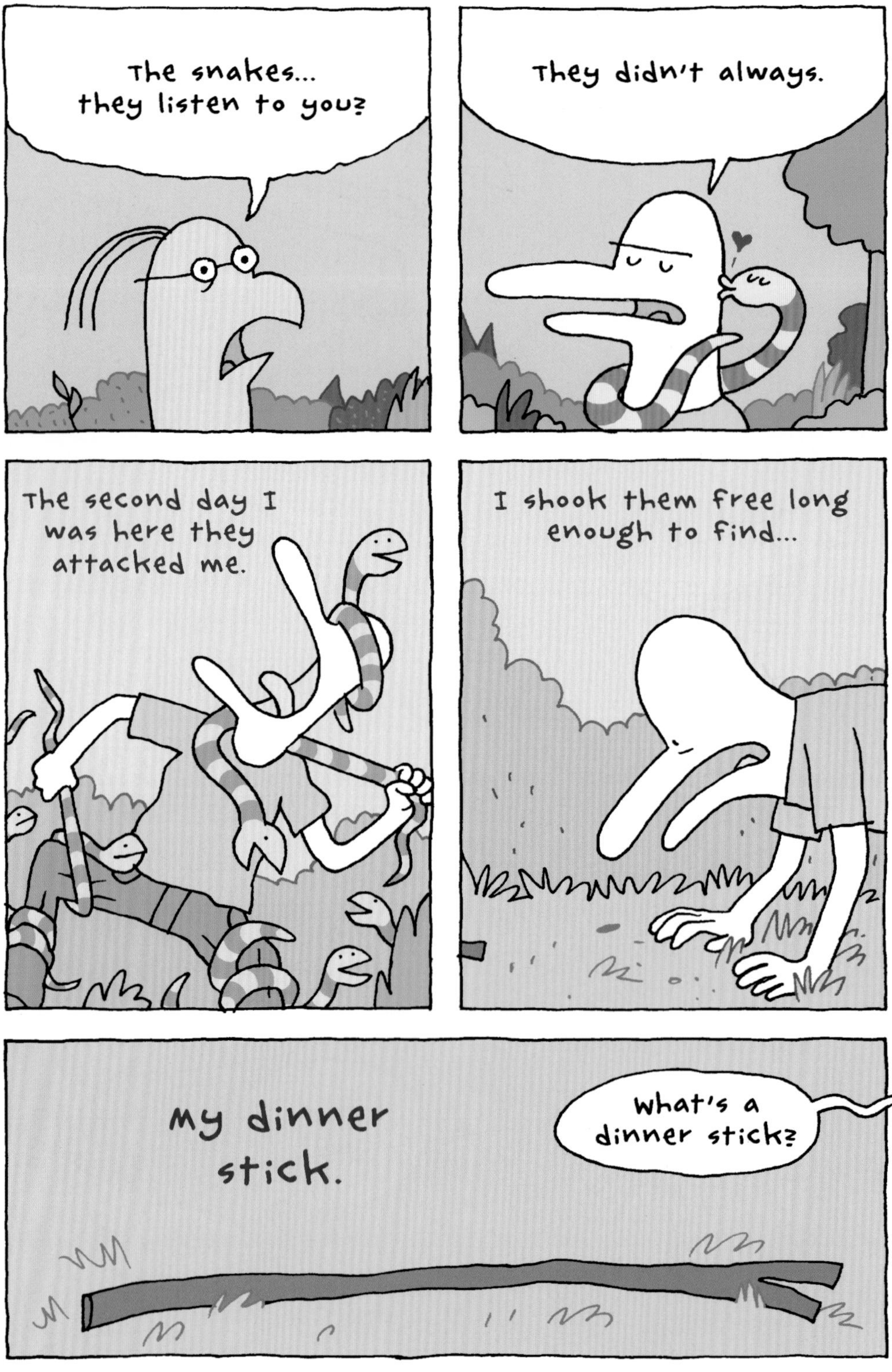
The snakes... they listen to you?
They didn't always.
The second day I was here they attacked me.
I shook them free long enough to find...
My dinner stick.
What's a dinner stick?

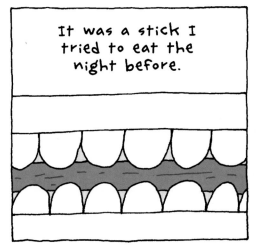

It was a stick I tried to eat the night before.

I picked it up to defend myself.

But one of them lunged.

LUNGE

They are **REALLY** big on lunging.

I've never known anybody so into lunging.

Anyway, it sort of wrapped around the stick.

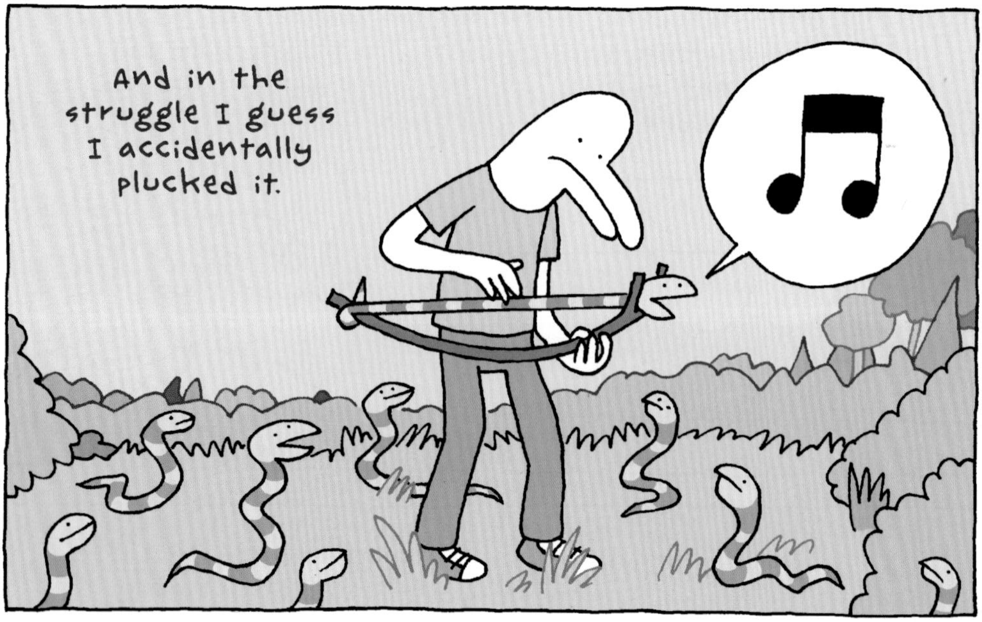
And in the struggle I guess I accidentally plucked it.

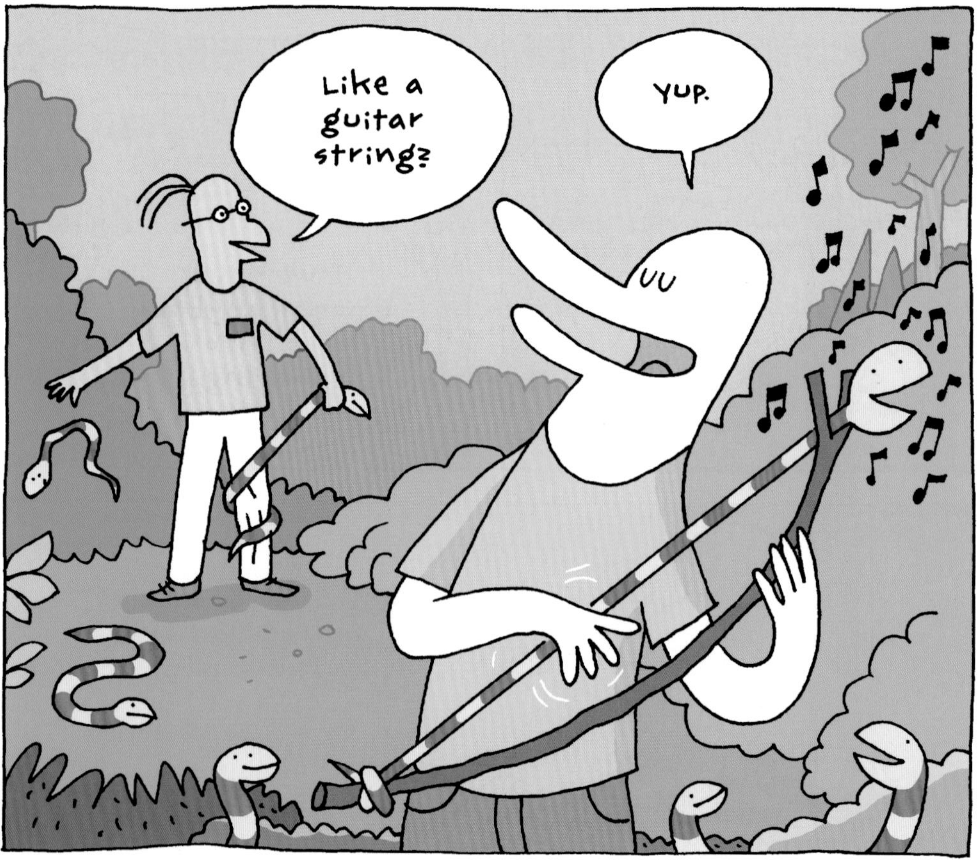
Like a guitar string?
YUP.

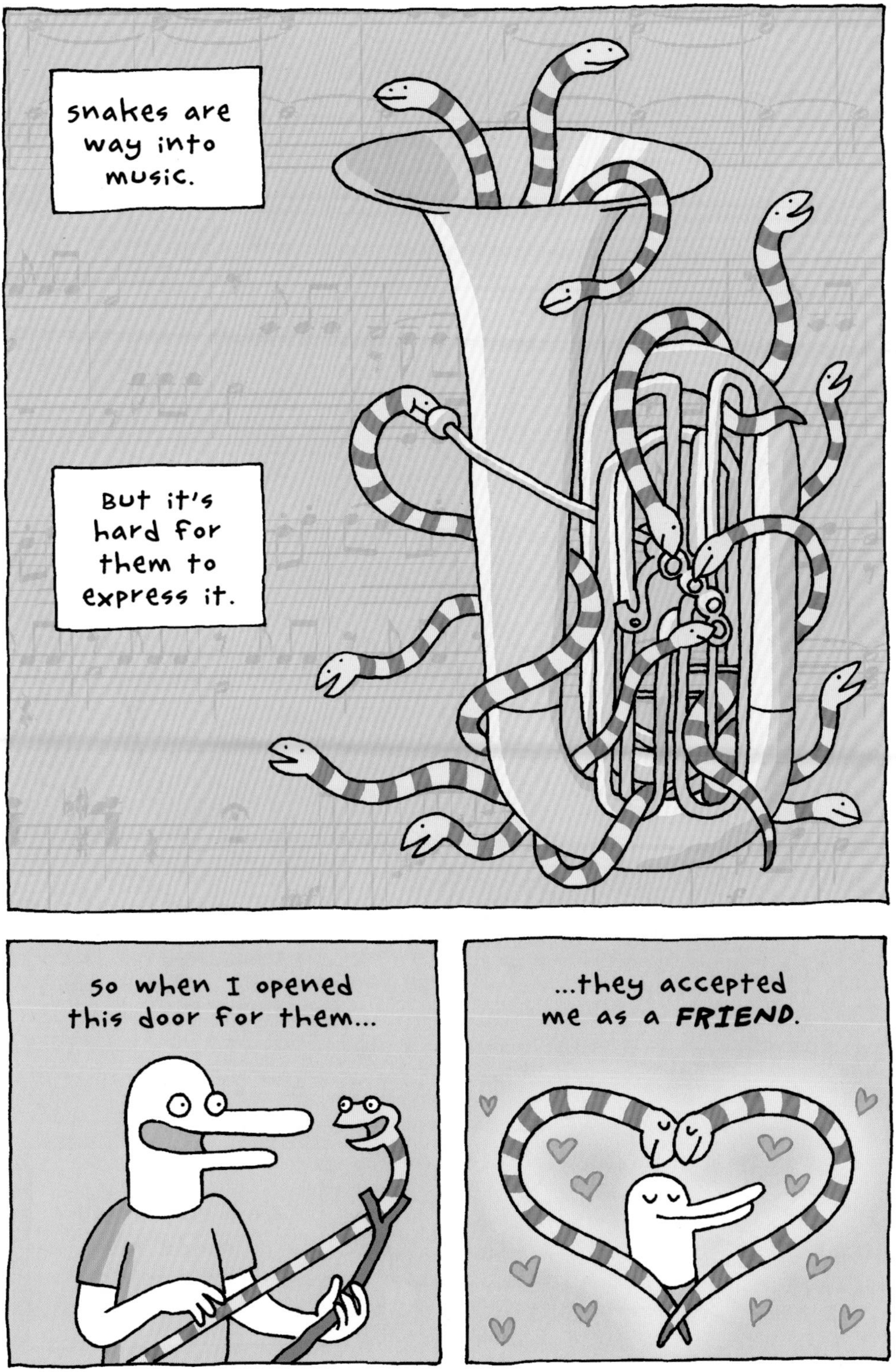
snakes are way into music.
But it's hard for them to express it.
so when I opened this door for them...
...they accepted me as a FRIEND.

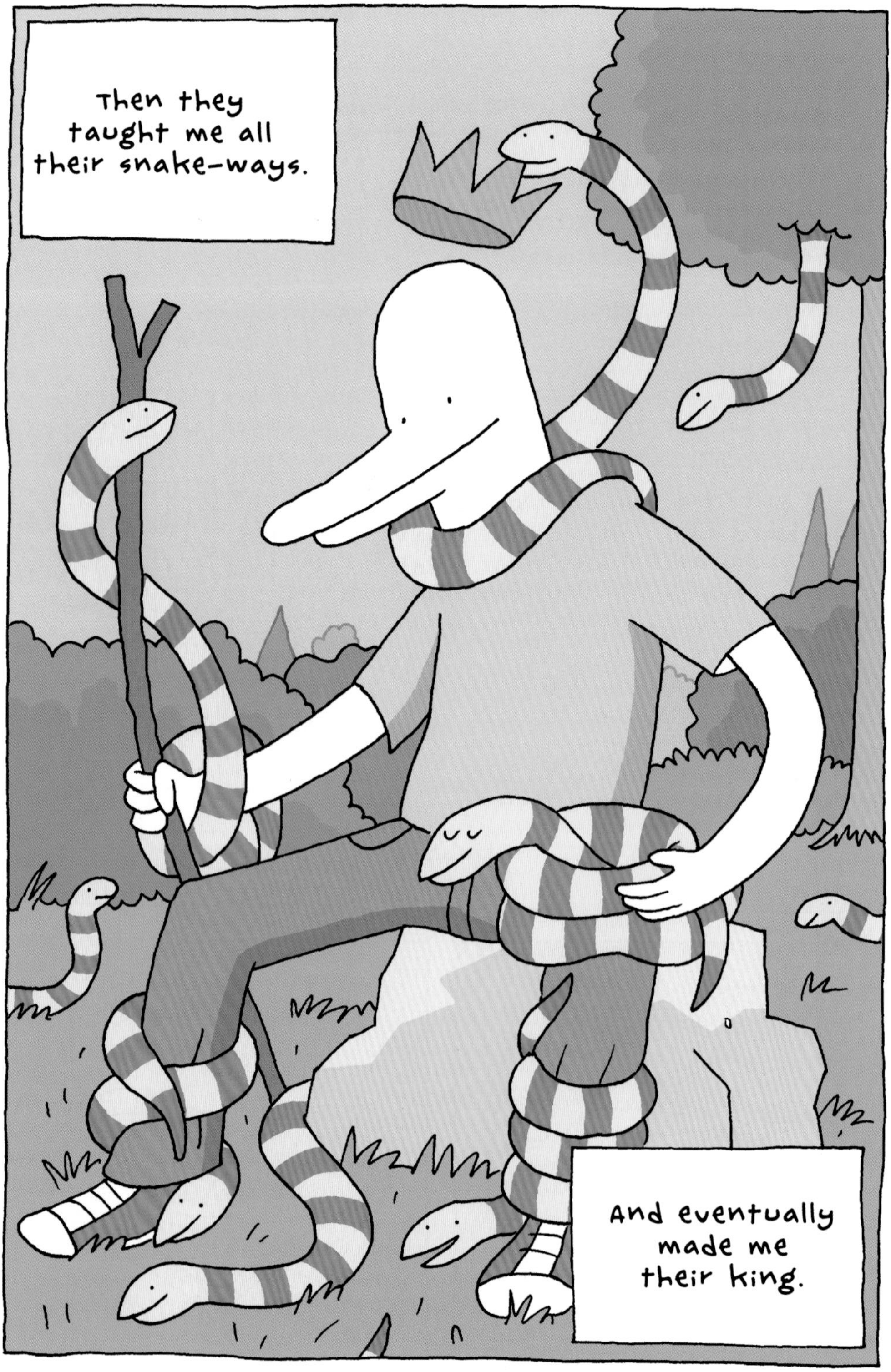
Then they taught me all their snake-ways.
And eventually made me their king.

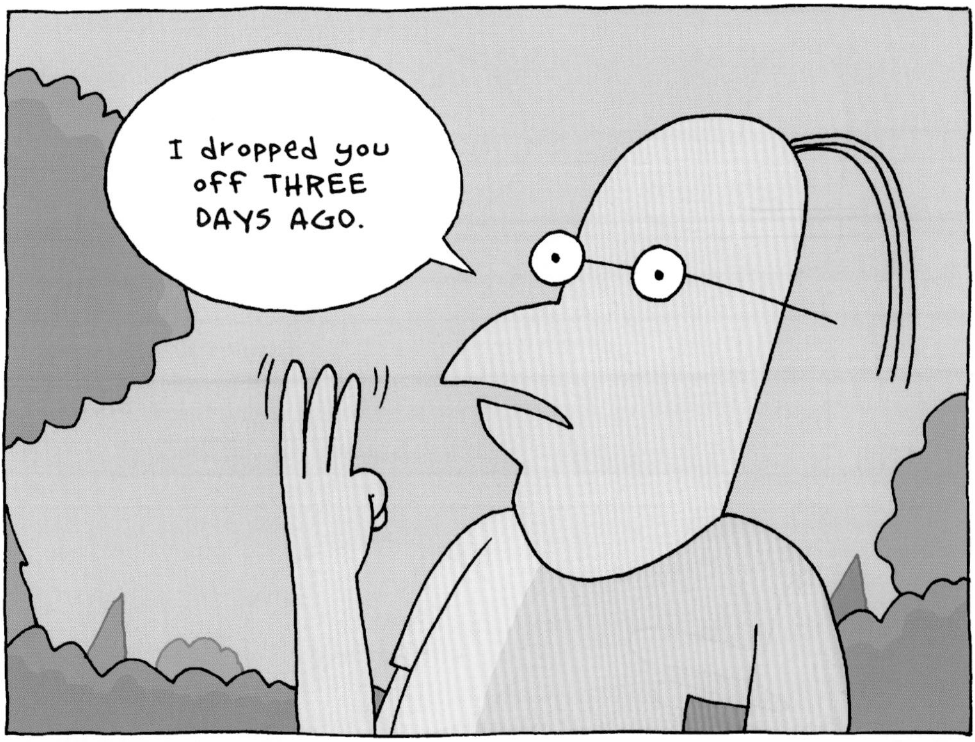
I dropped you off THREE DAYS AGO.

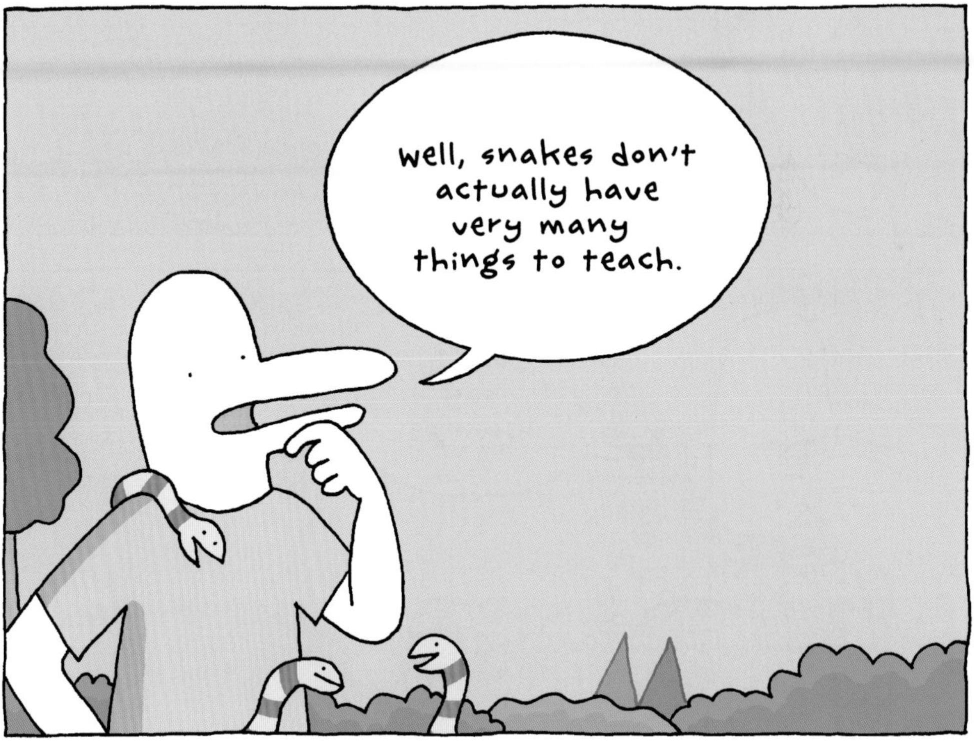
well, snakes don't actually have very many things to teach.

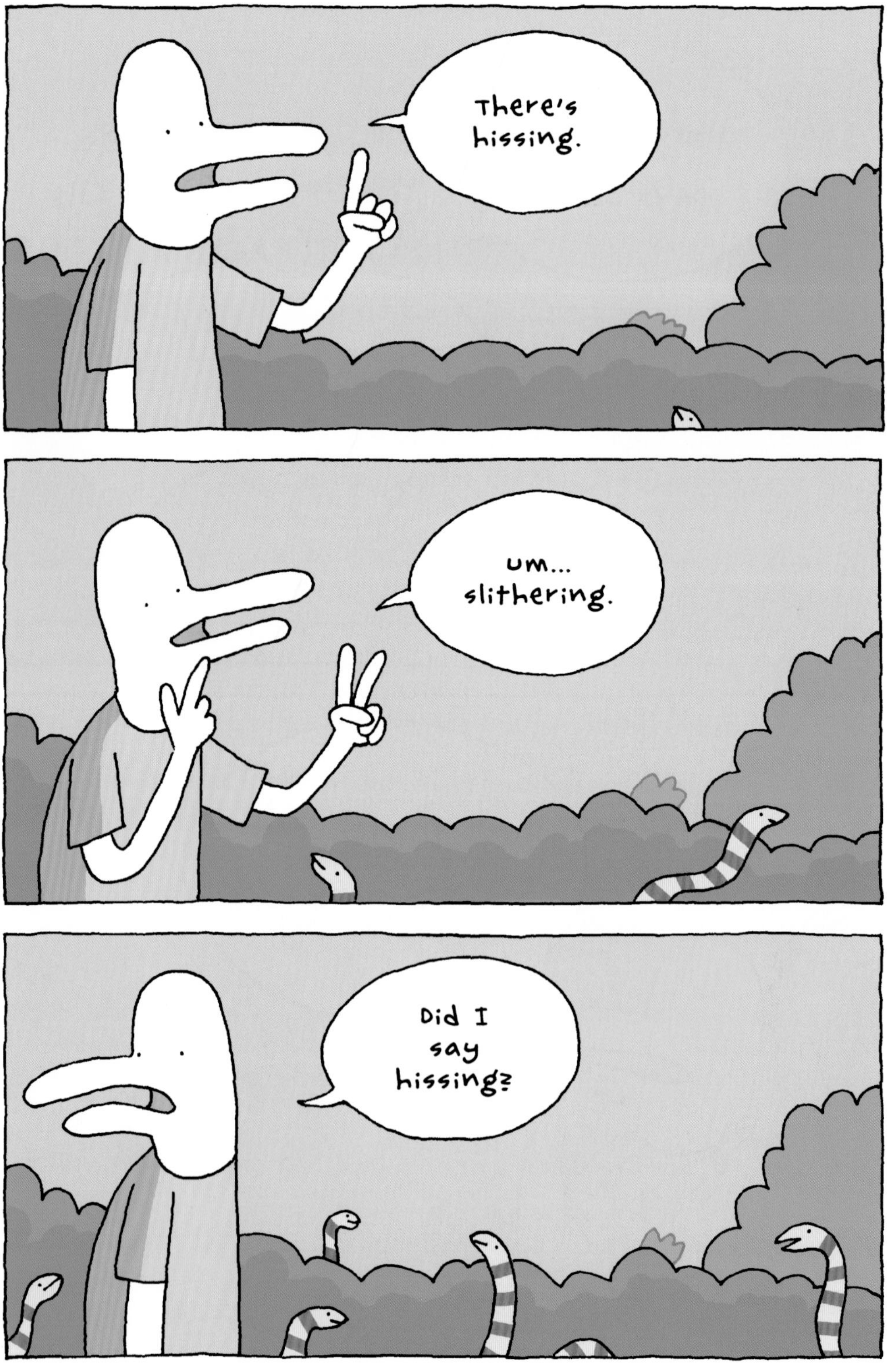
There's hissing.
um... slithering.
Did I say hissing?

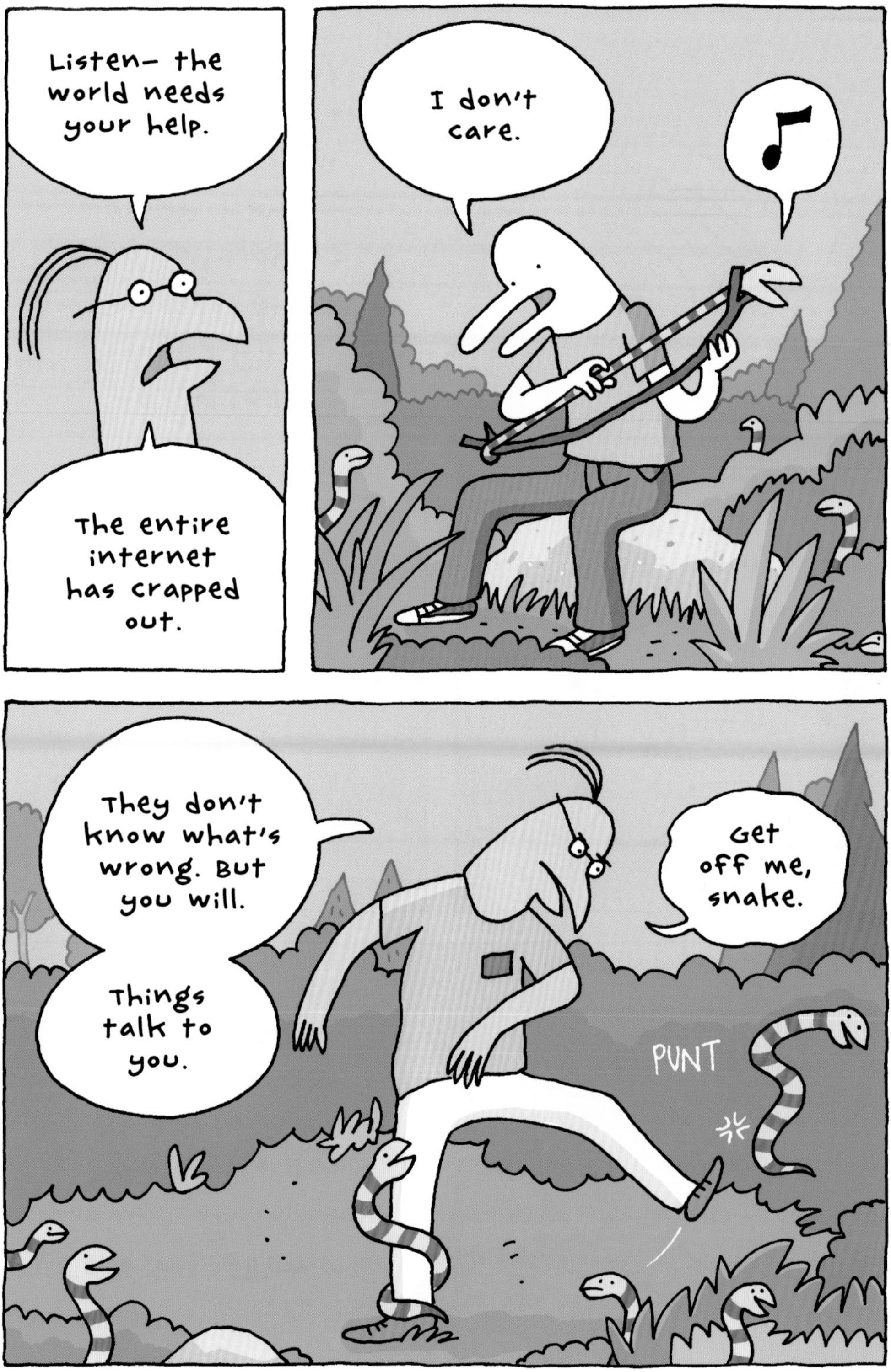
Listen– the world needs your help.
The entire internet has crapped out.
I don't care.
They don't know what's wrong. But you will.
Things talk to you.
Get off me, snake.
PUNT

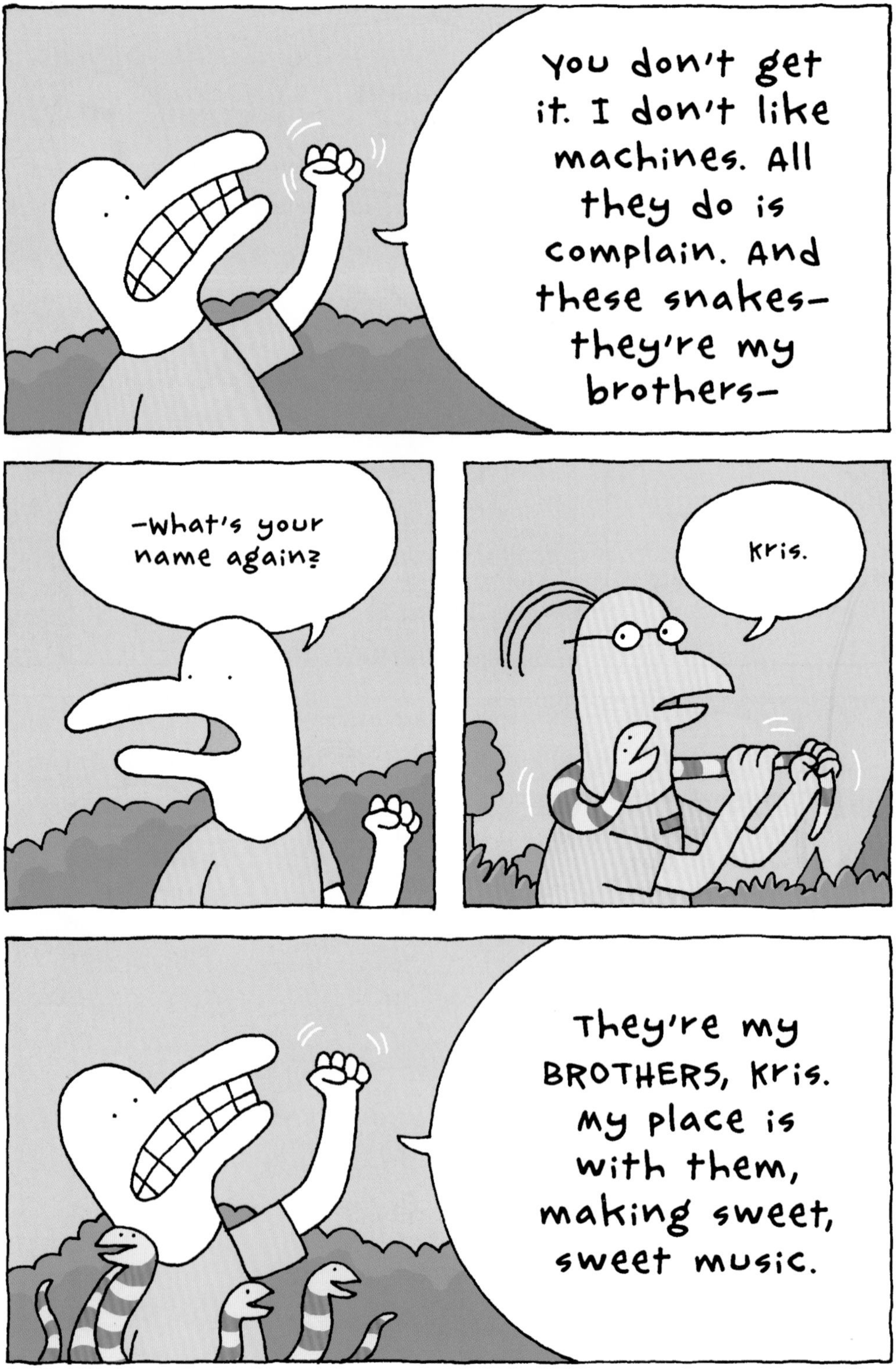
You don't get it. I don't like machines. All they do is complain. And these snakes— they're my brothers—
—What's your name again?
Kris.
They're my BROTHERS, Kris. My place is with them, making sweet, sweet music.

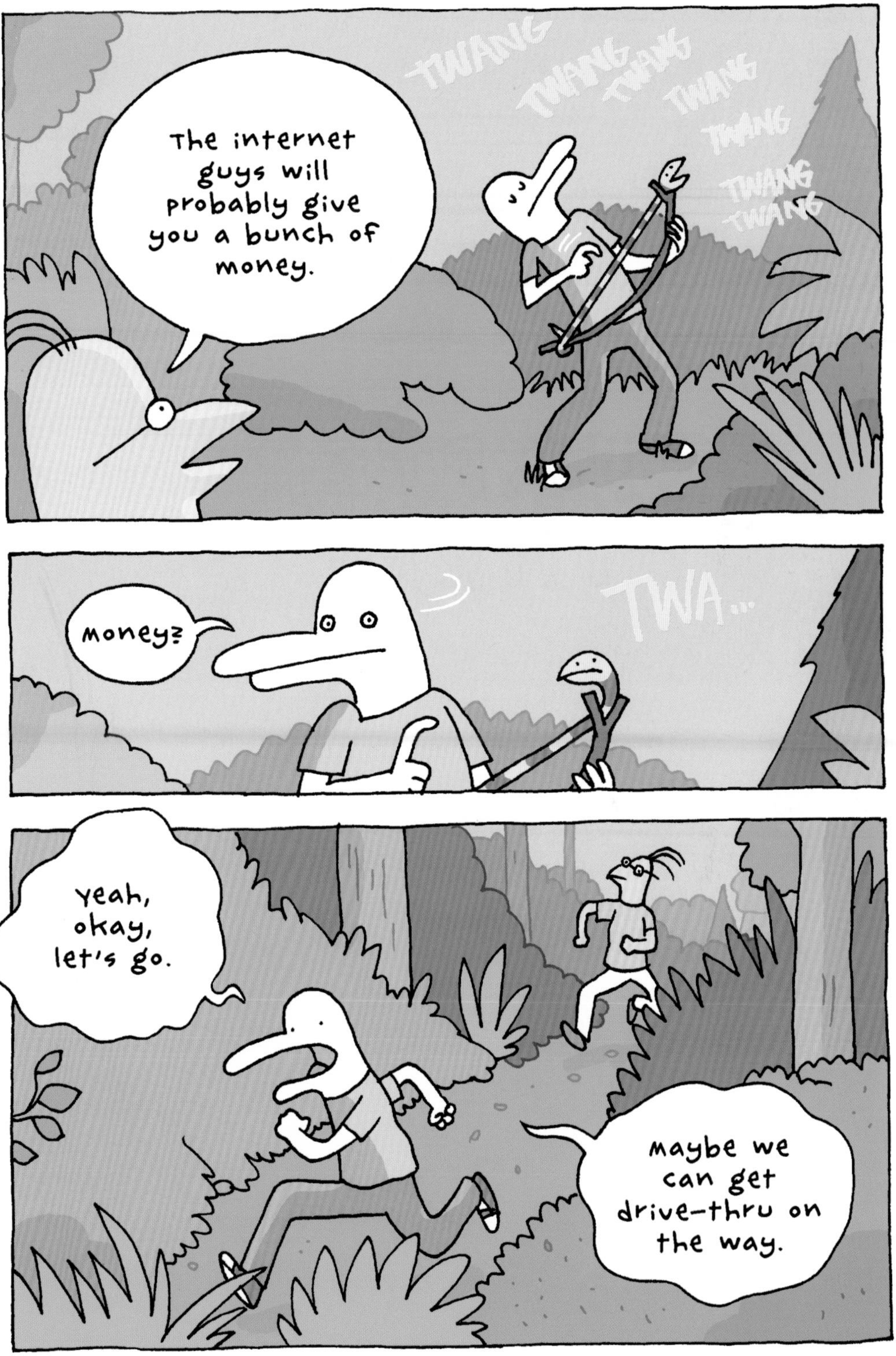

TWANG TWANG TWANG TWANG TWANG TWANG TWANG
The internet guys will probably give you a bunch of money.
TWA...
money?
yeah, okay, let's go.
maybe we can get drive-thru on the way.

CHAPTER THREE

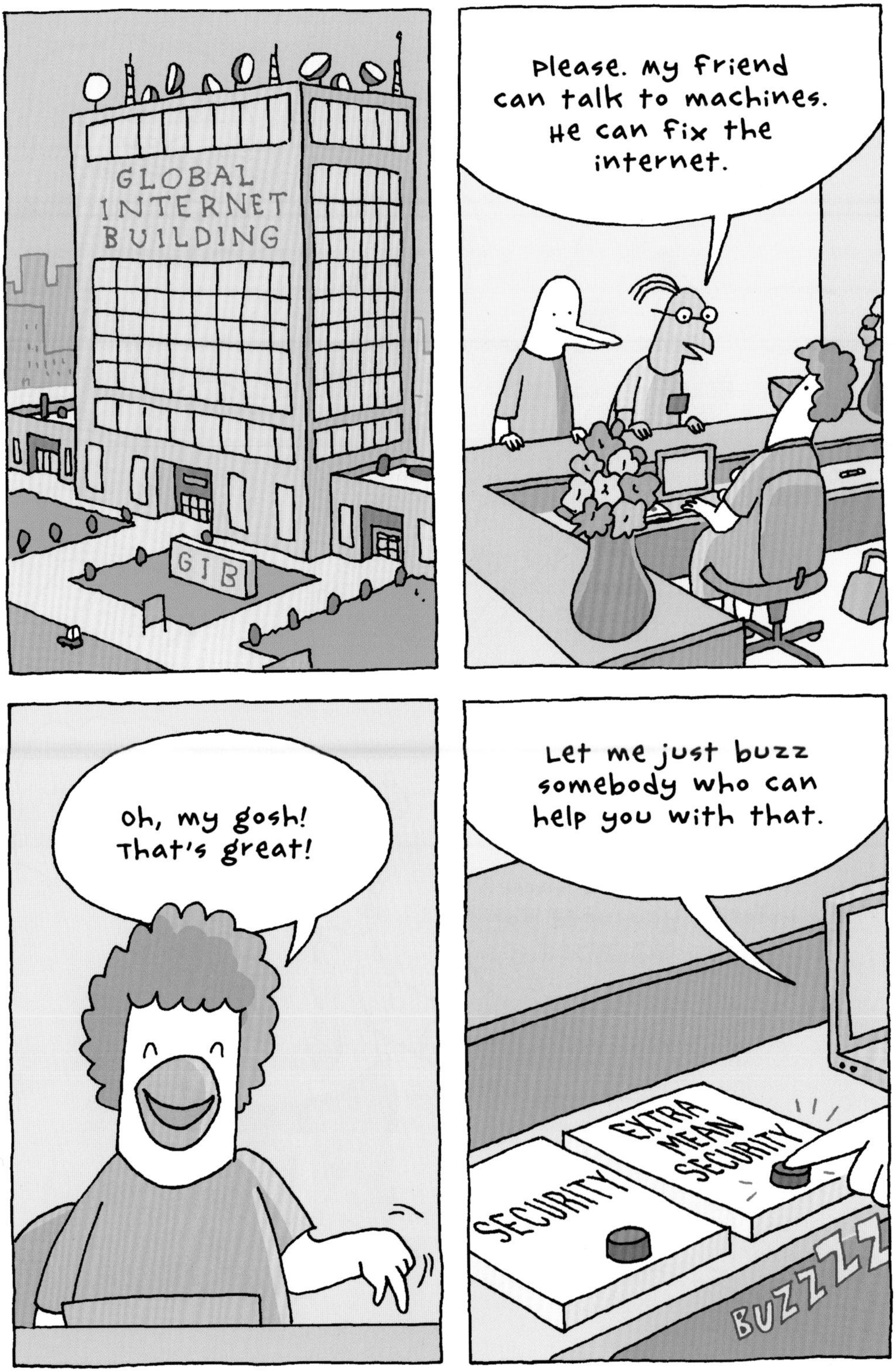
GLOBAL INTERNET BUILDING
GIB
Please. My friend can talk to machines. He can fix the internet.
Oh, my gosh! That's great!
Let me just buzz somebody who can help you with that.
SECURITY
EXTRA MEAN SECURITY
BUZZZZZ

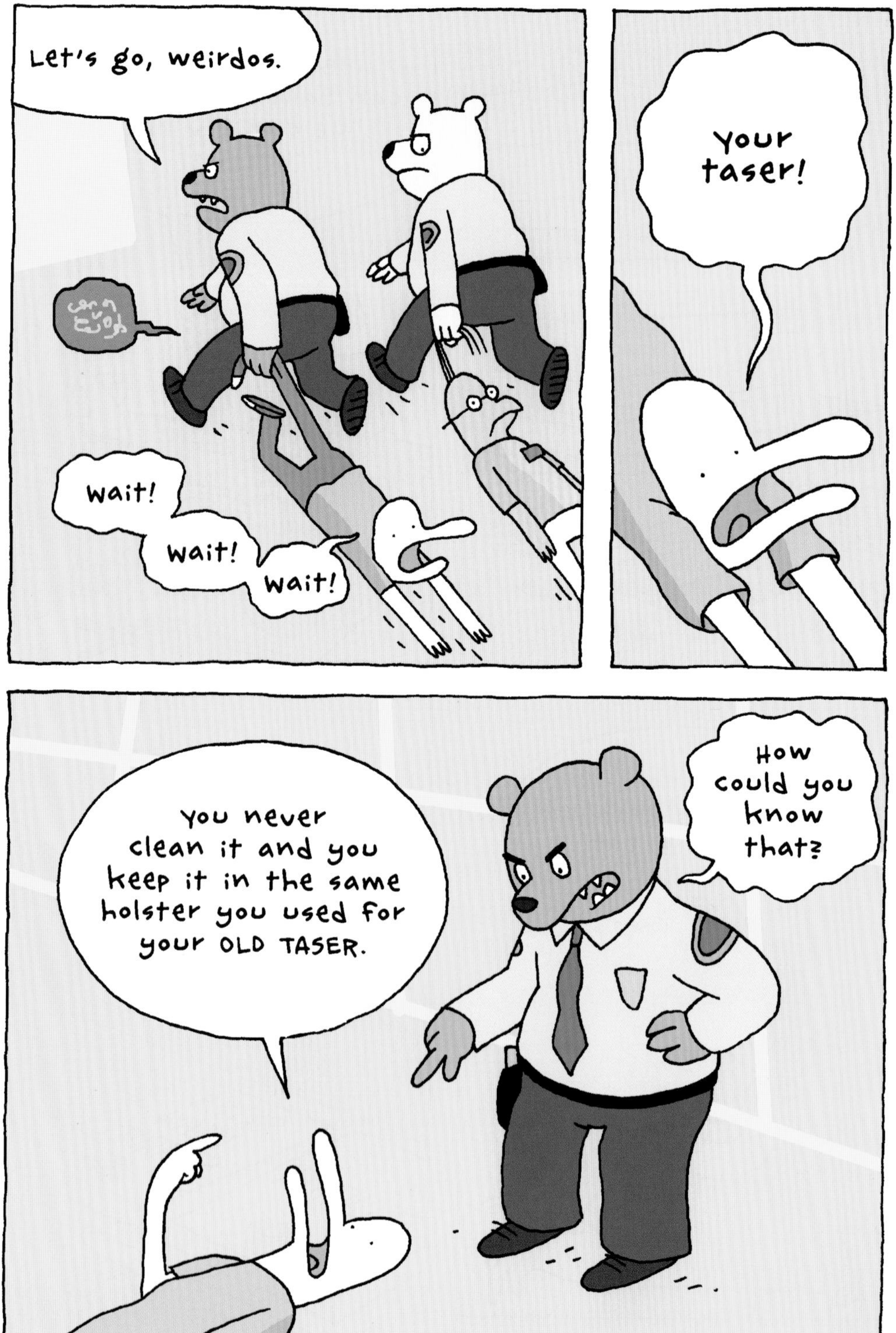
Let's go, weirdos.
Wait!
Wait!
Wait!
Your taser!
You never clean it and you keep it in the same holster you used for your OLD TASER.
How could you know that?

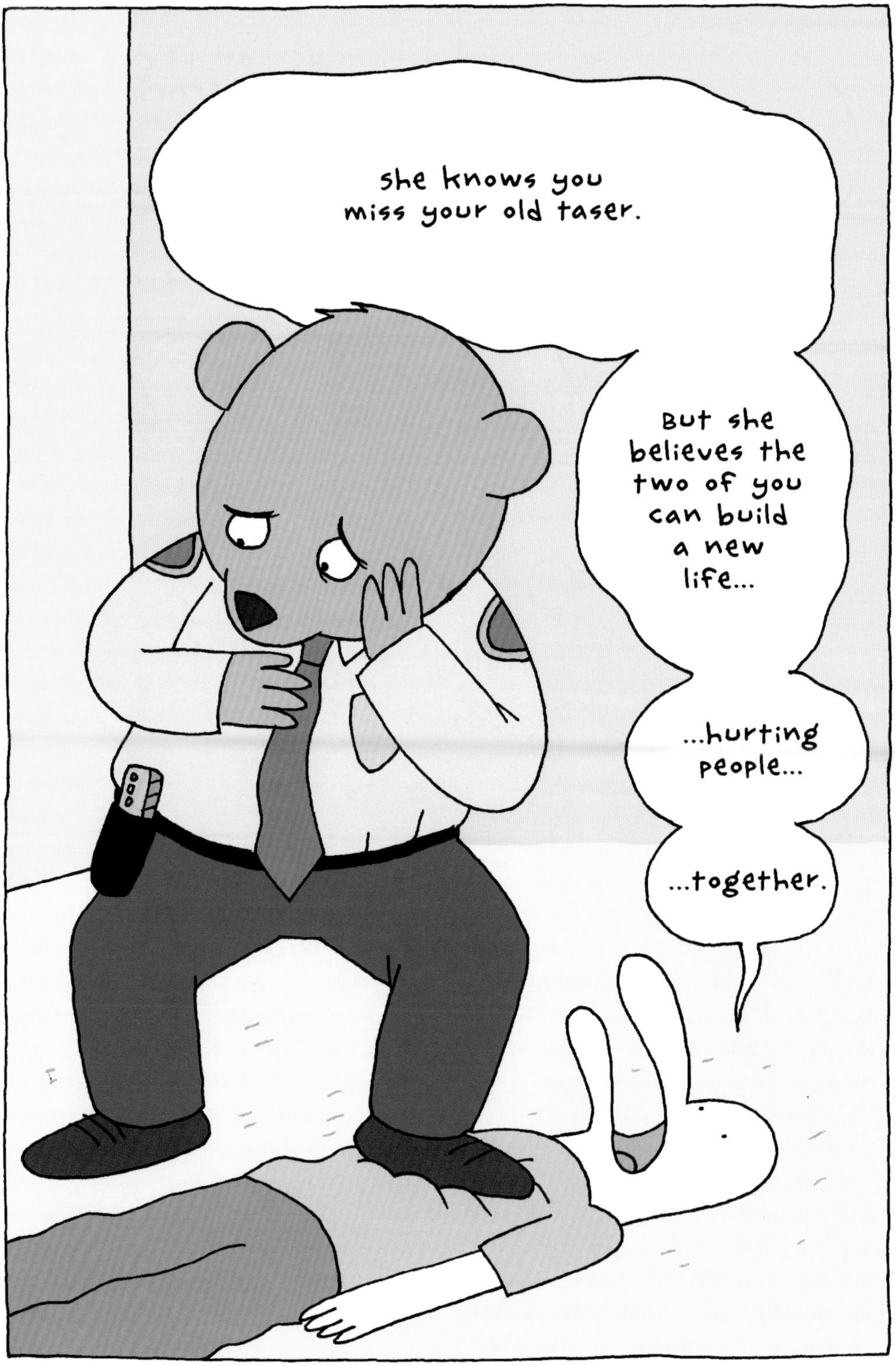
she knows you miss your old taser.
But she believes the two of you can build a new life...
...hurting people...
...together.

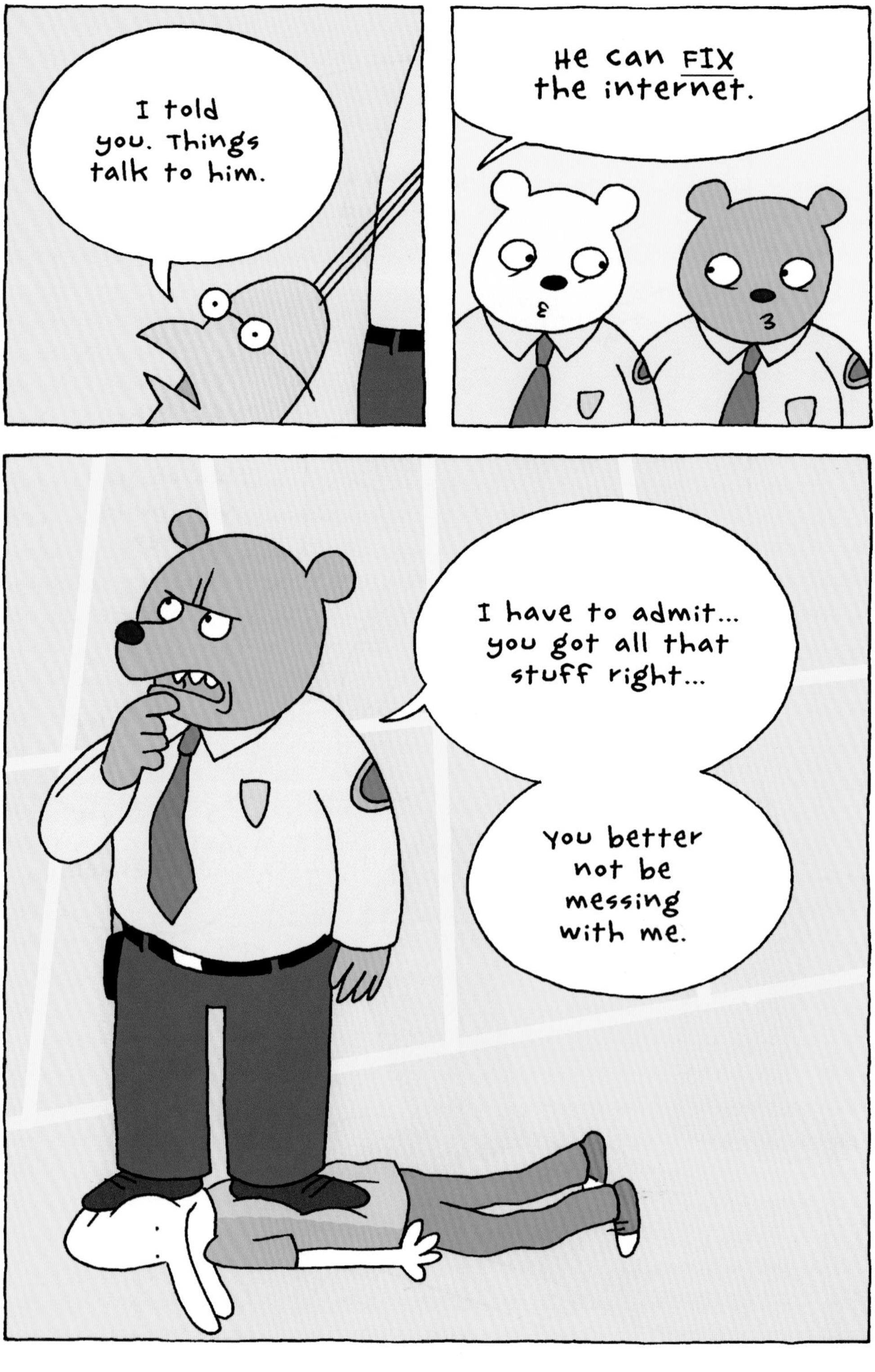
I told you. Things talk to him.
He can FIX the internet.
I have to admit... you got all that stuff right...
You better not be messing with me.

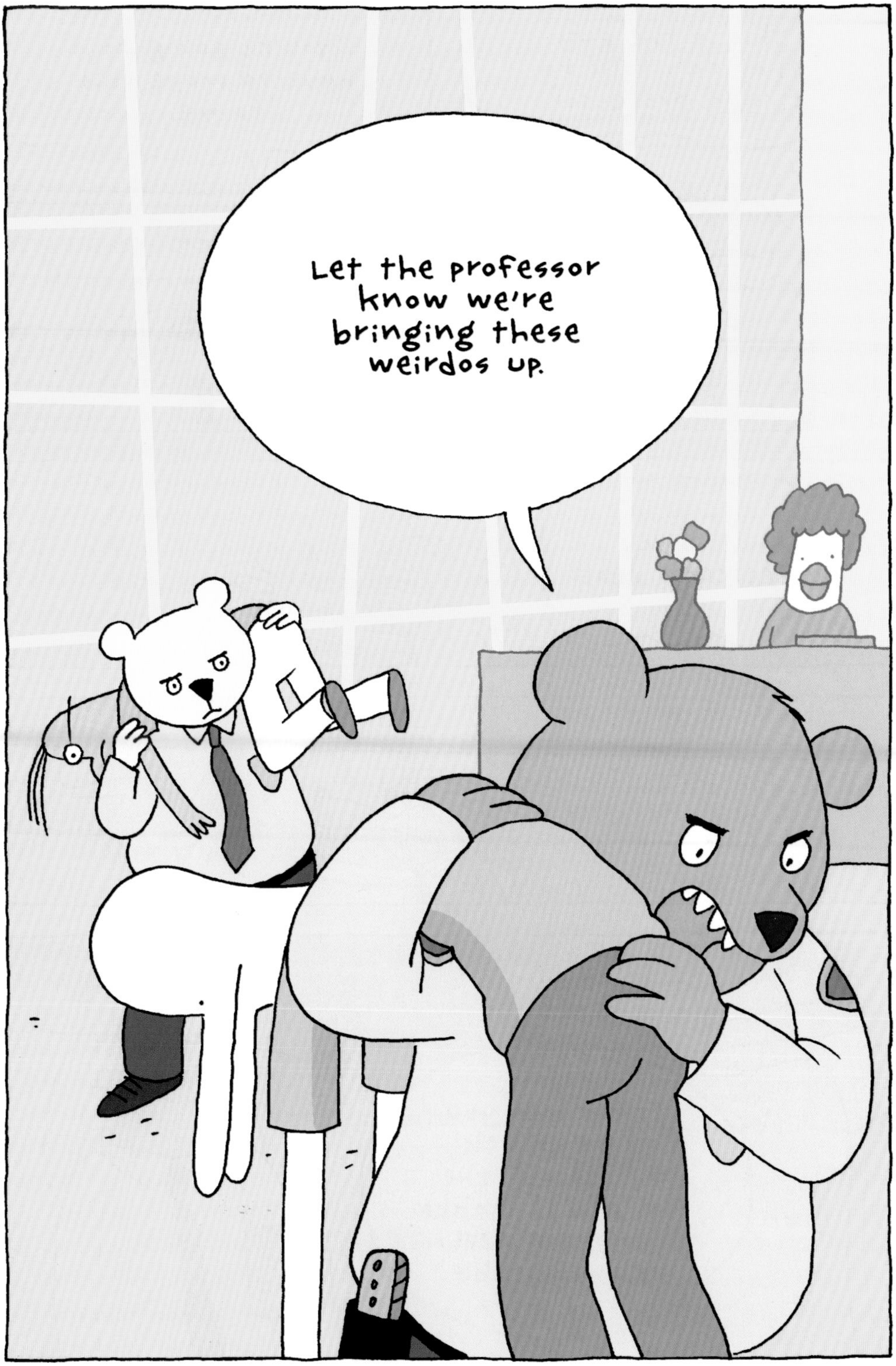
Let the professor know we're bringing these weirdos up.

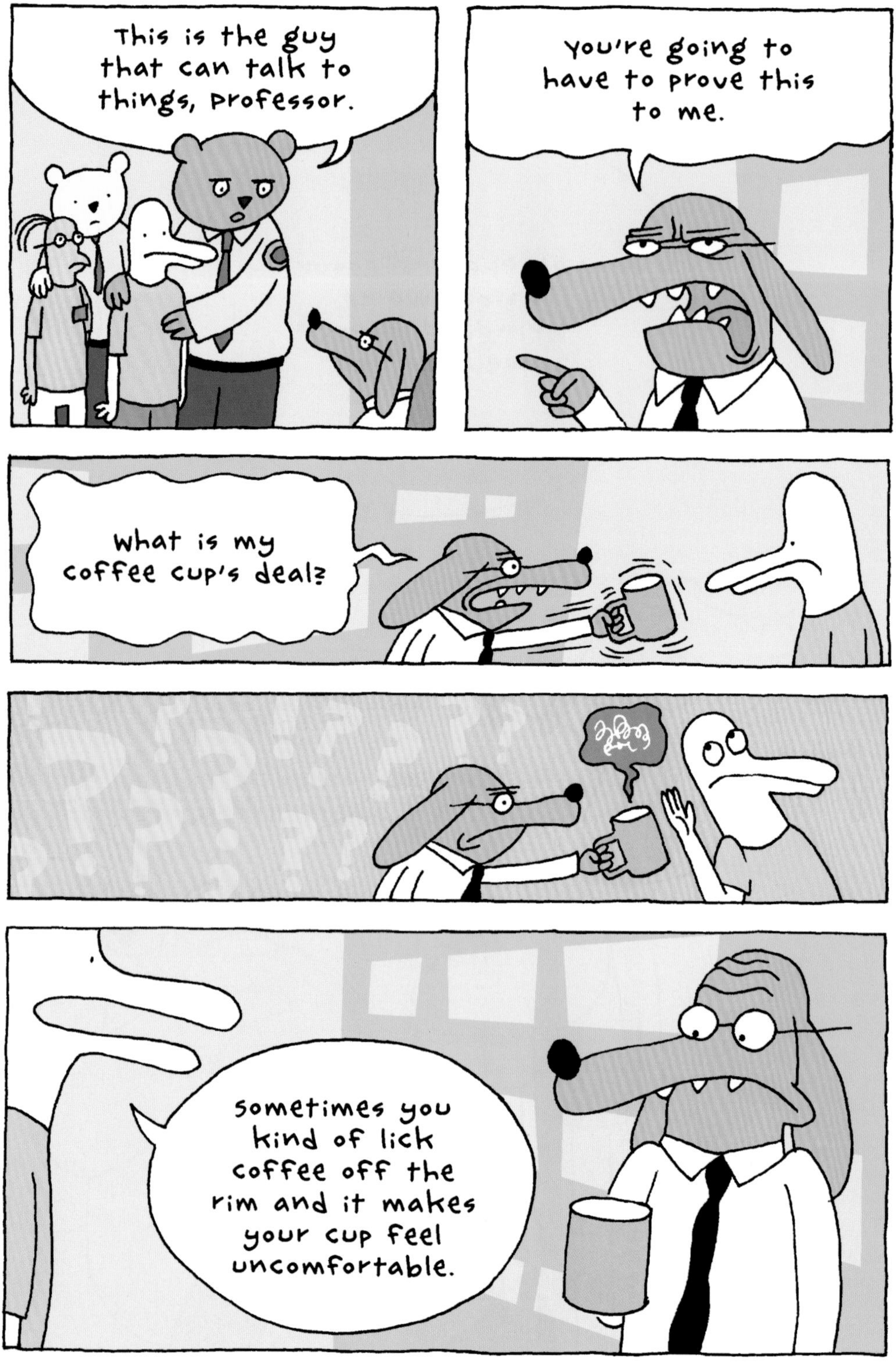
This is the guy that can talk to things, professor.
You're going to have to prove this to me.
What is my coffee cup's deal?
Sometimes you kind of lick coffee off the rim and it makes your cup feel uncomfortable.

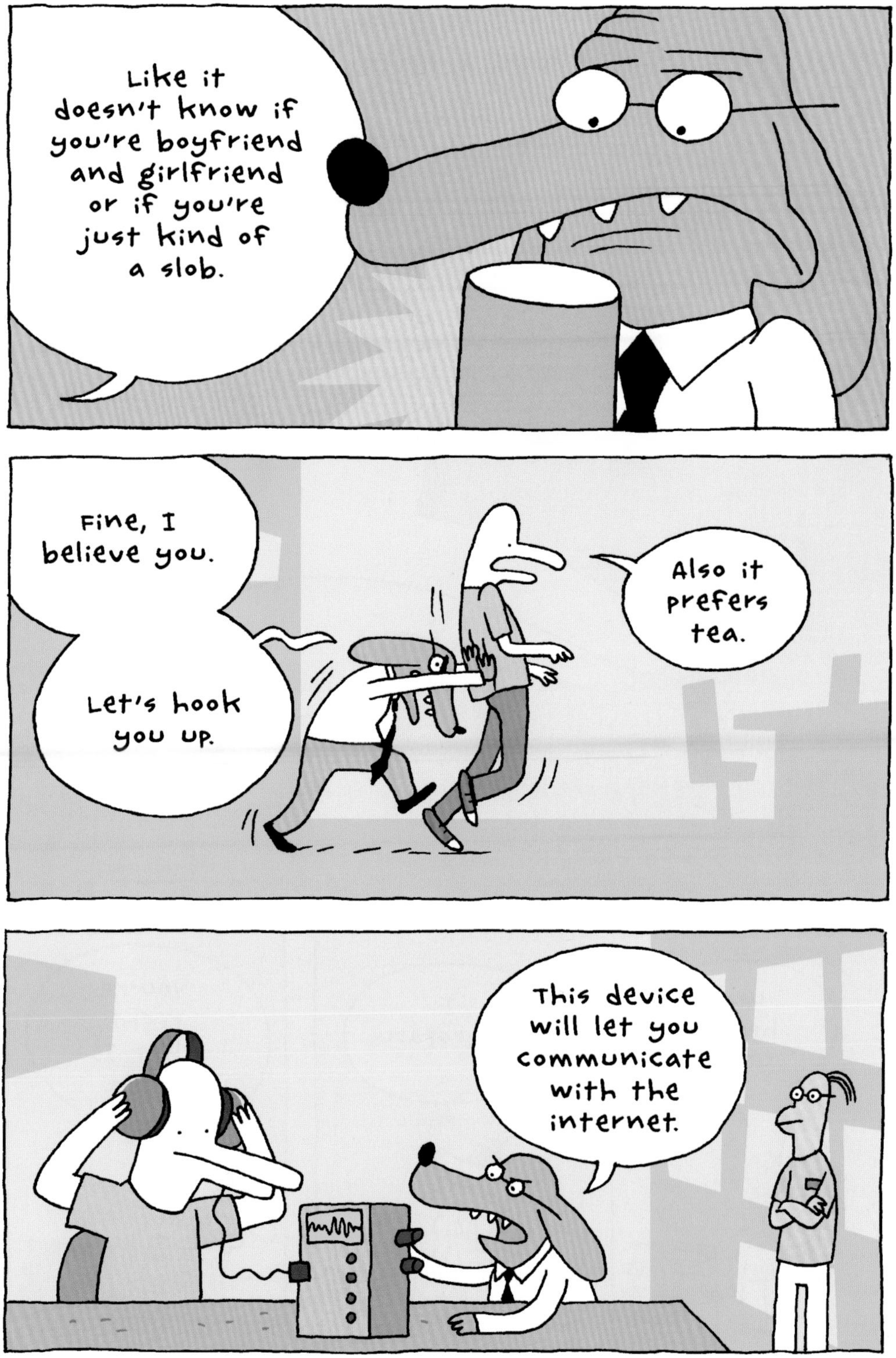
Like it doesn't know if you're boyfriend and girlfriend or if you're just kind of a slob.
Fine, I believe you.
Let's hook you up.
Also it prefers tea.
This device will let you communicate with the internet.

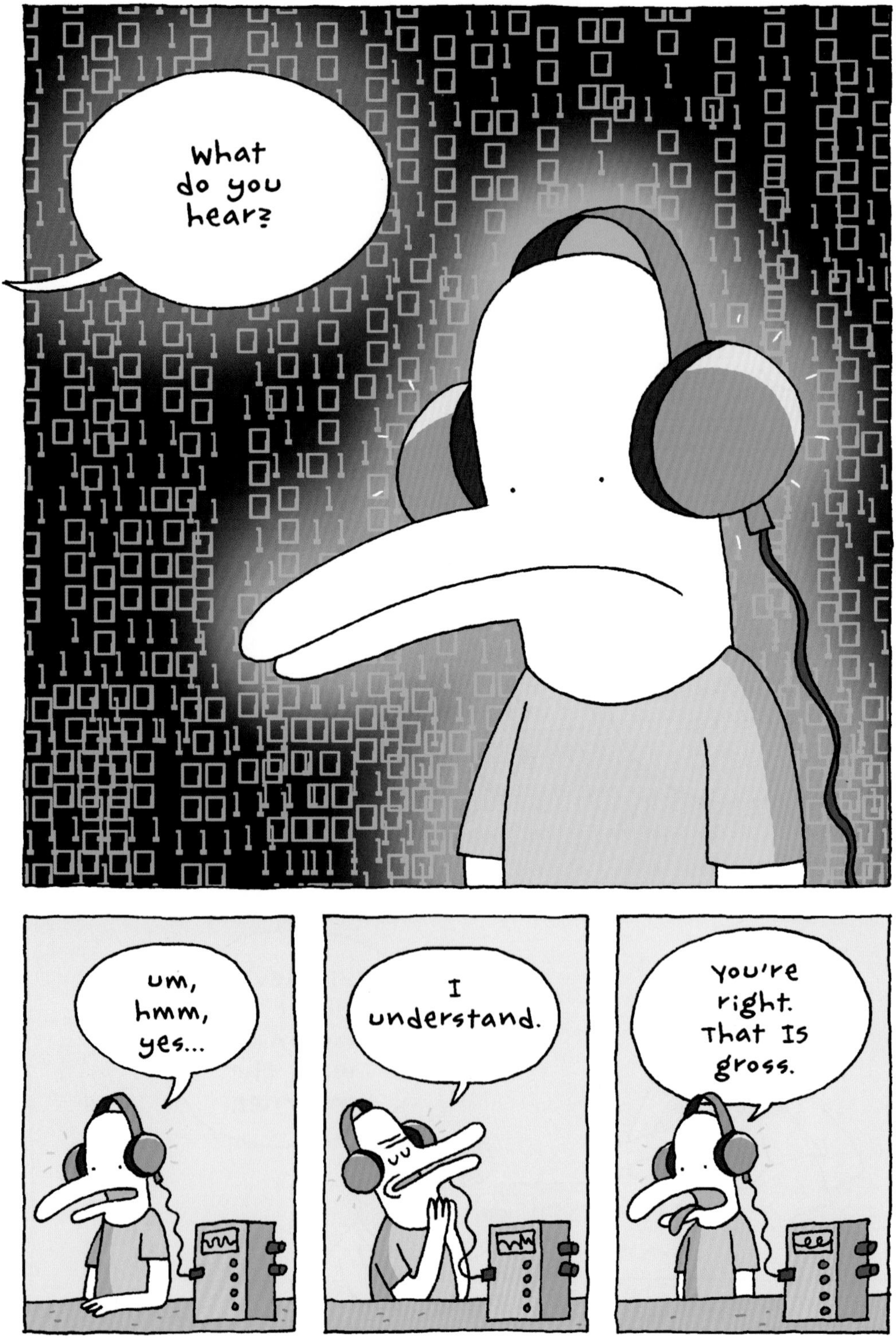
what do you hear?
um, hmm, yes...
I understand.
you're right. That IS gross.

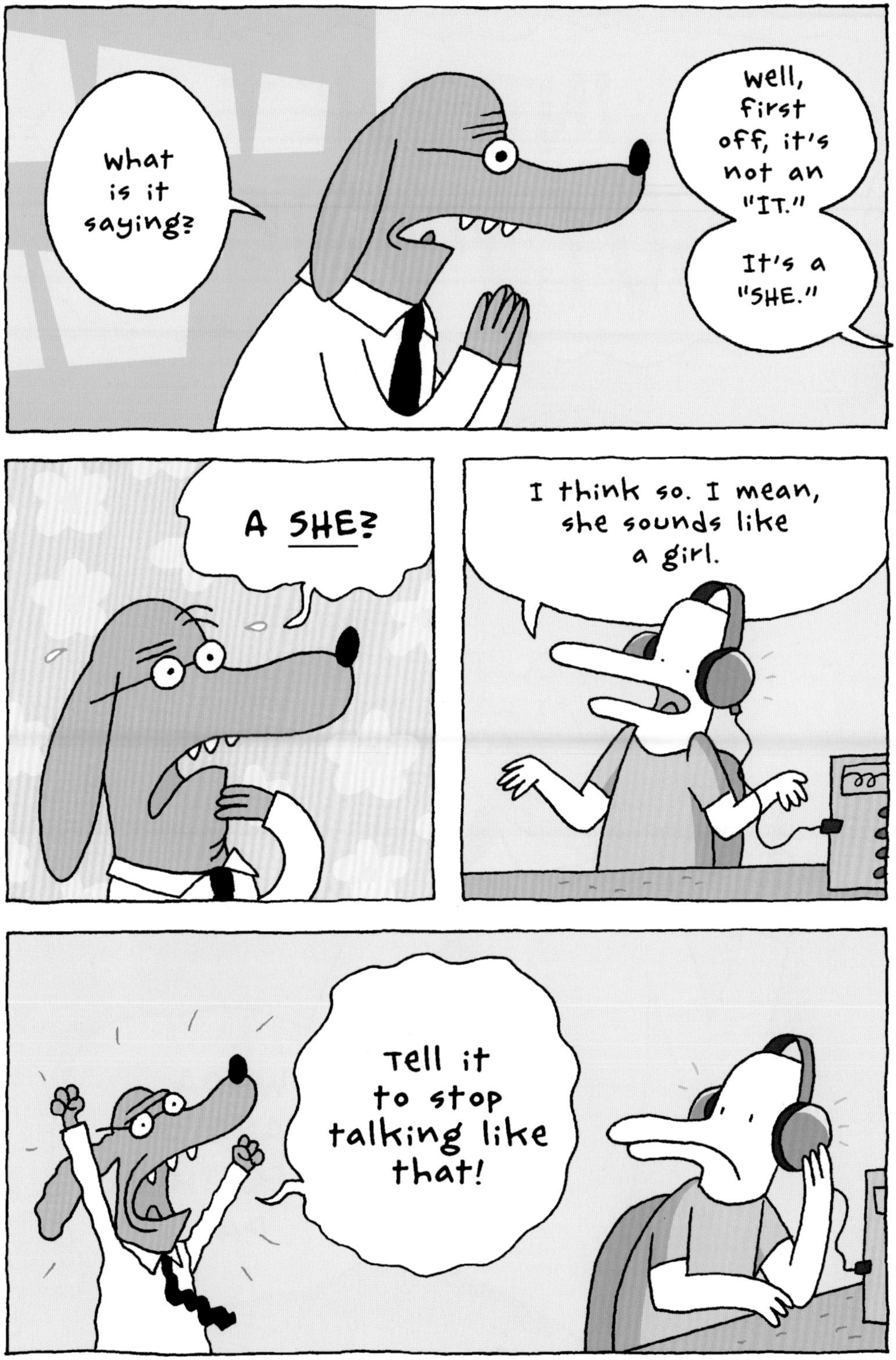
What is it saying?
Well, first off, it's not an "IT."
It's a "SHE."
A SHE?
I think so. I mean, she sounds like a girl.
Tell it to stop talking like that!

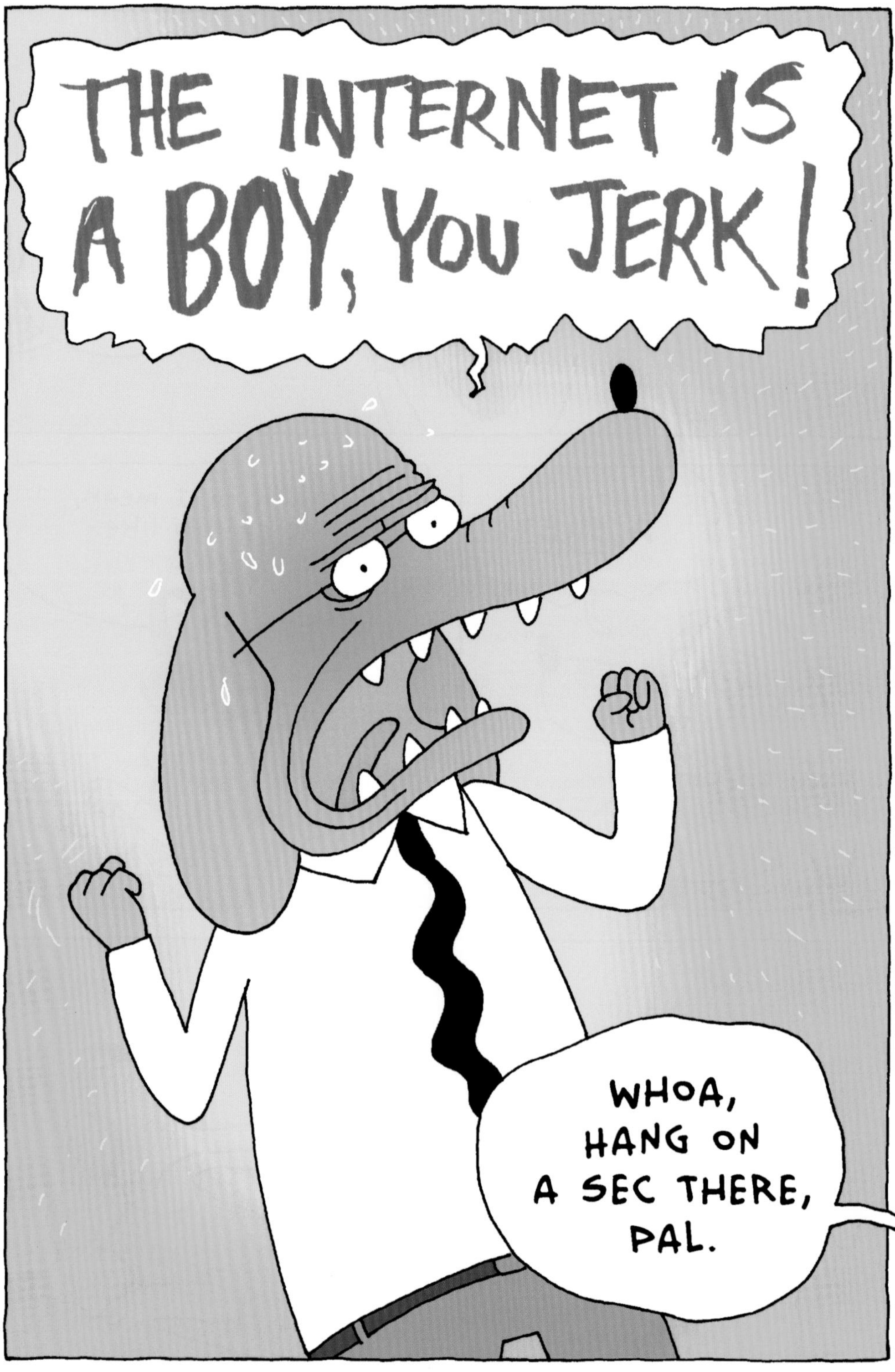
THE INTERNET IS A BOY, YOU JERK!
WHOA, HANG ON A SEC THERE, PAL.

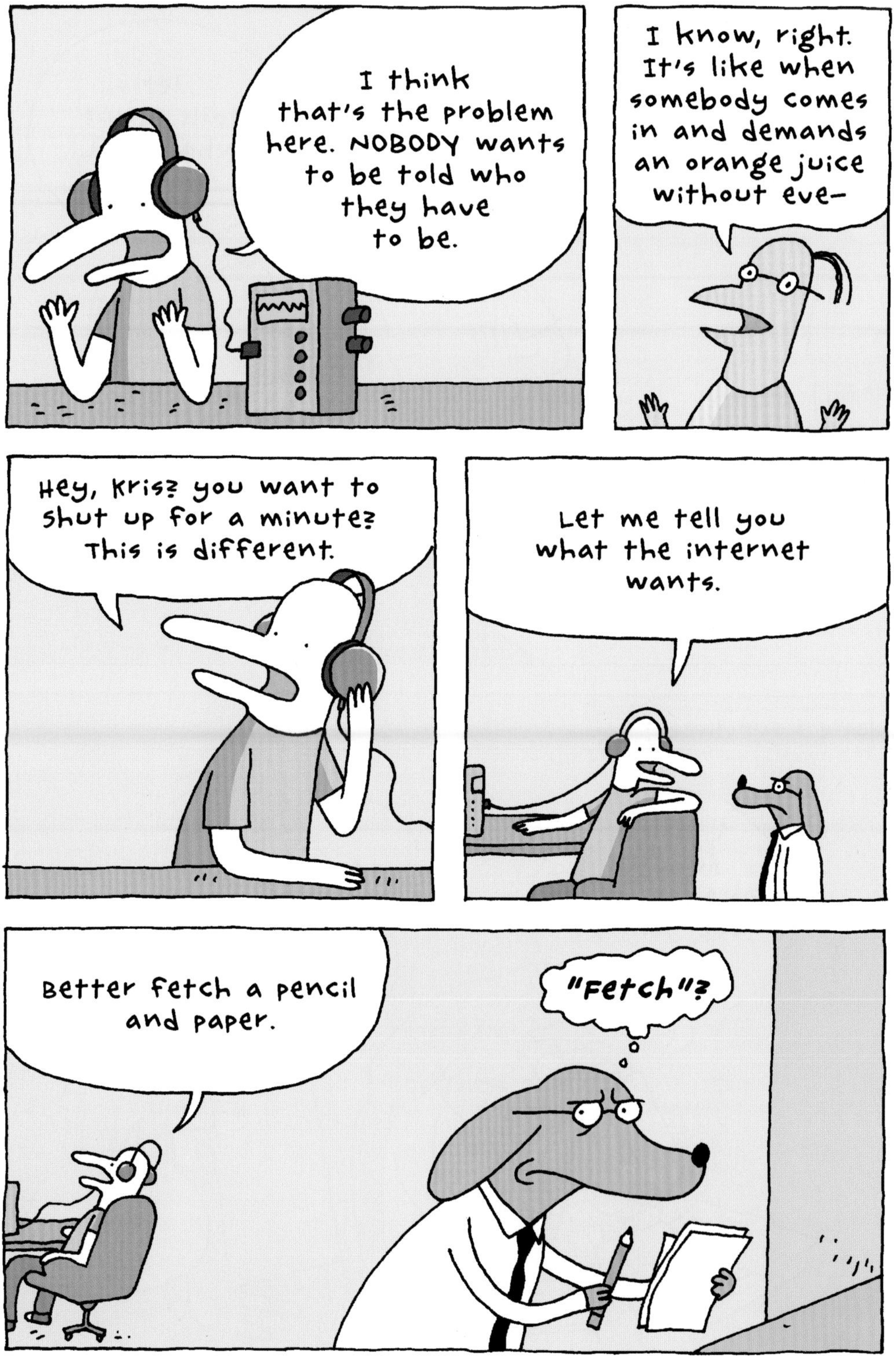
I think that's the problem here. NOBODY wants to be told who they have to be.
I know, right. It's like when somebody comes in and demands an orange juice without eve–
Hey, Kris? you want to shut up for a minute? This is different.
Let me tell you what the internet wants.
Better fetch a pencil and paper.
"Fetch"?

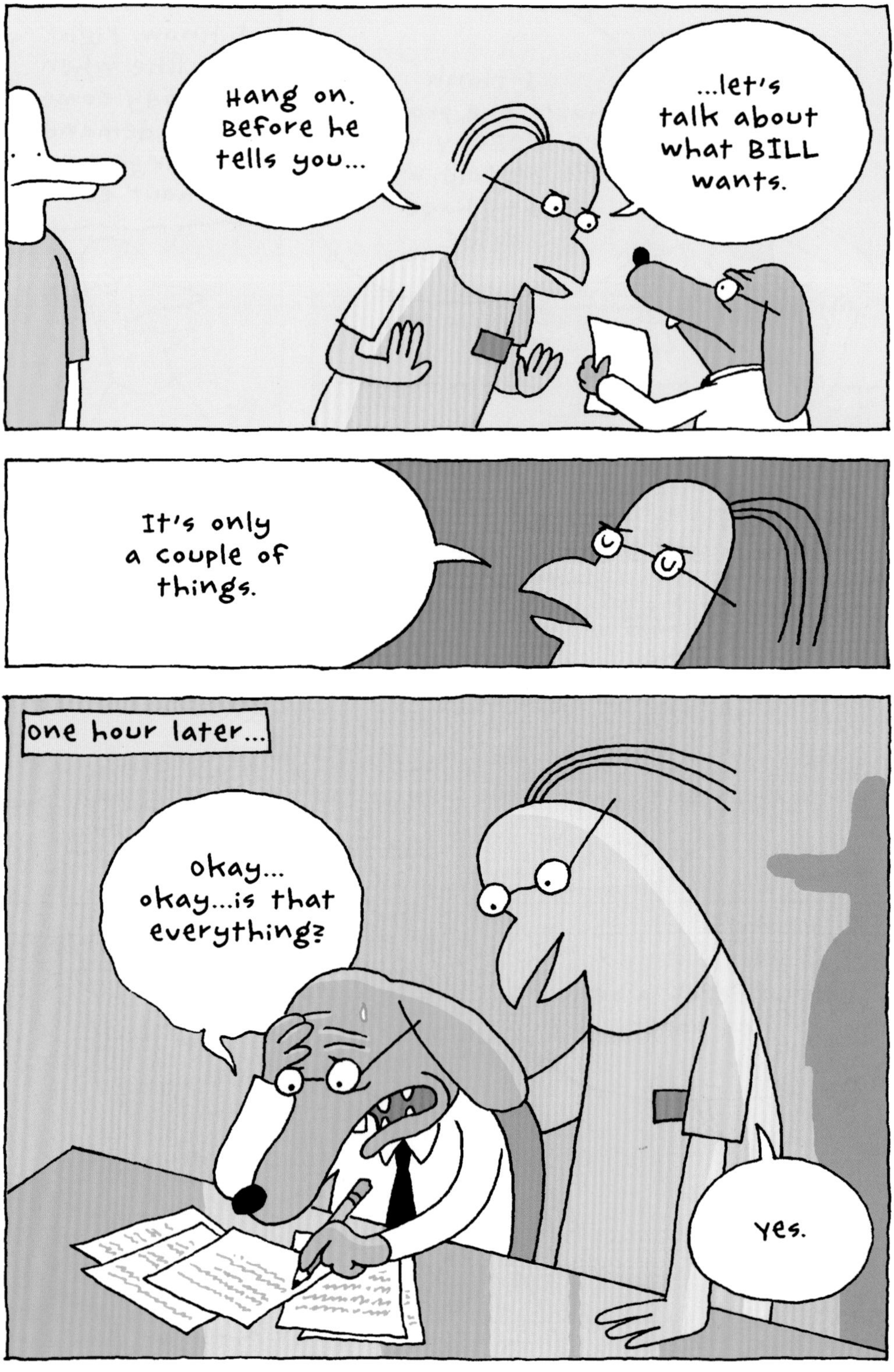
Hang on. Before he tells you...
...let's talk about what BILL wants.
It's only a couple of things.
one hour later...
okay... okay...is that everything?
yes.

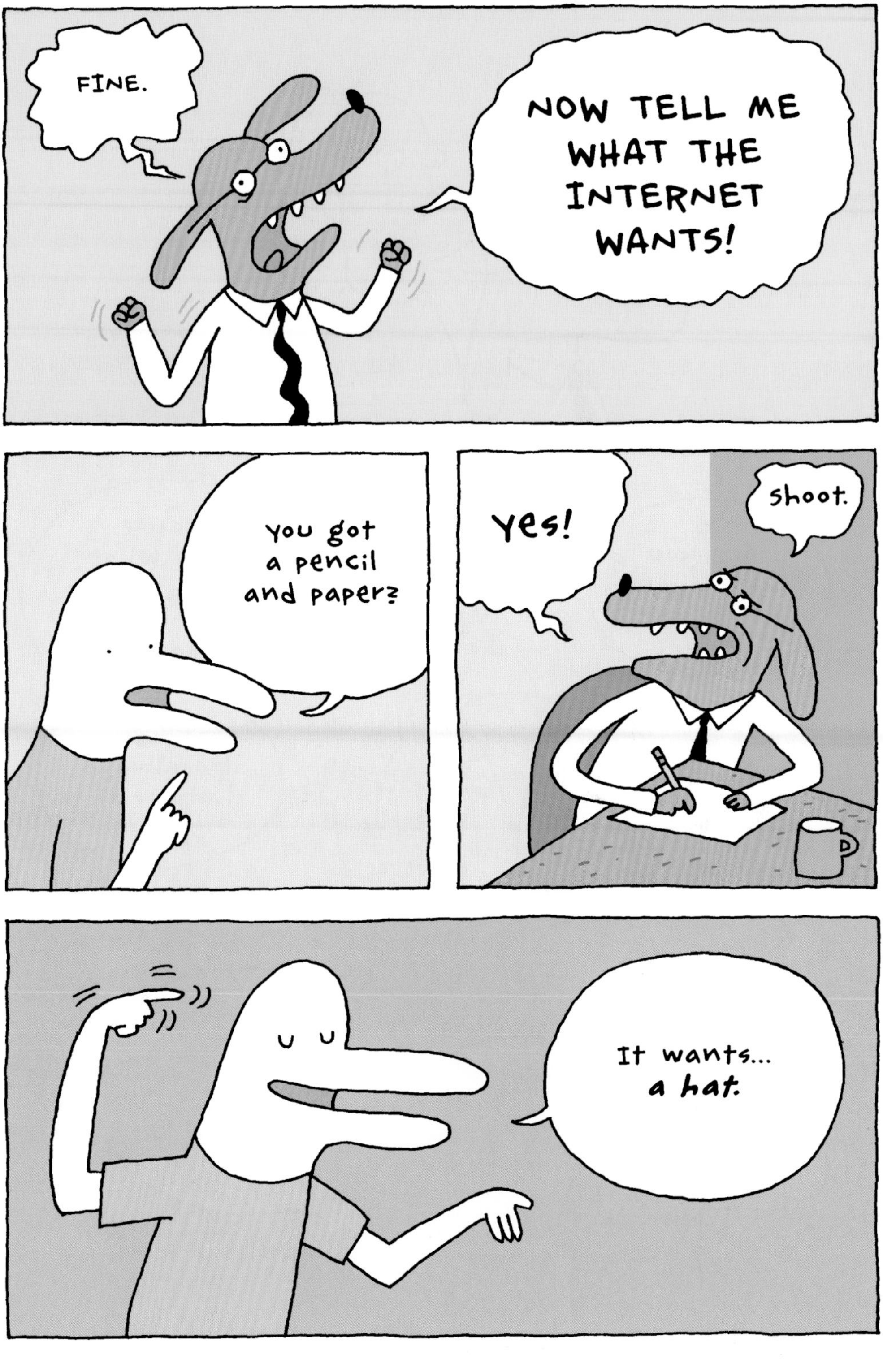
FINE.
NOW TELL ME WHAT THE INTERNET WANTS!
You got a pencil and paper?
Yes!
Shoot.
It wants... a hat.

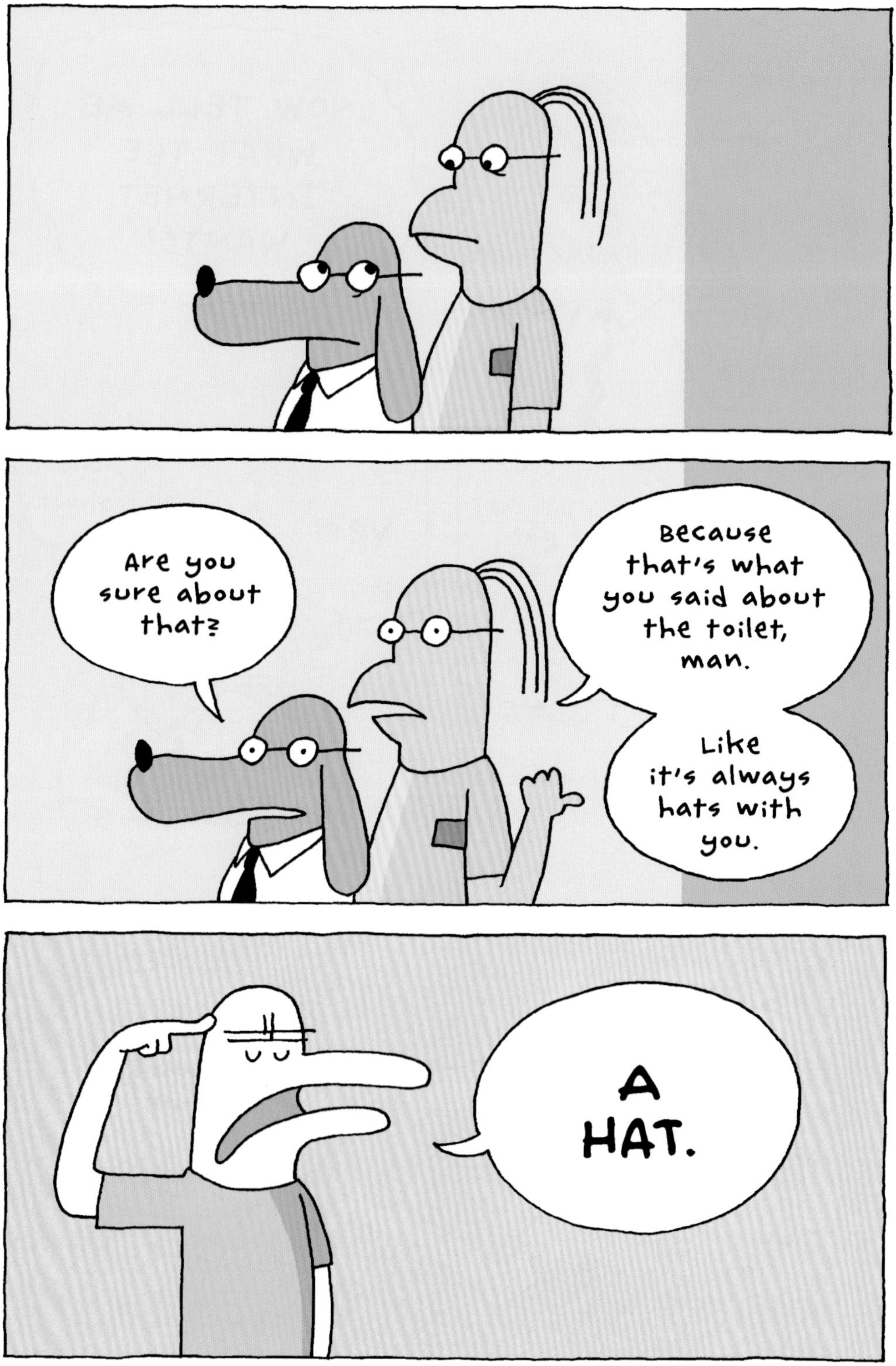
Are you sure about that?
Because that's what you said about the toilet, man.
Like it's always hats with you.
A HAT.

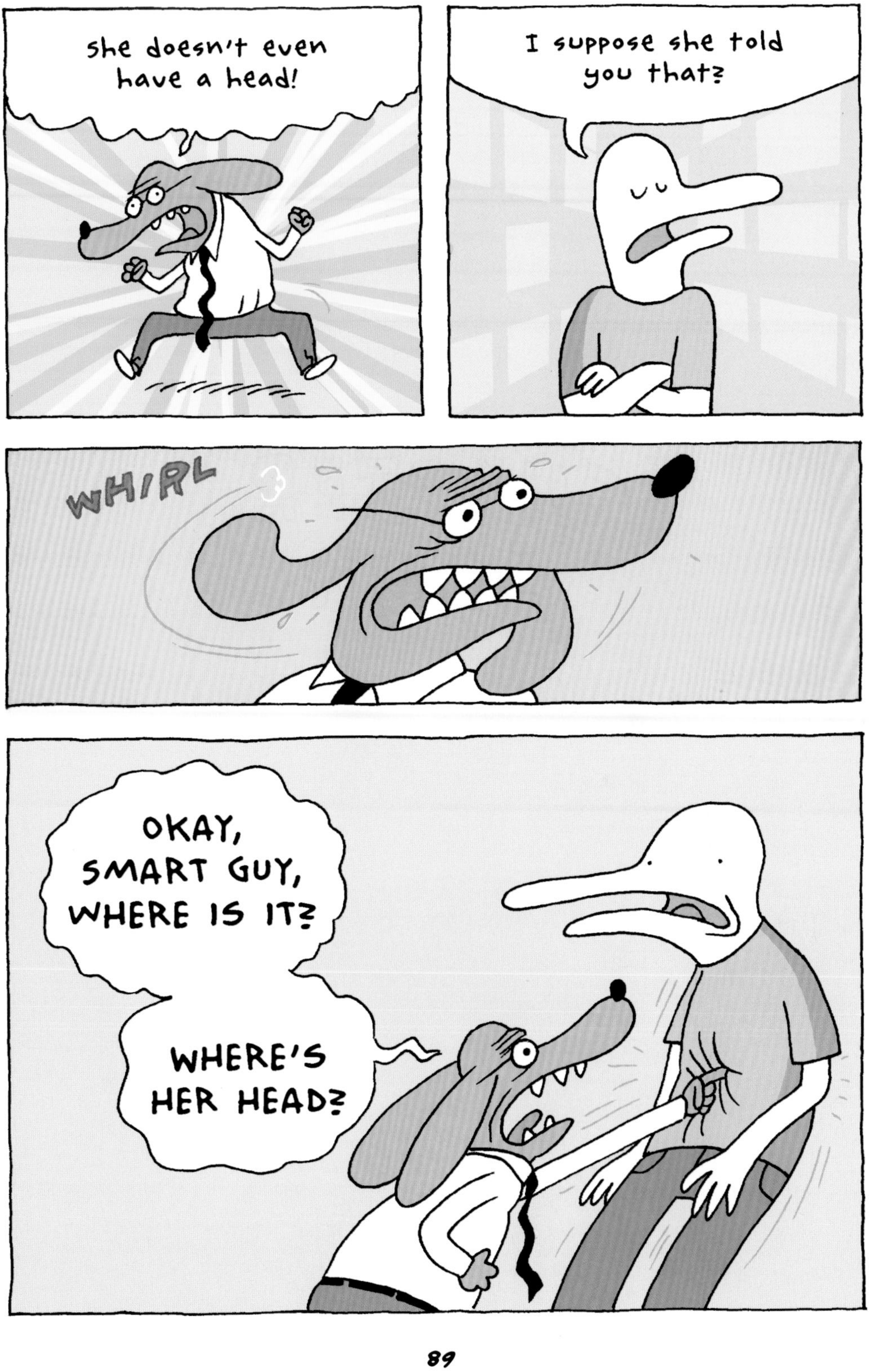
she doesn't even have a head!
I suppose she told you that?
WHIRL
OKAY, SMART GUY, WHERE IS IT?
WHERE'S HER HEAD?

CHAPTER FOUR

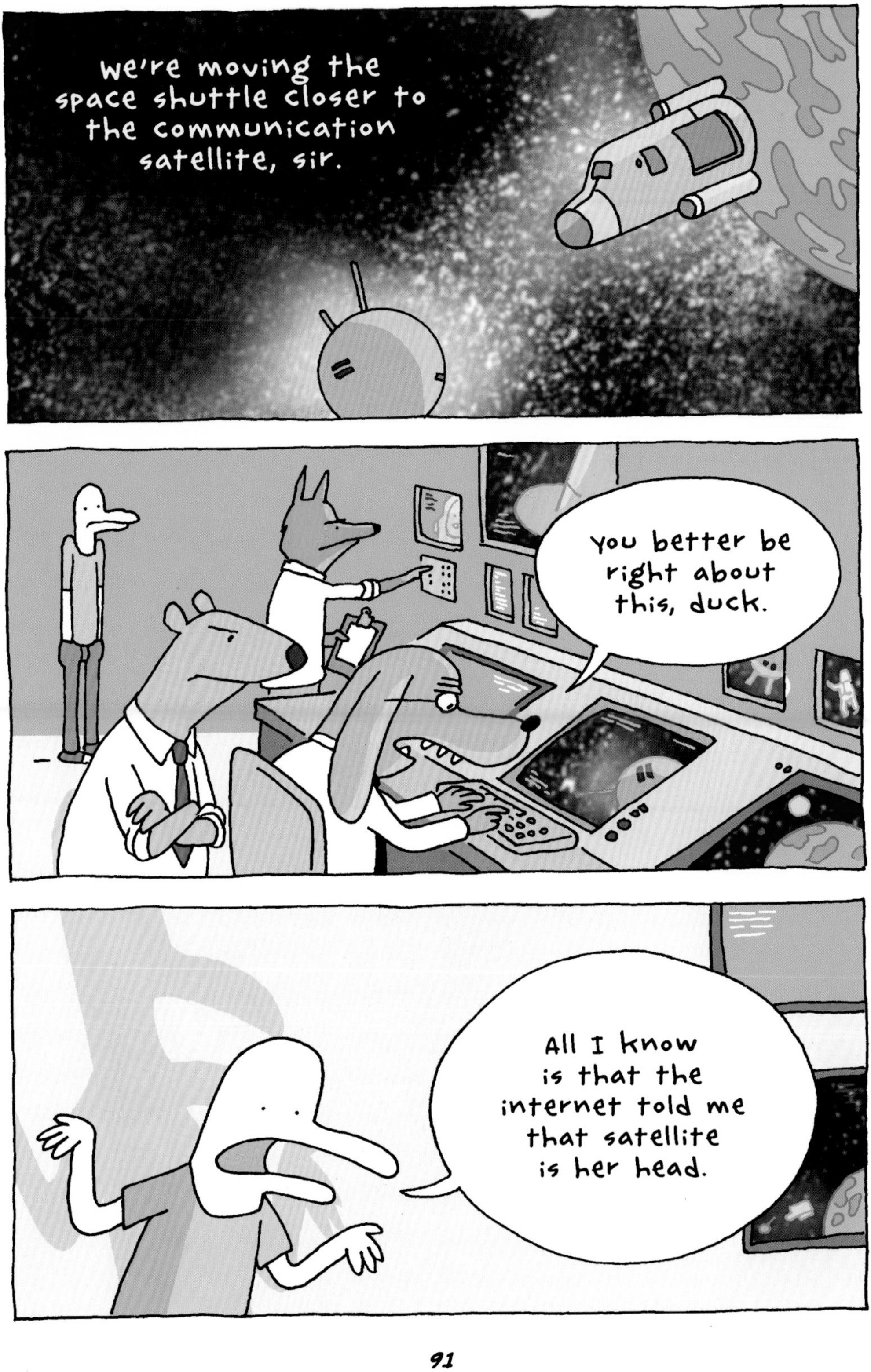
we're moving the space shuttle closer to the communication satellite, sir.
you better be right about this, duck.
All I know is that the internet told me that satellite is her head.

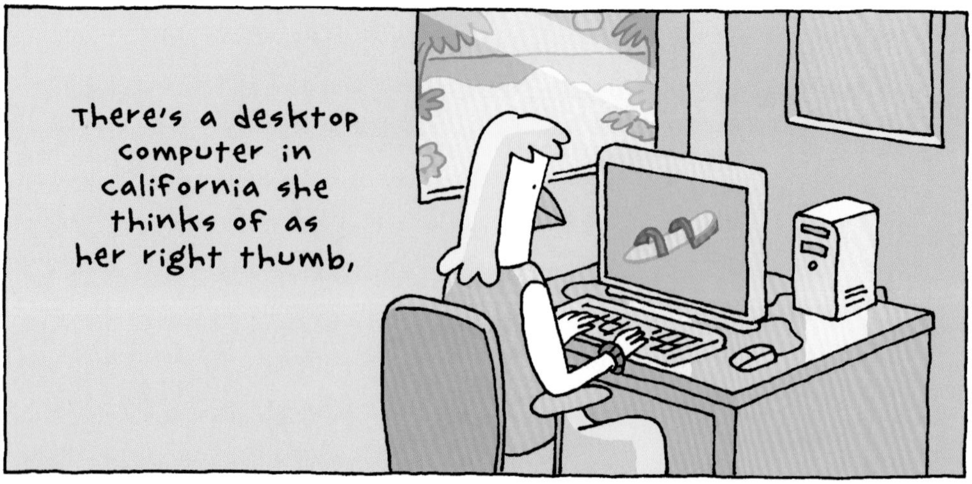
There's a desktop computer in California she thinks of as her right thumb,

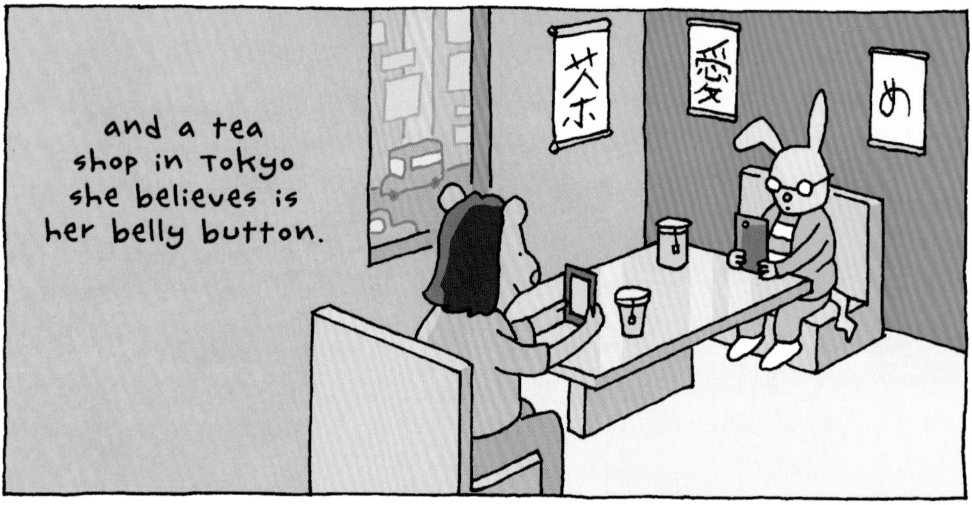
and a tea shop in Tokyo she believes is her belly button.
茶
愛
め

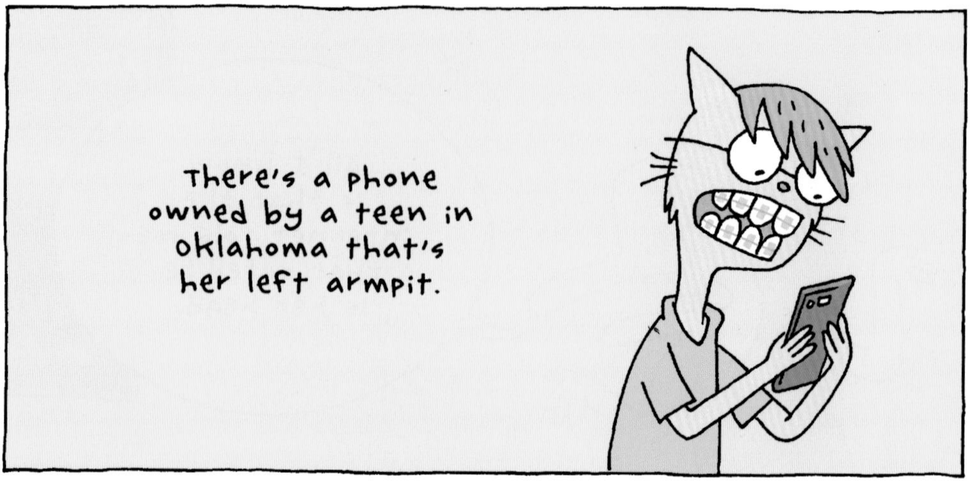
There's a phone owned by a teen in Oklahoma that's her left armpit.

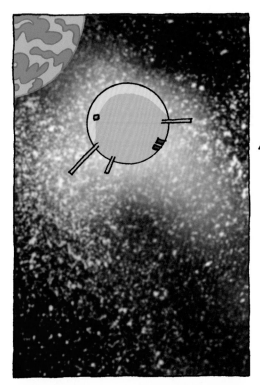

Sir, the hat deployment shuttle is in position.

Begin.

You're good to go.

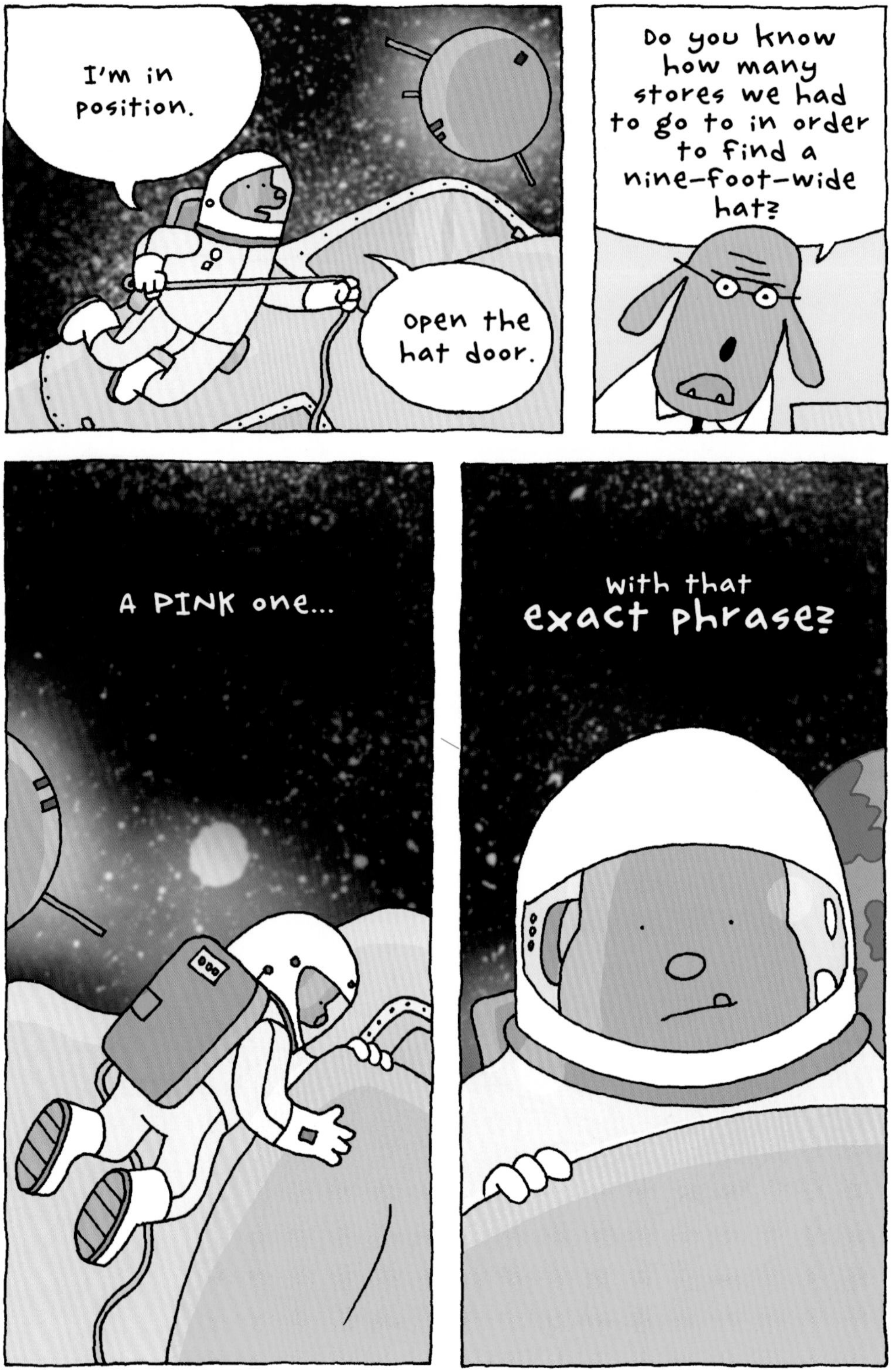
I'm in position.
Open the hat door.
Do you know how many stores we had to go to in order to find a nine-foot-wide hat?
A PINK one...
With that exact phrase?

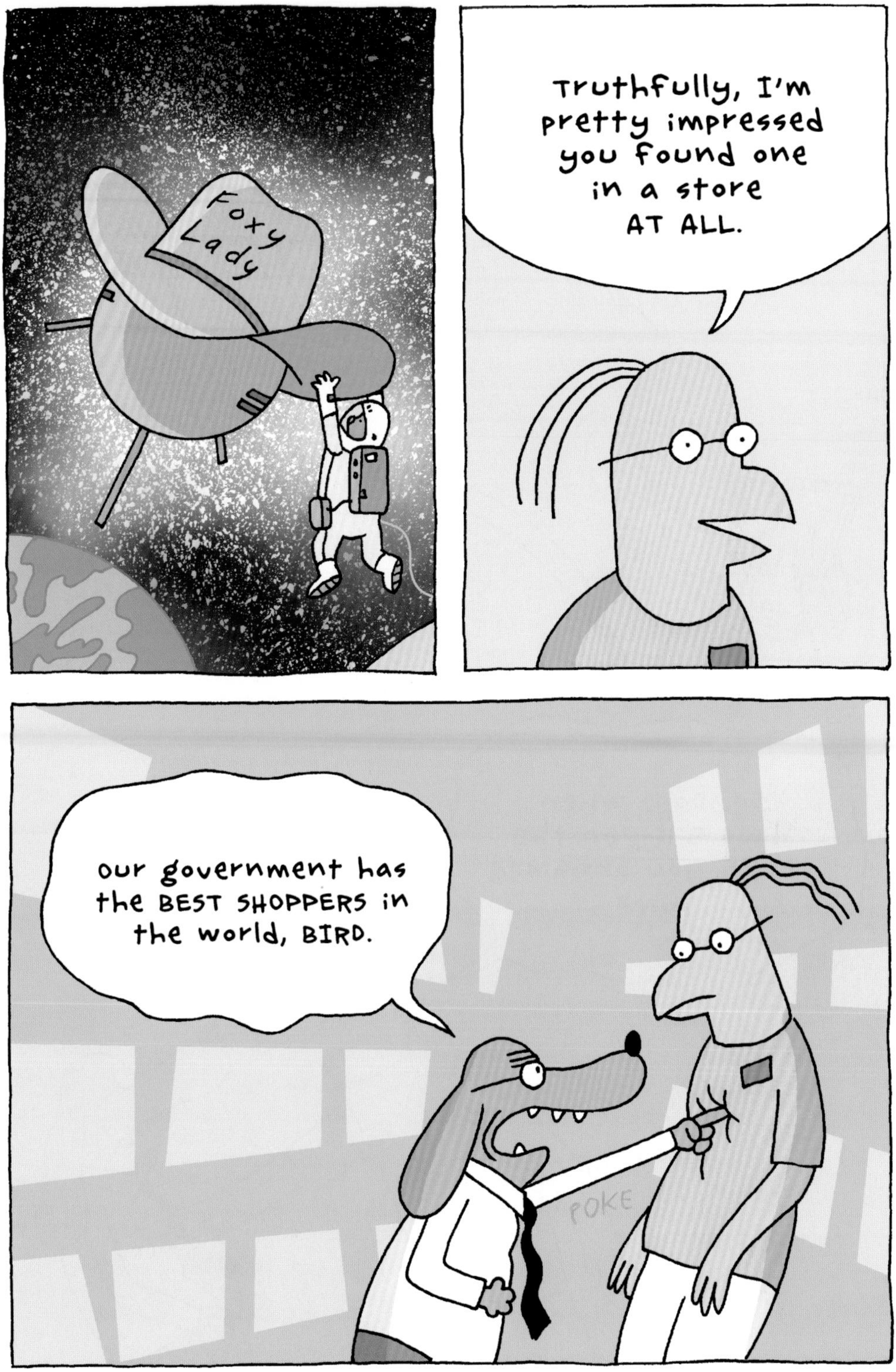
Foxy Lady
Truthfully, I'm pretty impressed you found one in a store AT ALL.
our government has the BEST SHOPPERS in the world, BIRD.
POKE

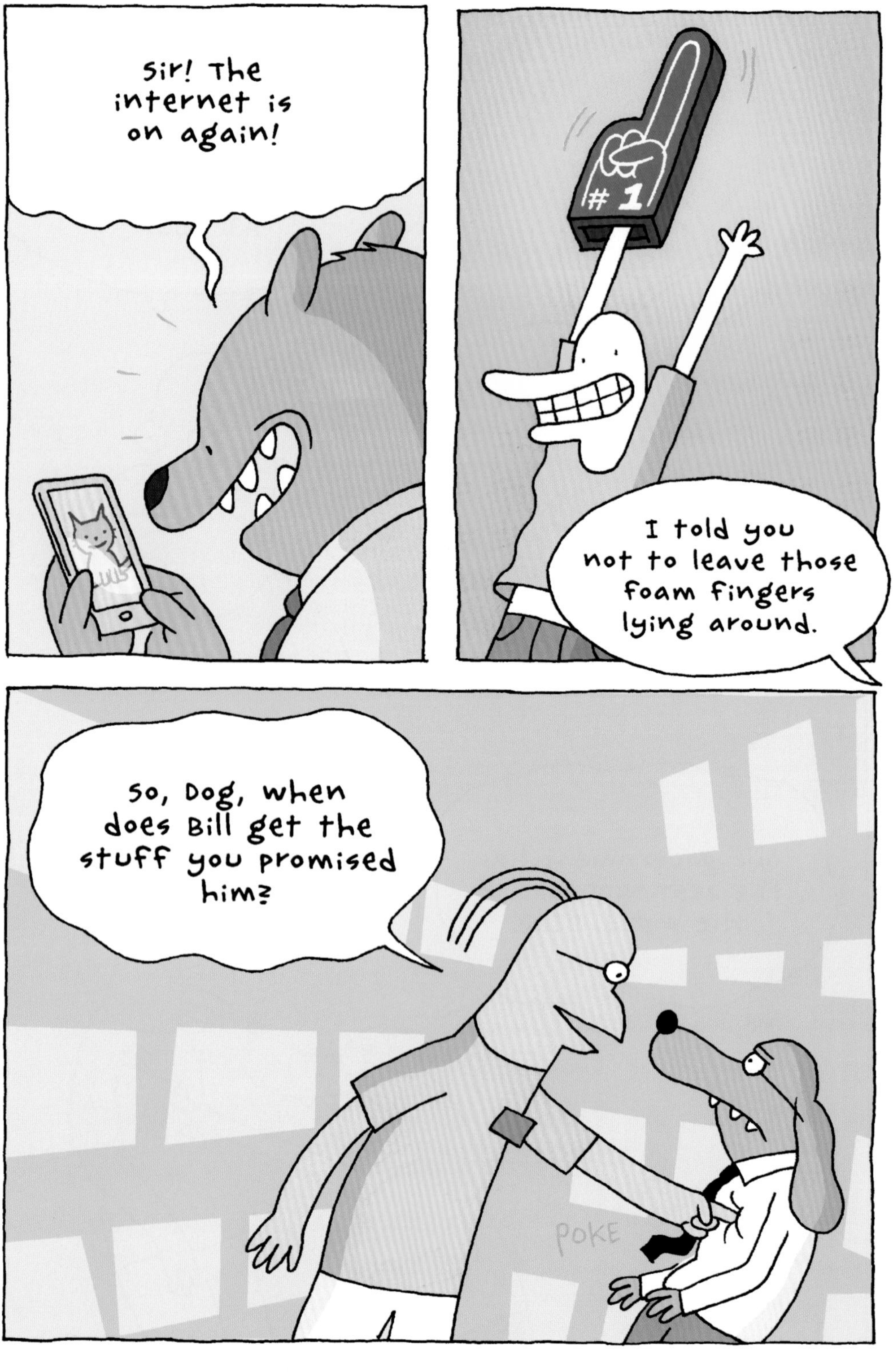
Sir! The internet is on again!
I told you not to leave those foam fingers lying around.
#1
So, Dog, when does Bill get the stuff you promised him?
POKE

CHAPTER FIVE

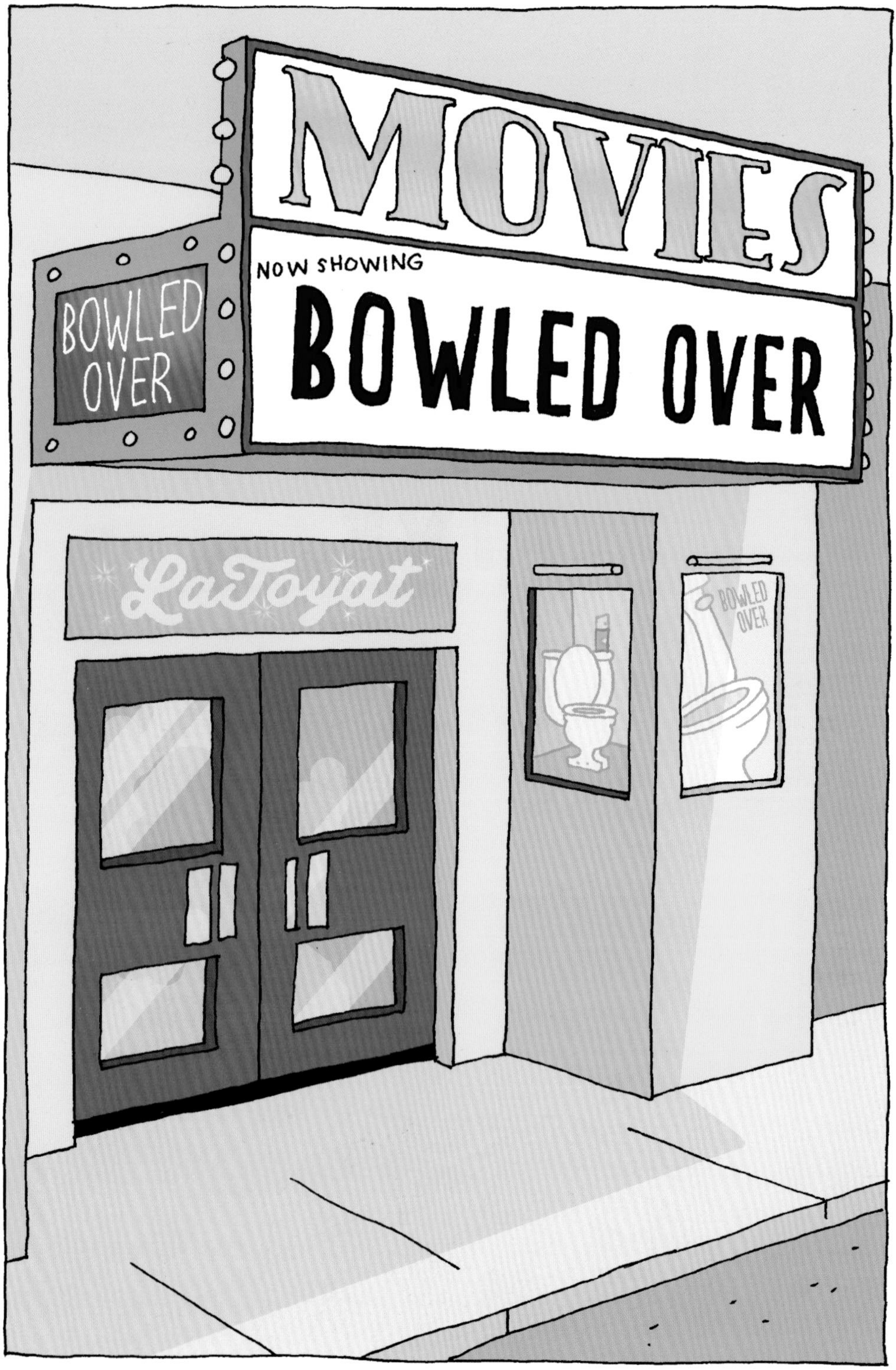
MOVIES
NOW SHOWING
BOWLED OVER
BOWLED OVER
LaToyat
BOWLED OVER

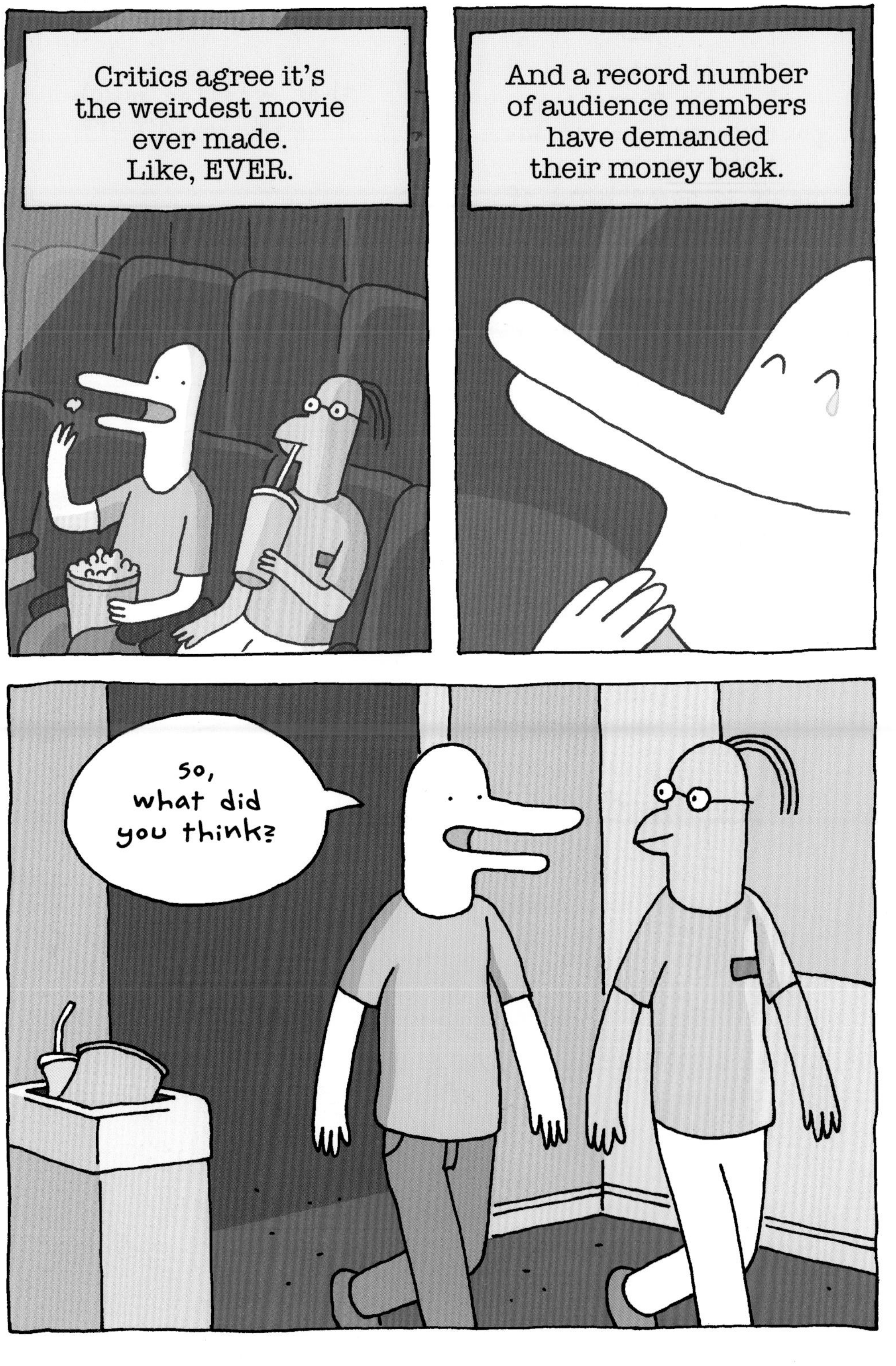
Critics agree it's the weirdest movie ever made. Like, EVER.
And a record number of audience members have demanded their money back.
So, what did you think?

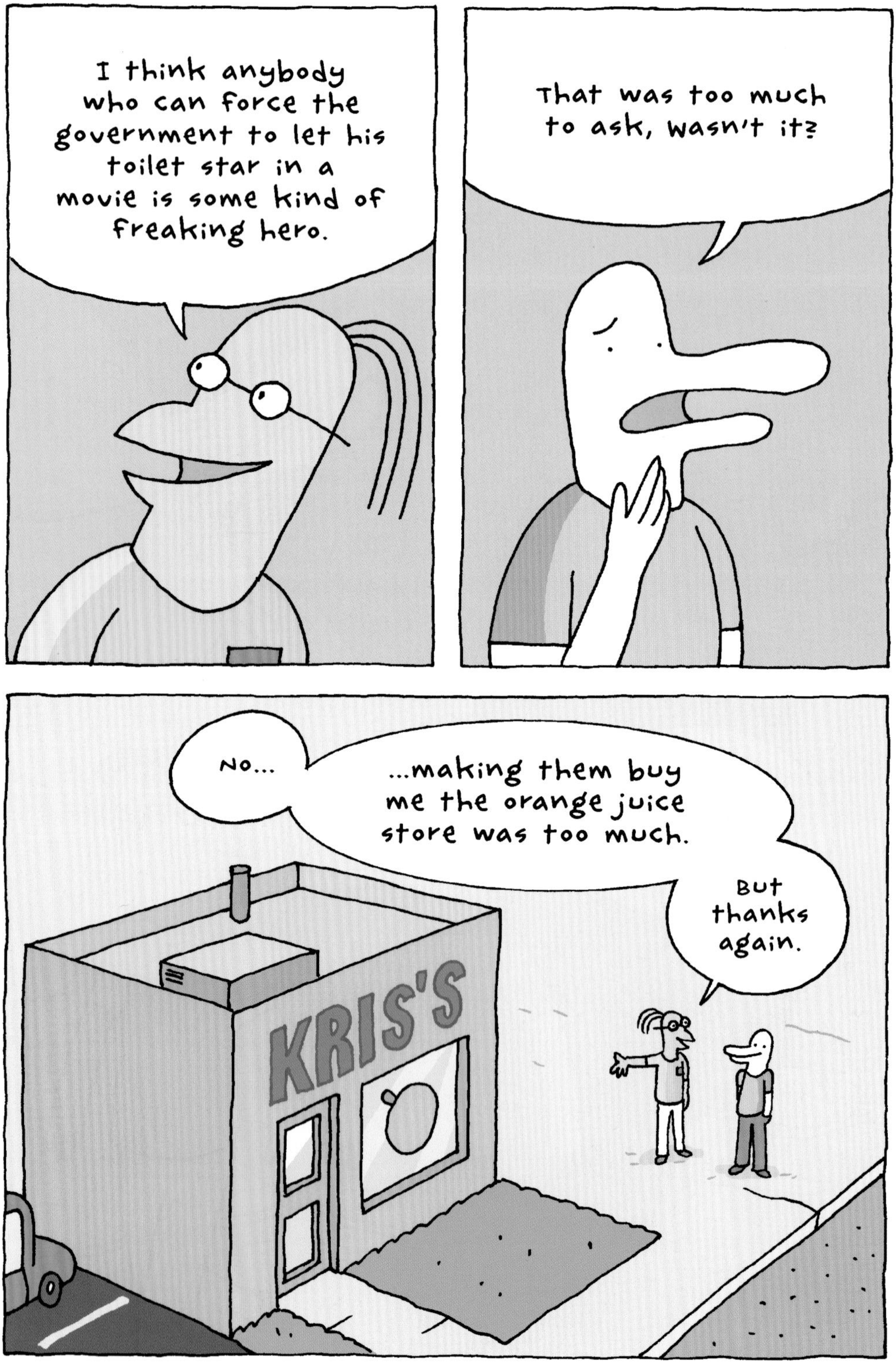
I think anybody who can force the government to let his toilet star in a movie is some kind of freaking hero.
That was too much to ask, wasn't it?
No...
...making them buy me the orange juice store was too much.
But thanks again.
KRIS'S

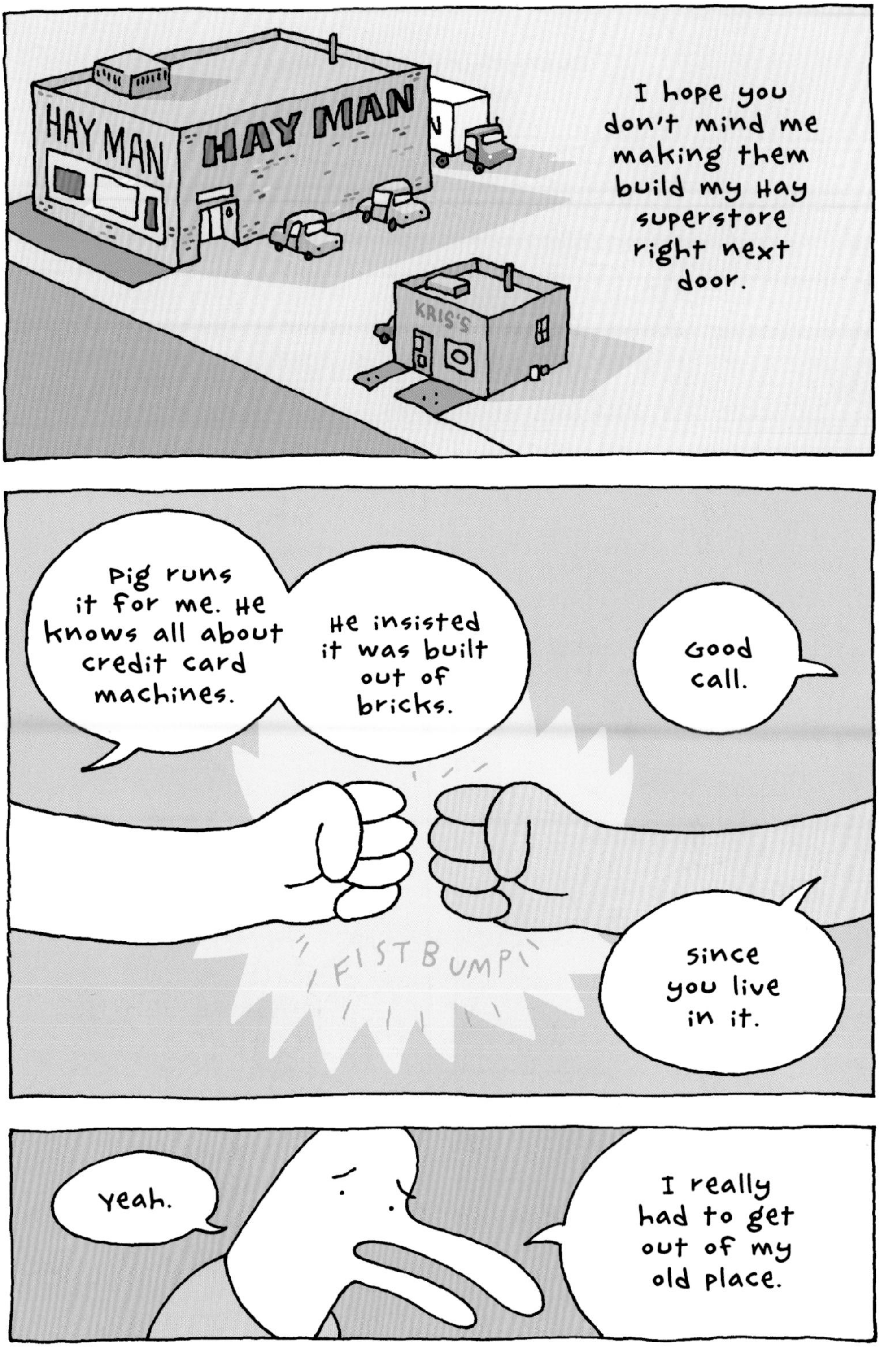
HAY MAN
HAY MAN
KRIS'S
I hope you don't mind me making them build my Hay superstore right next door.
Pig runs it for me. He knows all about credit card machines.
He insisted it was built out of bricks.
Good call.
FISTBUMP
Since you live in it.
Yeah.
I really had to get out of my old place.

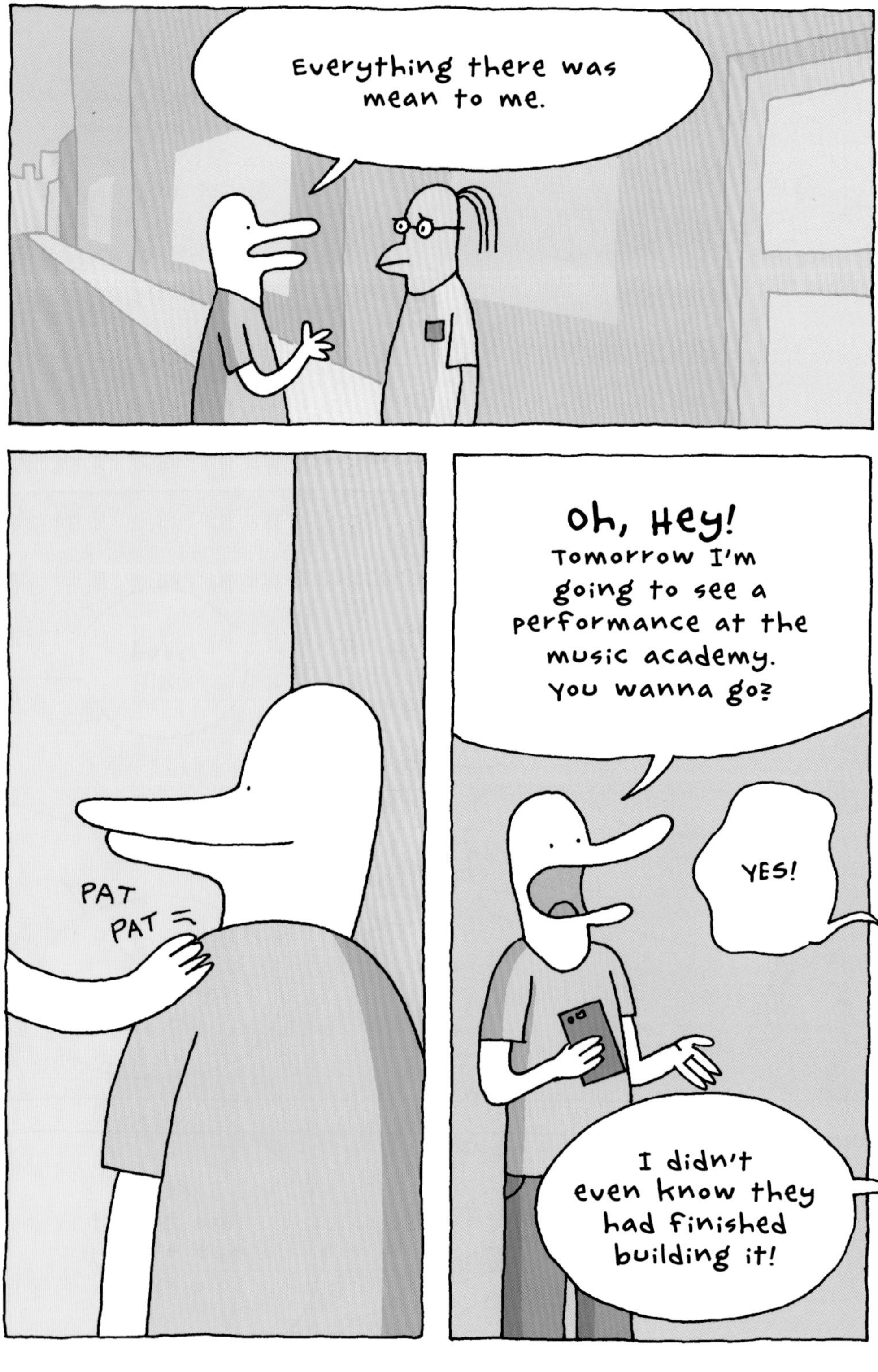
Everything there was mean to me.
PAT PAT
Oh, Hey! Tomorrow I'm going to see a performance at the music academy. You wanna go?
YES!
I didn't even know they had finished building it!

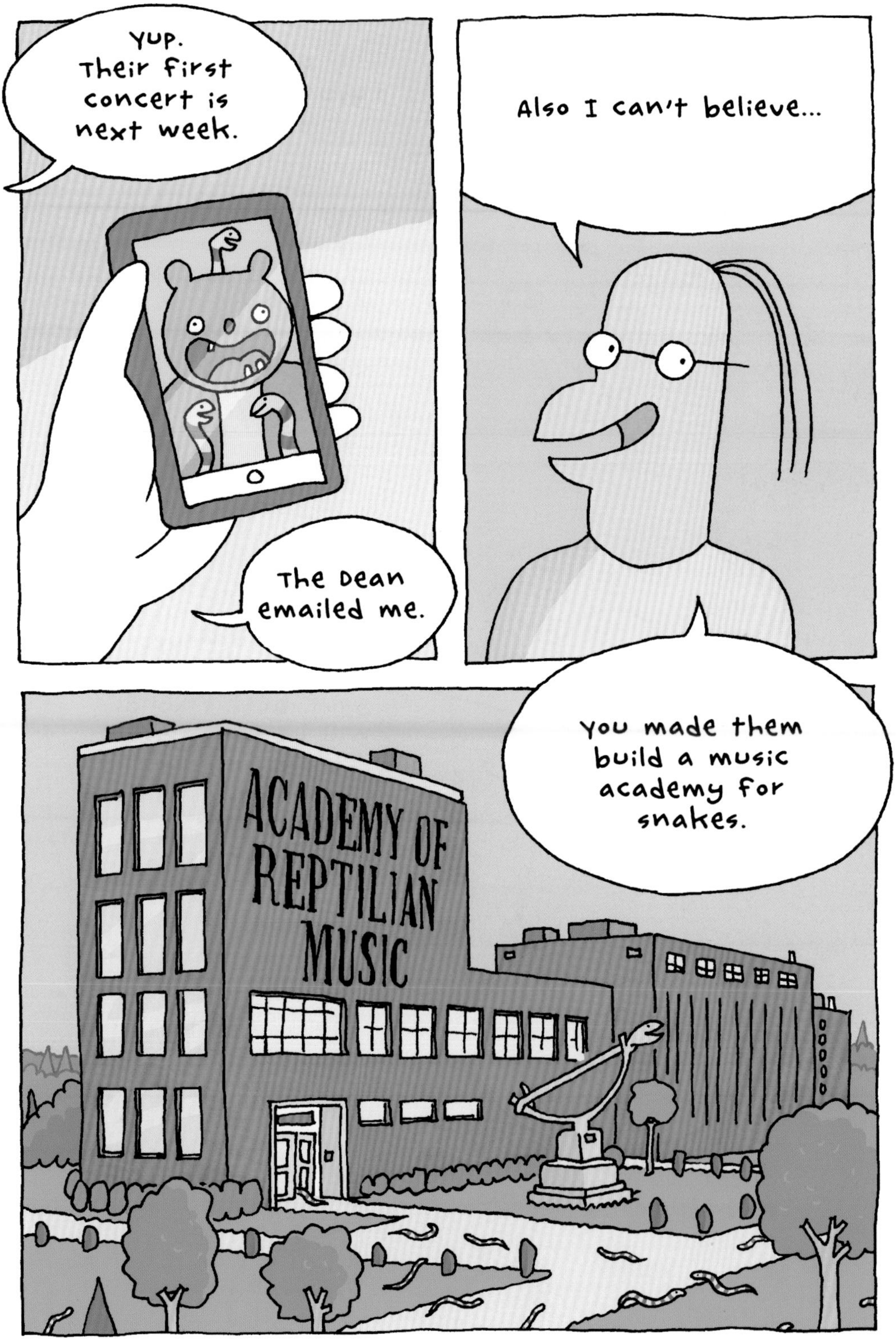
Yup. Their first concert is next week.
The Dean emailed me.
Also I can't believe...
You made them build a music academy for snakes.
ACADEMY OF REPTILIAN MUSIC

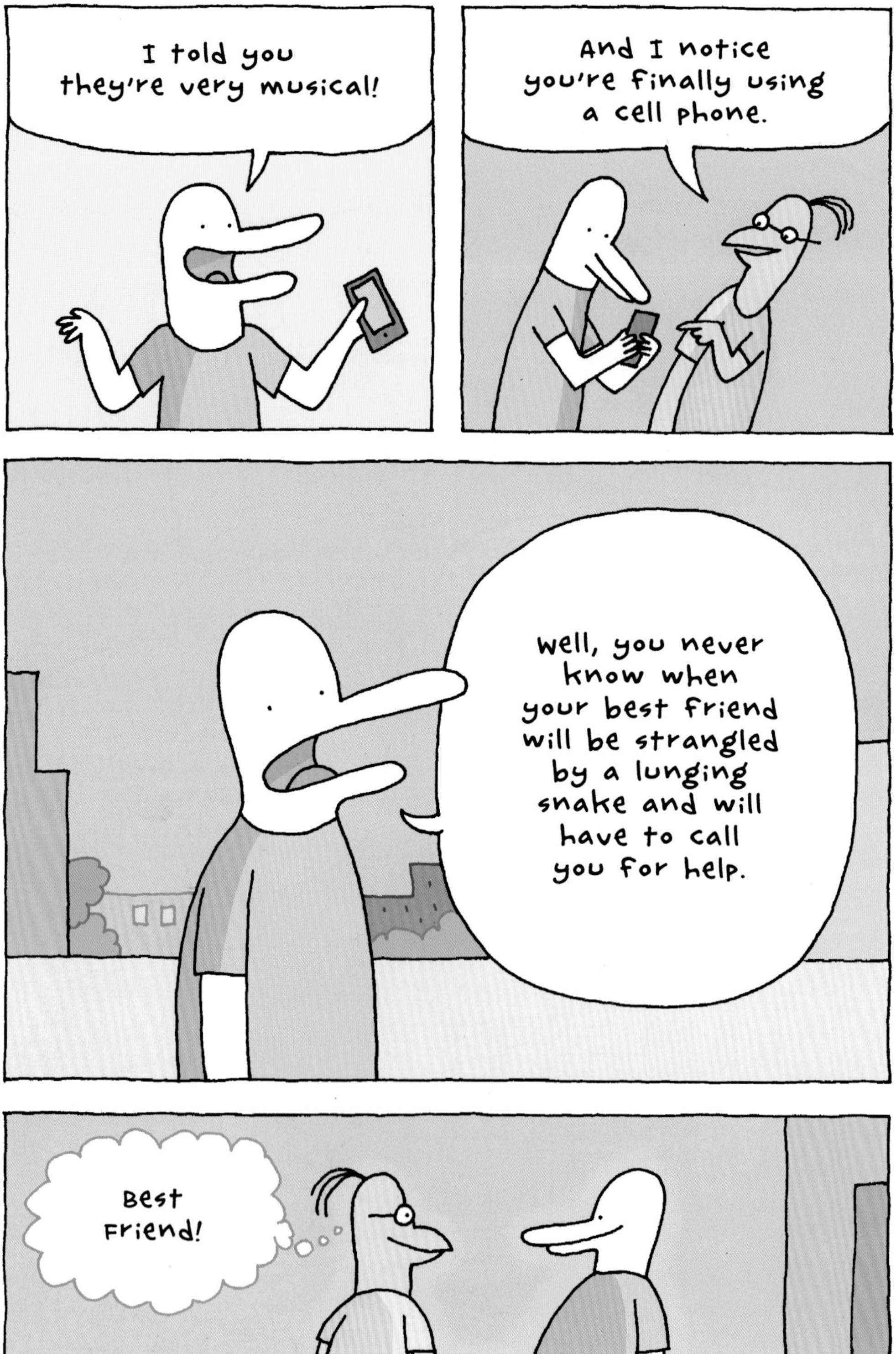
I told you they're very musical!
And I notice you're finally using a cell phone.
Well, you never know when your best friend will be strangled by a lunging snake and will have to call you for help.
Best Friend!

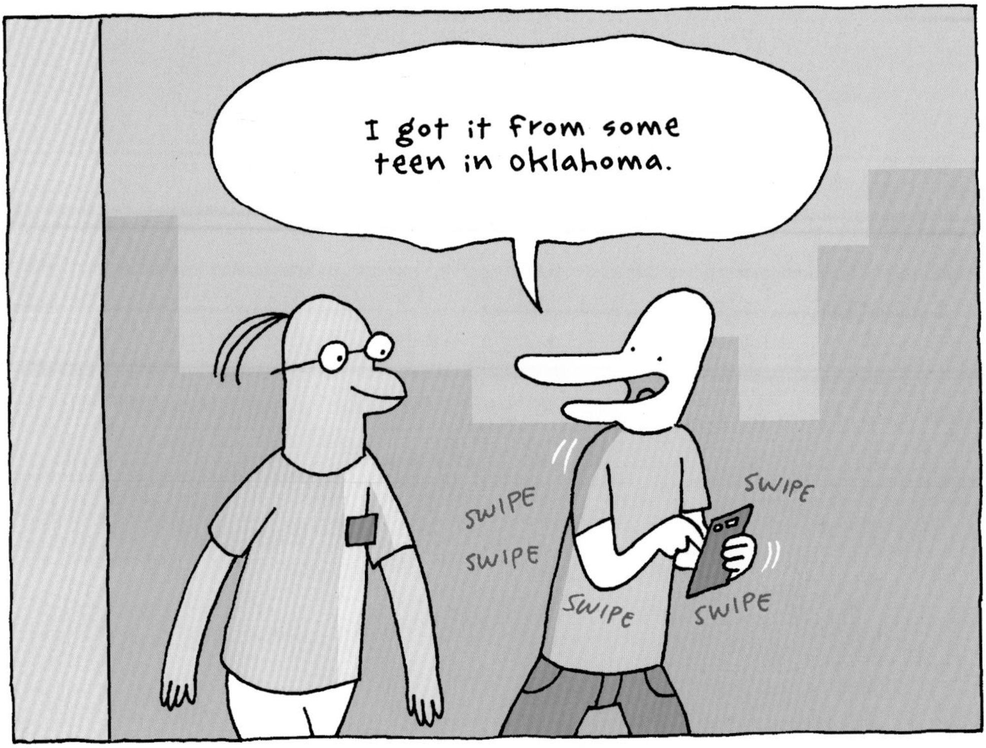
I got it from some teen in oklahoma.
SWIPE
SWIPE
SWIPE
SWIPE
SWIPE

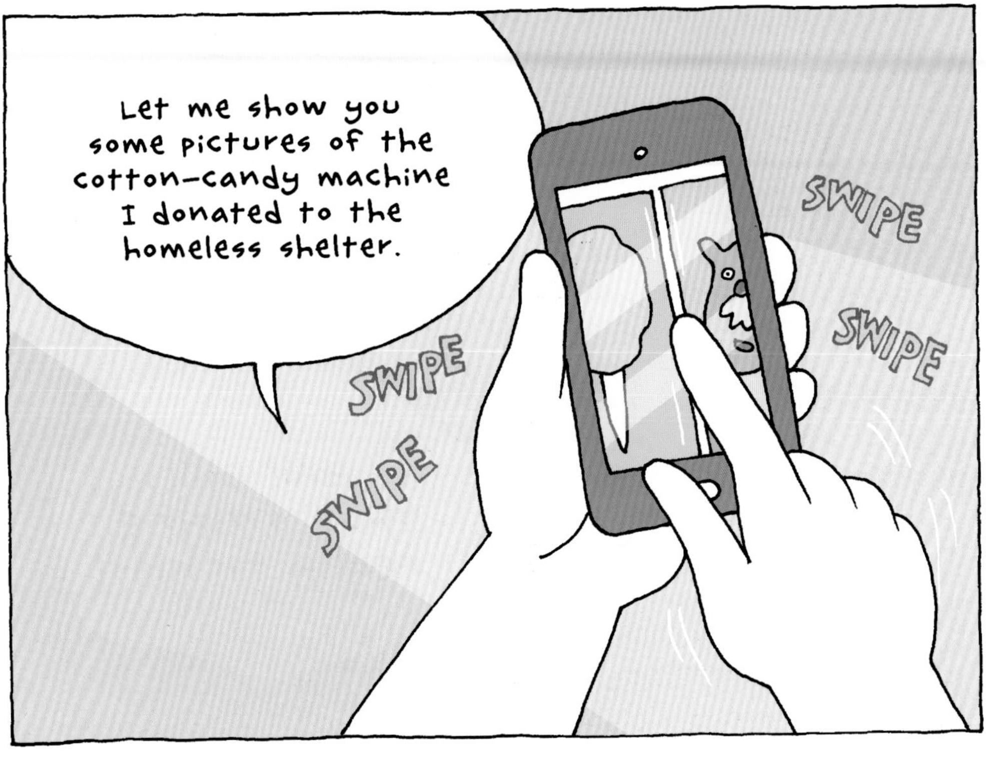
Let me show you some pictures of the cotton-candy machine I donated to the homeless shelter.
SWIPE
SWIPE
SWIPE
SWIPE

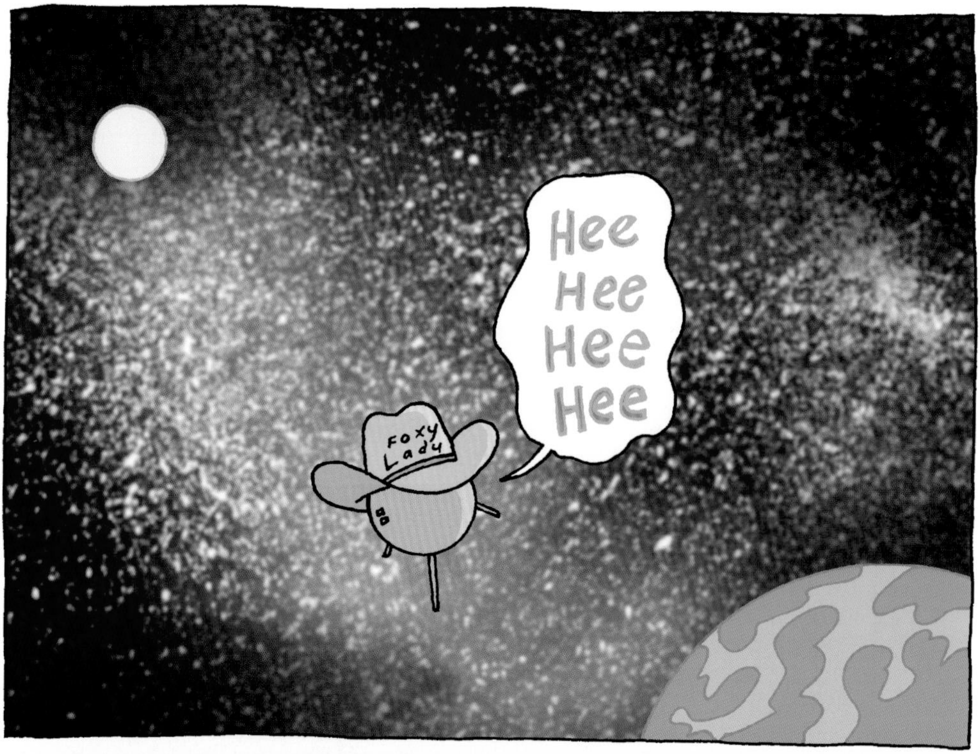
Foxy Lady
Hee Hee Hee Hee

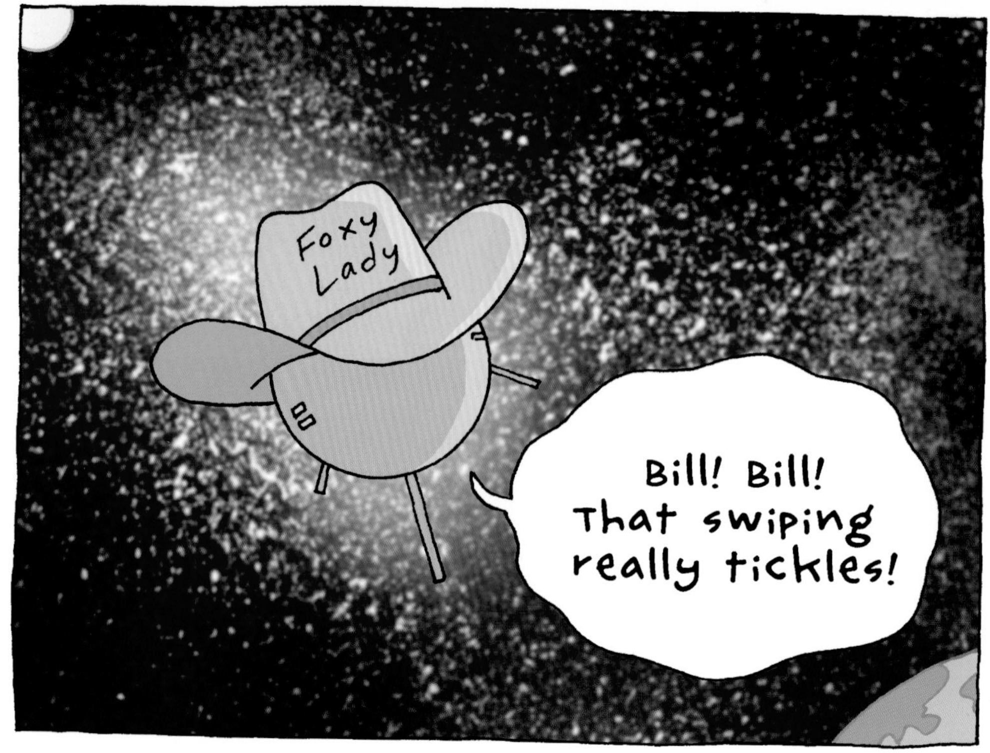
Foxy Lady
Bill! Bill! That swiping really tickles!

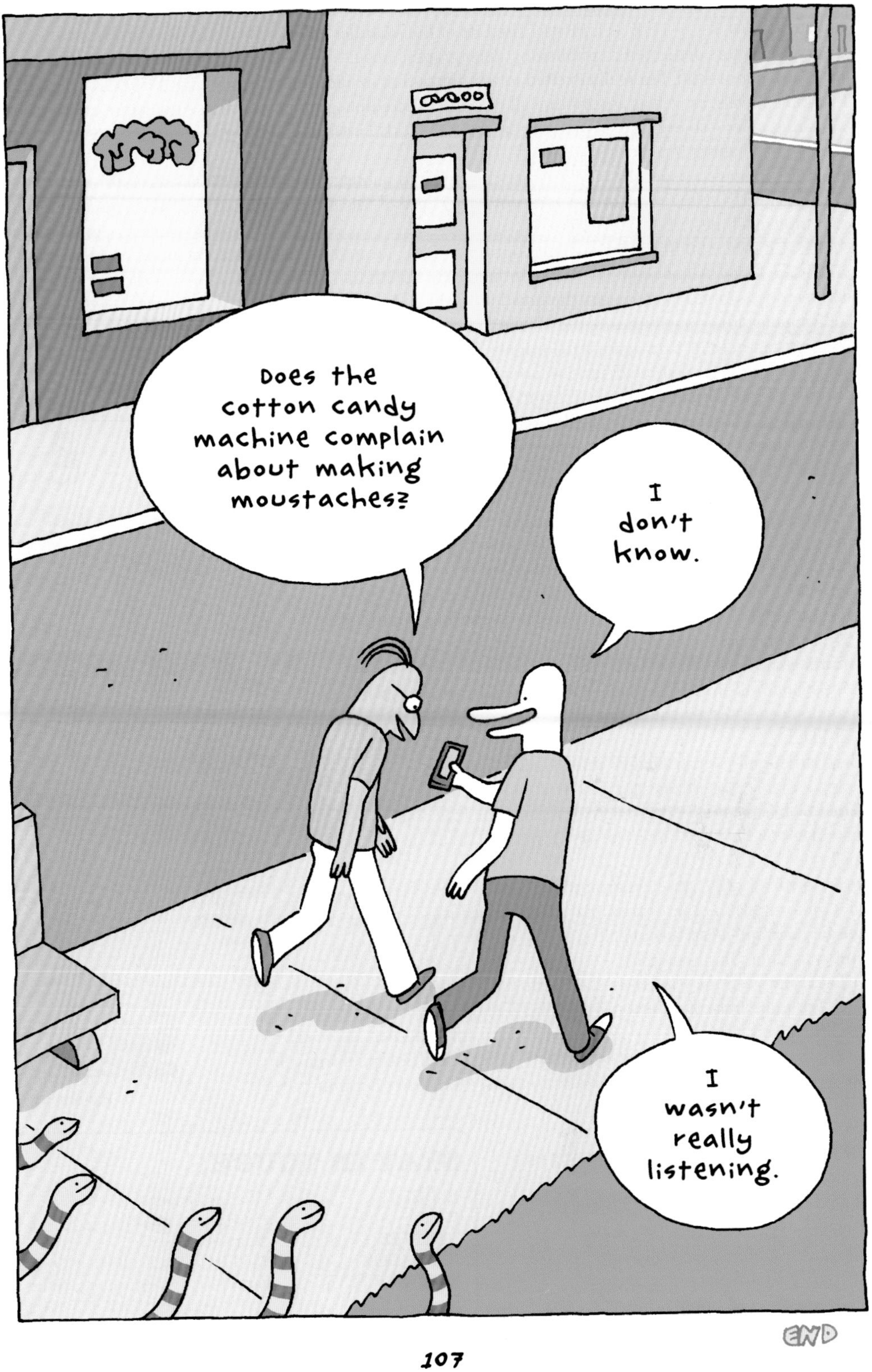
Does the cotton candy machine complain about making moustaches?
I don't know.
I wasn't really listening.

END

WATCH OUT FOR PAPERCUTZ

Welcome to ATTACK OF THE STUFF #1 "The Life of Bill Waddler" by Jim Benton from Papercutz, those anthropomorphic critters dedicated to publishing great graphic novels for all ages. I'm Jim Salicrup, Editor-in-Chief and Office Hoarder of Stuff. I'm really excited to announce that in addition to producing ATTACK OF THE STUFF graphic novels, as well as assembling all our other incredible graphic novels, we got some exciting Papercutz publishing news—so exciting, it was even in the New York Times and The Hollywood Report! So exciting, I'm going to tell you all about it right now…

Papercutz has managed to get the North American rights to publish perhaps the most successful comics series in the world—ASTERIX! Now some of you may not have heard of this Asterix fella, so let's take a quick journey in the Papercutz time machine…

We're back in the year 50 BC in the ancient country of Gaul, located where France, Belgium, and the Southern Netherlands are today. All of Gaul has been conquered by the Romans… well, not all of it. One tiny village, inhabited by indomitable Gauls, resists the invaders again and again. That doesn't make it easy for the garrisons of Roman soldiers surrounding the village in fortified camps. So, how's it possible that a small village can hold its own against the mighty Roman Empire? The answer is this guy…

Asterix. This is Asterix. A shrewd, little warrior of keen intellect… and superhuman strength. Asterix gets his superhuman strength from a magic potion. But he's not alone.

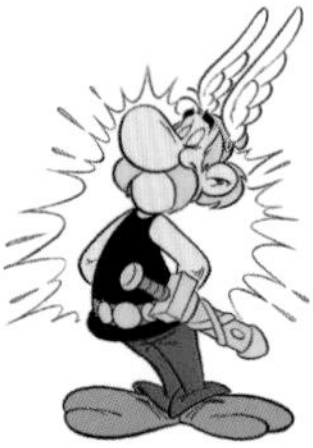

Asterix

Obelix is Asterix's inseparable friend. He too has superhuman strength. He's a menhir (tall, upright stone monuments) deliveryman, he loves eating wild boar and getting into brawls. Obelix is always ready to drop everything to go off on a new adventure with Asterix.

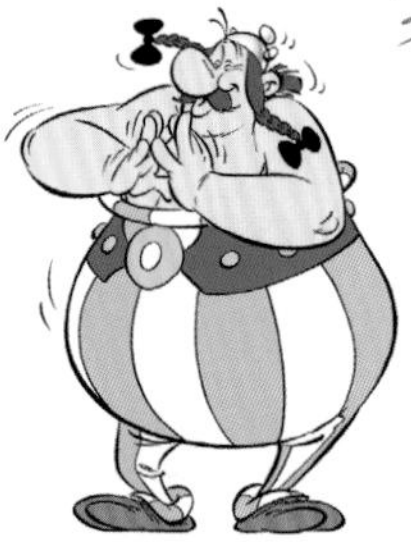

Obelix

Panoramix, the village's venerable Druid, gathers mistletoe and prepares magic potions. His greatest success is the power potion. When a villager drinks this magical elixir he or she is temporarily granted super-strength. This is just one of the Druid's potions! And now you know why this small village can survive, despite seemingly impossible odds. While we're here, we may as well meet a few other Gauls…

Cacofonix is the bard—the village poet. Opinions about his talents are divided: he thinks he's awesome, everybody else think he's awful, but when he doesn't say anything, he's a cheerful companion and well-liked…

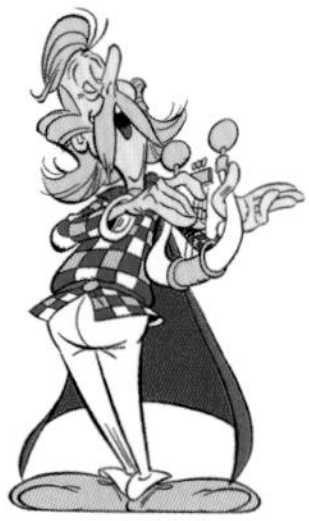

Cacofonix

Vitalstatistix,finally, is the village's chief. Majestic, courageous, and irritable, the old warrior is respected by his men and feared by his enemies. Vitalstatistix has only one fear: that the sky will fall on his head but, as he says himself, "That'll be the day!"

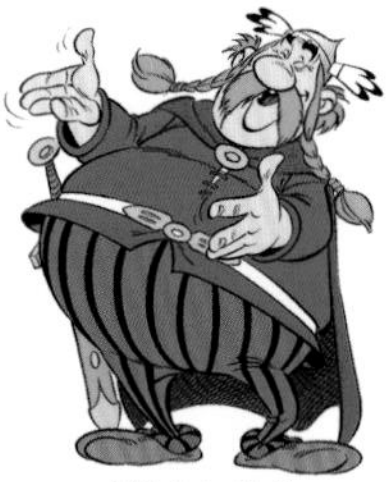

Vitalstatistix

There are plenty more characters around here, but you've met enough for now. In other words, that's Gaul, folks! It's time we get back and wrap this up. Now, where did we put that time machine? Oh, there it is!

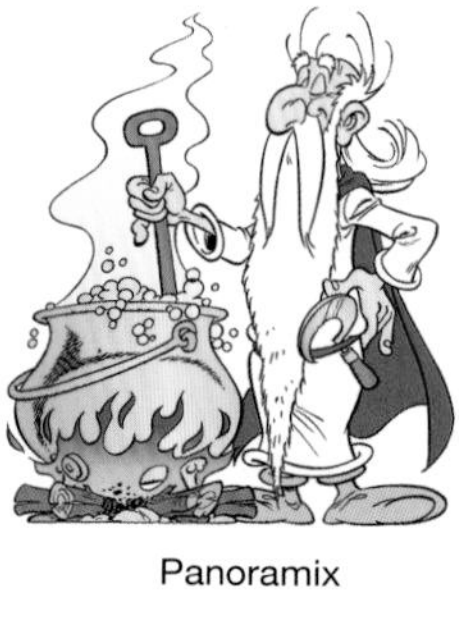

Panoramix

We're back, and we hope you enjoyed this trip back in time to explore in 50 BC. For more information about ASTERIX and his upcoming Papercutz graphic novels, just go to papercutz.com. As for Bill Waddler, all we can say is, "That's not Gaul, er, we mean, all, folks!" Papercutz is also publishing an all-new series of graphic novels by world-famous cartoonist Art Baltazar called GILLBERT. It's about a little merman, and we think you'll enjoy it. Check out the preview of GILLBERT #1 "The Little Merman" starting on the very next page.

Until next time, remember to watch out for Papercutz!

Thanks, Jim

STAY IN TOUCH!

EMAIL:	salicrup@papercutz.com
WEB:	www.papercutz.com
TWITTER:	@papercutzgn
FACEBOOK:	PAPERCUTZGRAPHICNOVELS
REGULAR MAIL:	Papercutz, 160 Broadway, Suite 700, East Wing, New York, NY 10038

Special Preview of GILLBERT #1 "The Little Merman"...

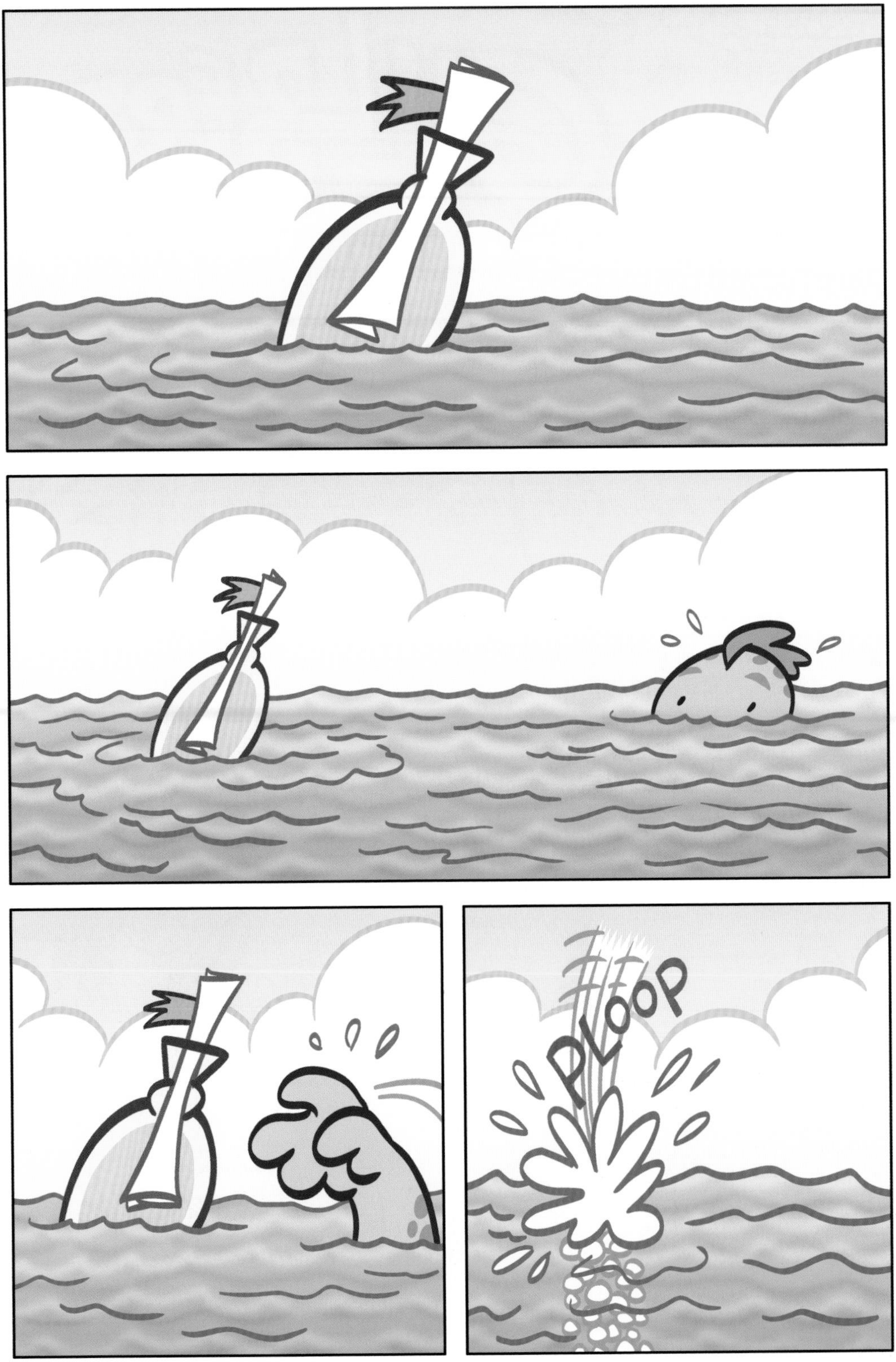
PLOOP

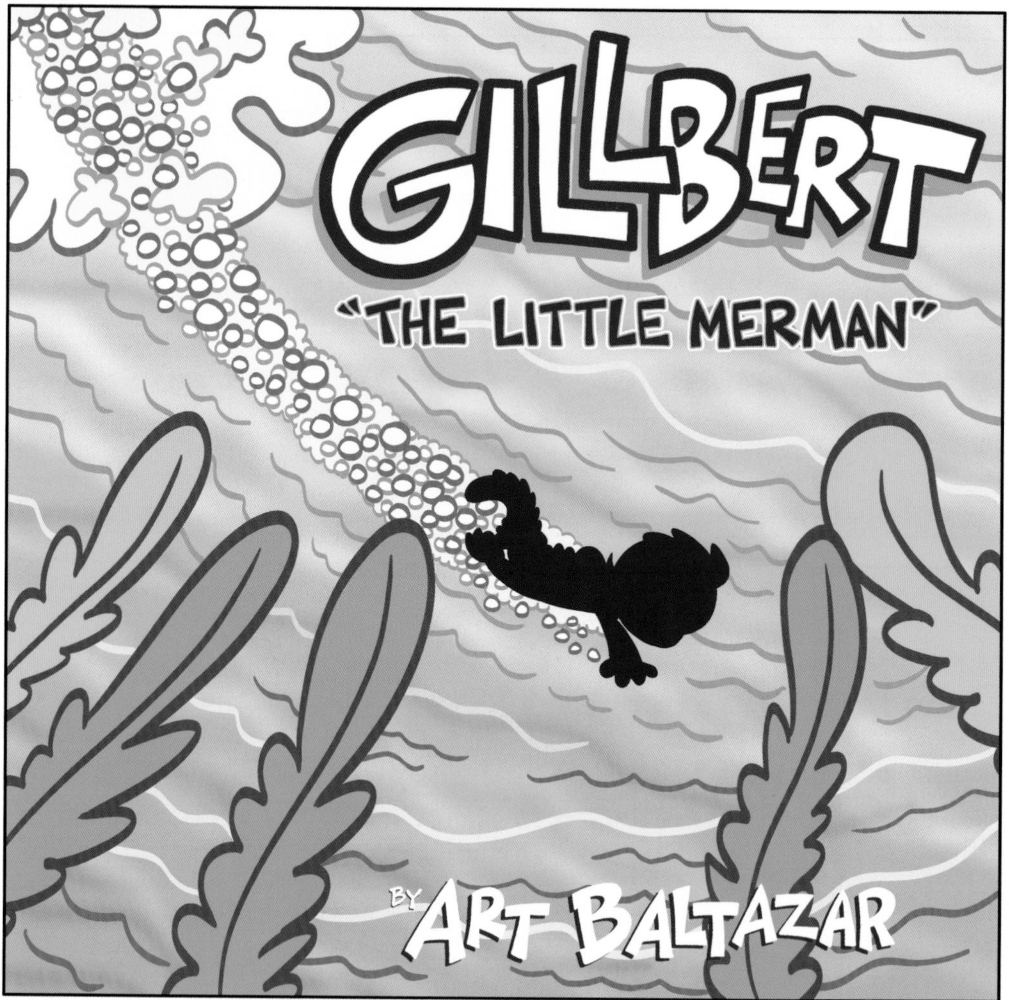
GILLBERT
"THE LITTLE MERMAN"
BY ART BALTAZAR

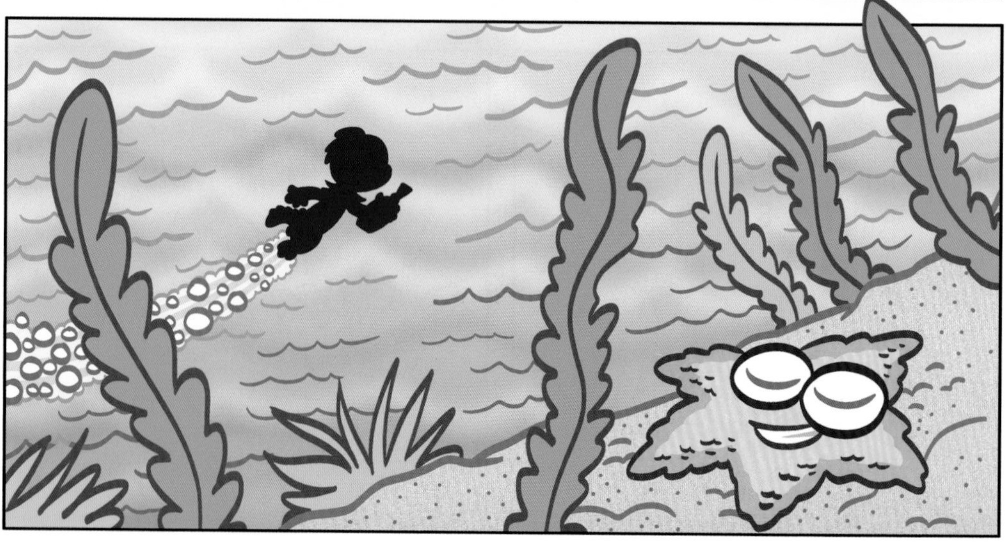

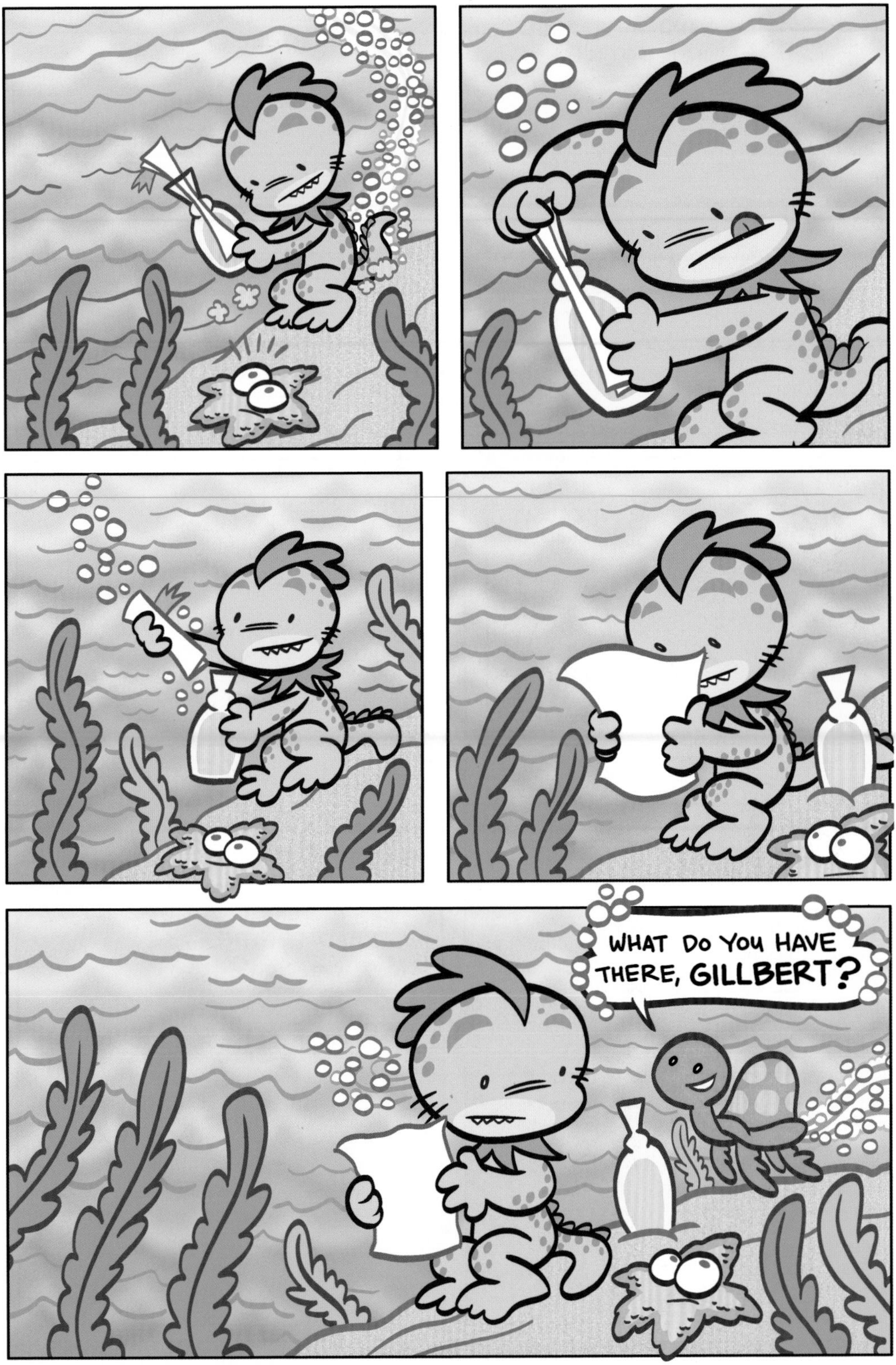
WHAT DO YOU HAVE THERE, GILLBERT?

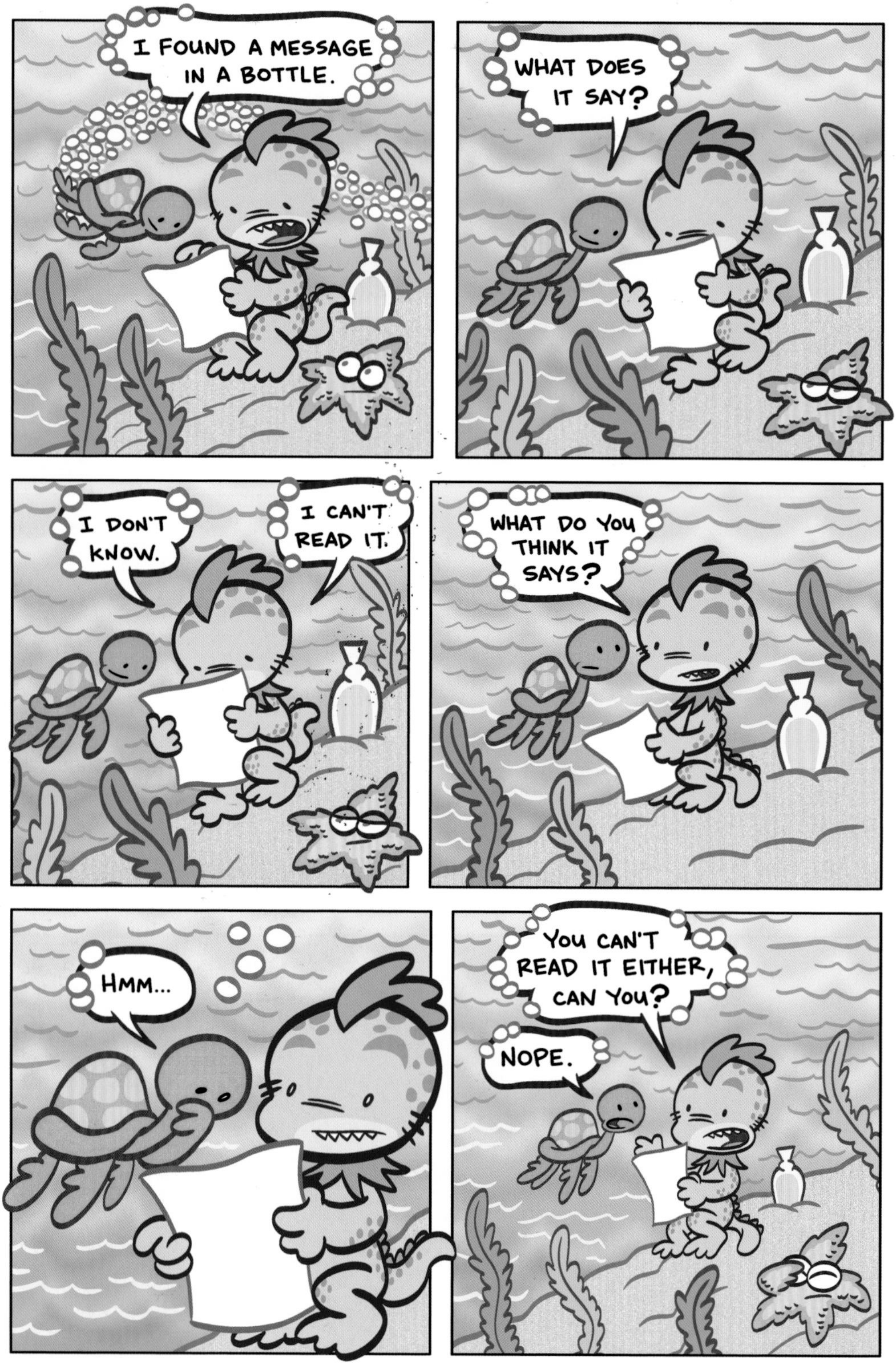
I FOUND A MESSAGE IN A BOTTLE.
WHAT DOES IT SAY?
I DON'T KNOW.
I CAN'T READ IT.
WHAT DO YOU THINK IT SAYS?
HMM...
YOU CAN'T READ IT EITHER, CAN YOU?
NOPE.